10/
1

GAYLORD MG

# Harrowing
# the Dragon

*Ace Books by Patricia A. McKillip*

THE FORGOTTEN BEASTS OF ELD
THE SORCERESS AND THE CYGNET
THE CYGNET AND THE FIREBIRD
THE BOOK OF ATRIX WOLFE
WINTER ROSE
SONG FOR THE BASILISK
RIDDLE-MASTER: THE COMPLETE TRILOGY
THE TOWER AT STONY WOOD
OMBRIA IN SHADOW
IN THE FORESTS OF SERRE
ALPHABET OF THORN
OD MAGIC
HARROWING THE DRAGON

# Harrowing the Dragon

PATRICIA A. MCKILLIP

ACE BOOKS, NEW YORK

**THE BERKLEY PUBLISHING GROUP**
**Published by the Penguin Group**
**Penguin Group (USA) Inc.**
**375 Hudson Street, New York, New York 10014, USA**
Penguin Group (Canada), 90 Eglinton Avenue East, Suite 700, Toronto, Ontario M4P 2Y3, Canada
(a division of Pearson Penguin Canada Inc.)
Penguin Books Ltd., 80 Strand, London WC2R 0RL, England
Penguin Group Ireland, 25 St. Stephen's Green, Dublin 2, Ireland (a division of Penguin Books Ltd.)
Penguin Group (Australia), 250 Camberwell Road, Camberwell, Victoria 3124, Australia
(a division of Pearson Australia Group Pty. Ltd.)
Penguin Books India Pvt. Ltd., 11 Community Centre, Panchsheel Park, New Delhi—110 017, India
Penguin Group (NZ), Cnr. Airborne and Rosedale Roads, Albany, Auckland 1310, New Zealand
(a division of Pearson New Zealand Ltd.)
Penguin Books (South Africa) (Pty.) Ltd., 24 Sturdee Avenue, Rosebank, Johannesburg 2196, South
Africa

Penguin Books Ltd., Registered Offices: 80 Strand, London WC2R 0RL, England

This is a work of fiction. Names, characters, places, and incidents either are the product of the author's imagination or are used fictitiously, and any resemblance to actual persons, living or dead, business establishments, events, or locales is entirely coincidental. The publisher does not have any control over and does not assume any responsibility for author or third-party websites or their content.

Copyright © 2005 by Patricia A. McKillip.
*For a complete listing of individual copyrights and acknowledgments please see page 309.*
Text design by Kristin del Rosario.

First edition: November 2005

Library of Congress Cataloging-in-Publication Data

McKillip, Patricia A.
    Harrowing the dragon / Patricia A. McKillip.— 1st ed.
      p. cm.
    Contents: The harrowing of the dragon of Hoarsbreath—A matter of music—A troll and two roses—Baba Yaga and the sorcerer's son—The fellowship of the dragon—Lady of the skulls—The snow queen—Ash, wood, fire—The stranger—Transmutations—The lion and the lark—The witches of junket—Star-crossed—Voyage into the heart—Toad.
    ISBN 0-441-01360-0
    1. Fantasy fiction, American. I. Title.

PS3563.C38H37 2005
813'.54—dc22

                           2005051311

PRINTED IN THE UNITED STATES OF AMERICA

10  9  8  7  6  5  4  3  2  1

*for Dave*

# Contents

# The Harrowing
# of the Dragon of Hoarsbreath

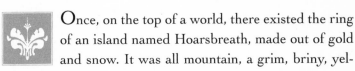 Once, on the top of a world, there existed the ring of an island named Hoarsbreath, made out of gold and snow. It was all mountain, a grim, briny, yellowing ice-world covered with winter twelve months out of thirteen. For one month, when the twin suns crossed each other at the world's cap, the snow melted from the peak of Hoarsbreath. The hardy trees shrugged the snow off their boughs and sucked in light and mellow air, pulling themselves toward the suns. Snow and icicles melted off the roofs of the miners' village; the snow-tunnels they had dug from house to tavern to storage barn to mine shaft sagged to the ground; the dead white river flowing down from the mountain to the sea turned blue and began to move again. Then the

miners gathered the gold they had dug by firelight out of the chill, harsh darkness of the deep mountain and took it down-river, across the sea to the mainland, to trade for food and furs, tools and a liquid fire called wormspoor because it was gold and bitter, like the leavings of dragons. After three swallows of it, in a busy city with a harbor frozen only part of the year, with people who wore rich furs, kept horses and sleds to ride in during winter, and who knew the patterns of the winter stars since they weren't buried alive by the snow, the miners swore they would never return to Hoarsbreath. But the gold waiting in the dark secret places of the mountain-island drew at them in their dreaming, lured them back.

For two hundred years after the naming of Hoarsbreath, winter followed winter, and the miners lived their rich, iso-lated, precarious lives on the pinnacle of ice and granite, cursing the cold and loving it, for it kept lesser folk away. They mined, drank, spun tales, raised children who were sent to the mainland when they were half-grown, to receive their education, and find easier, respectable lives. But always a few children found their way back, born with a gnawing in their hearts for fire, ice, stone, and the solitary pursuit of gold in the dark.

Then two miners' children came back from the great world and destroyed the island.

They had no intention of doing that. The younger of them was Peka Krao. After spending five years on the mainland, boring herself with schooling, she came back to Hoarsbreath to mine. At seventeen, she was good-natured and sturdy, with dark eyes, and dark, braided hair. She loved every part of Hoarsbreath, even its chill, damp shafts at midwinter and the bone-jarring work of hewing through darkness and stone to unbury its gold. Her instincts for gold were uncanny; she seemed to sense it through her fingertips touching bare rock. The miners called her their good luck. She could make wormspoor, too, one of the few useful things she had learned on the mainland. It lost its bitterness, somehow, when she made it: it aged into a rich, smoky gold that made the miners forget their sore muscles and inspired marvelous tales out of them that whittled away at the endless winter.

She met the Dragon-Harrower one evening at a cross section of tunnel between her mother's house and the tavern. She knew all the things to fear in her world: a rumble in the mountain, a guttering torch in the mines, a crevice in the snow, a crack of ice underfoot. There was little else she couldn't handle with a soft word or her own right arm. So when he loomed out of the darkness unexpectedly into her taper-light, she wasn't afraid. But he made her stop instinctively, like an animal might stop, faced with something that puzzled its senses.

His hair was dead white, with strands bright as wormspoor running through it; his eyes were the light, hard blue of dawn during suns-crossing. Rich colors flashed out of him everywhere in her light: from a gold knife hilt and a brass pack buckle; from the red ties of his cloak that were weighted with ivory, and the blue-and-silver threads in his gloves. His heavy fur cloak was closed, but she felt that if he shifted, other colors would escape from it into the cold, dark air. At first she thought he must be ancient: the taper-fire showed her a face that was shadowed and scarred, remote with strange experience, but no more than a dozen years older than hers.

"Who are you?" she breathed. Nothing on Hoarsbreath

glittered like that in midwinter; its colors were few and simple: snow, damp fur and leather, fire, gold.

"I can't find my father," he said. "Lule Yarrow."

She stared at him, amazed that his colors had their beginnings on Hoarsbreath. "He's dead." His eyes widened slightly, losing some of their hardness. "He fell in a crevice. They chipped him out of the ice at suns-crossing, and buried him six years ago."

He looked away from her a moment, down at the icy ridges of tramped snow. "Winter." He broke the word in two, like an icicle. Then he shifted his pack, sighing. "Do they still have wormspoor on this ice-tooth?"

"Of course. Who are you?"

"Ryd Yarrow. Who are you?"

"Peka Krao."

"Peka. I remember. You were squalling in somebody's arms when I left."

"You look a hundred years older than that," she commented, still puzzling, holding him in her light, though she was beginning to feel the cold. "Seventeen years you've been gone. How could you stand it, being away from Hoarsbreath so long? I couldn't stand five years of it. There are so many people whose names you don't know, trying to tell you about things that don't matter, and the flat earth and the blank sky are everywhere. Did you come back to mine?"

He glanced up at the gray-white ceiling of the snow-tunnel, barely an inch above his head. "The sky is full of stars, and the gold wake of dragon-flights," he said softly. "I am a Dragon-Harrower. I am trained and hired to trouble dragons out of their lairs. That's why I came back here."

"Here. There are no dragons on Hoarsbreath."

His smile touched his eyes like a reflection of fire across ice. "Hoarsbreath is a dragon's heart."

She shifted, her own heart suddenly chilled. She said tolerantly, "That sounds like a marvelous tale to me."

"It's no tale. I know. I followed this dragon through centuries, through ancient writings, through legends, through rumors of terror and deaths. It is here, sleeping, coiled around the treasures of Hoarsbreath. If you on Hoarsbreath rouse it, you are dead. If I rouse it, I will end your endless winter."

"I like winter." Her protest sounded very small, muted within the thick snow-walls, but he heard it. He lifted his hand, held it lightly against the low ceiling above his head.

"You might like the sky beyond this. At night it is a mine of lights and hidden knowledge."

She shook her head. "I like close places, full of fire and darkness. And faces I know. And tales spun out of wormspoor. If you come with me to the tavern, they'll tell you where your father is buried and give you lodgings, and then you can leave."

"I'll come to the tavern. With a tale."

Her taper was nearly burned down, and she was beginning to shiver. "A dragon." She turned away from him. "No one will believe you anyway."

"You do."

She listened to him silently, warming herself with wormspoor, as he spoke to the circle of rough, fire-washed faces in the tavern. Even in the light, he bore little resemblance to his father, except for his broad cheekbones and the threads of gold in his hair. Under his bulky cloak, he was dressed as plainly as any miner, but stray bits of color still glinted from him, suggesting wealth and distant places.

"A dragon," he told them, "is creating your winter. Have you ever asked yourselves why winter on this island is nearly twice as long as winter on the mainland twenty miles away? You live in dragon's breath, in the icy mist of its bowels, hoarfrost cold, that grips your land in winter the way another dragon's breath might burn it to flinders. One month out of the year, in the warmth of suns-crossing, it looses its ringgrip on your island, slides into the sea, and goes to mate. Its ice-kingdom begins to melt. It returns, loops its length around its mountain of ice and gold. Its breath freezes the air once more, locks the river into its bed, you into your houses, the gold into its mountain, and you curse the cold and drink until the next dragon-mating." He paused. There was not a sound around him. "I've been to strange places in this world, places even colder than this, where the suns never cross, and I have seen such monsters. They are ancient as rock, white as old ice, and their skin is like iron. They breed winter and they cannot be killed. But they can be driven away, into far corners of the world where they are dangerous to no one. I'm trained for this. I can rid you of your winter. Harrowing is dangerous work and usually I am highly paid. But I've been looking for this ice-dragon for many years, through its spoor of legend and destruction. I tracked it here, one of the oldest of its kind, to the place where I was born. All I ask from you is a guide."

He stopped, waiting. Peka, her hands frozen around her glass, heard someone swallow. A voice rose and faded from

the tavern kitchen; sap hissed in the fire. A couple of the miners were smiling; the others looked satisfied and vaguely ex-
pectant, wanting the tale to continue. When it didn't, Kor
Flynt, who had mined Hoarsbreath for fifty years, spat
wormspoor into the fire. The flame turned a baleful gold, and
then subsided. "Suns-crossing," he said politely, reminding a
scholar of a scrap of knowledge children acquired with their
first set of teeth, "causes the seasons."

"Not here," Ryd said. "Not on Hoarsbreath. I've seen. I
know."

Peka's mother Ambris leaned forward. "Why," she asked
curiously, "would a miner's son become a Dragon-Harrower?"
She had a pleasant, craggy face; her dark hair and her slow,
musing voice were like Peka's. Peka saw the Dragon-
Harrower ride between two answers in his mind. Meeting
Ambris's eyes, he made a choice, and his own eyes strayed to
the fire.

"I left Hoarsbreath when I was twelve. When I was fifteen, I saw a dragon in the mountains east of the city. Until
then, I had intended to come back and mine. I began to learn
about dragons. The first one I saw burned red and gold under the suns' fire; it swallowed small hills with its shadow. I
wanted to call it, like a hawk. I wanted to fly with it. I kept
studying, meeting other people who studied them, seeing
other dragons. I saw a night-black dragon in the northern
deserts; its scales were dusted with silver, and the flame that
came out of it was silver. I saw people die in that flame, and I
watched the harrowing of that dragon. It lives now on the
underside of the world, in shadow. We keep watch on all
known dragons. In the green midworld belt, rich with rivers

and mines, forests and farmland, I saw a whole mining town burned to the ground by a dragon so bright I thought at first it was sun-fire arching down to the ground. Someone I loved had the task of tracking that one to its cave, deep beneath the mine shafts. I watched her die, there. I nearly died. The dragon is sealed into the bottom of the mountain, by stone and by words. That is the dragon which harrowed me." He paused to sip wormspoor. His eyes lifted, not to Ambris, but to Peka. "Now do you understand what danger you live in? What if one year the dragon sleeps through its mating time, with the soft heat of the suns making it sluggish from dreaming? You don't know it's there, wrapped around your world. It doesn't know you're there, stealing its gold. What if you sail your boats full of gold downriver and find the great white bulk of it sprawled like a wall across your passage? Or worse, you find its eye opening like a third, dead sun to see your hands full of its gold? It would slide its length around the mountain, coil upward, and crush you all, then breathe over the whole of the island and turn it dead-white as its heart, and it would never sleep again."

There was another silence. Peka felt something play along her spine like the thin, quavering, arthritic fingers of wind. "It's getting better," she said, "your tale." She took a deep swallow of wormspoor and added, "I love sitting in a warm, friendly place listening to tales I don't have to believe."

Kor Flynt shrugged. "It rings true, lass."

"It is true," Ryd said.

"Maybe so," she said. "And it may be better if you just let the dragon sleep."

"And if it wakes unexpectedly? The winter killed my father. The dragon at the heart of winter could destroy you all."

"There are other dangers. Rockfalls, sudden floods, freezing winds. A dragon is simply one more danger to live with."

He studied her. "I saw a dragon once with wings as softly blue as a spring sky. Have you ever felt spring on Hoarsbreath? It could come."

She drank again. "You love them," she said. "Your voice loves them and hates them, Dragon-Harrower."

"I hate them," he said flatly. "Will you guide me down the mountain?"

"No. I have work to do."

He shifted, and the colors rippled from him again, red, gold, silver, spring-blue. She finished the wormspoor, felt it burn in her like liquid gold. "It's only a tale. All your dragons are just colors in our heads. Let the dragon sleep. If you wake it, you'll destroy the night."

"No," he said. "You will see the night. That's what you're afraid of."

Kor Flynt shrugged. "There probably is no dragon, anyway."

"Spring, though," Ambris said; her face had softened. "Sometimes I can smell it from the mainland, and I always wonder . . . Still, after a hard day's work, sitting beside a roaring fire sipping dragon-spit, you can believe anything. Especially this." She looked into her glass at the glowering liquid. "Is this some of yours, Peka? What did you put into it?"

"Gold." The expression in Ryd's eyes made her swallow sudden tears of frustration. She refilled her glass. "Fire, stone, dark, wood smoke, night air smelling like cold tree bark. You don't care, Ryd Yarrow."

"I do care," he said imperturbably. "It's the best wormspoor I've ever tasted."

"And I put a dragon's heart into it." She saw him start slightly; ice and hoarfrost shimmered from him. "If that's what Hoarsbreath is." A dragon beat into her mind, its wings of rime, its breath smoldering with ice, the guardian of winter. She drew breath, feeling the vast bulk of it looped around them all, dreaming its private dreams. Her bones seemed suddenly fragile as kindling, and the gold wormspoor in her hands a guilty secret. "It's a tale."

"Oh, go with him, lass," her mother said tolerantly. "There may be no dragon, but we can't have him swallowed up in the ice like his father. Besides, it may be a chance for spring."

"Spring is for flatlanders. There are things that shouldn't be wakened. I know."

"How?" Ryd asked.

She groped, wishing for the first time for a flatlander's skill with words. She said finally, "I feel it," and he smiled. She sat back in her chair, irritated and vaguely frightened. "Oh, all right, Ryd Yarrow, since you'll go with or without me. I'll lead you down to the shores in the morning. Maybe by then you'll listen to me."

"You can't see beyond your snow-world," he said implacably. "It is morning."

They followed one of the deepest mine shafts and clambered out of it to stand in the snow halfway down the mountain. The sky was lead gray; across the mists ringing the island's shores, they could see the ocean, a swirl of white, motionless ice. The mainland harbor was locked. Peka wondered if the ships were stuck like birds in the ice. The world looked empty and somber.

"At least in the dark mountain there is fire and gold. Here, there isn't even a sun." She took out a skin of wormspoor, sipped it to warm her bones. She held it out to Ryd, but he shook his head.

"I need all my wits. So do you, or we'll both end up preserved in ice at the bottom of a crevice."

"I know. I'll keep you safe." She corked the skin and added, "In case you were wondering."

But he looked at her, startled out of his remoteness. "I wasn't. Do you feel that strongly?"

"Yes."

"So did I, when I was your age. Now I feel very little." He moved again. She stared after him, wondering how he kept her smoldering and on edge.

She said abruptly, catching up with him, "Ryd Yarrow."

"Yes."

"You have two names. Ryd Yarrow and Dragon-Harrower. One is a plain name this mountain gave you. The other you got from the world, the name that gives you color. One name I can talk to, the other is the tale at the bottom of a bottle of wormspoor. Maybe you could understand me if you hadn't brought your past back to Hoarsbreath."

"I do understand you," he said absently. "You want to sit in the dark all your life and drink wormspoor."

She drew breath and held it. "You talk but you don't listen," she said finally. "Just like all the other flatlanders." He didn't answer. They walked in silence a while, following the empty bed of an old river. The world looked dead, but she could tell by the air, which was not even freezing spangles of breath on her hood fur, that the winter was drawing to an end. "Suns-crossing must be only two months away," she commented surprisedly.

"Besides, I'm not a flatlander," he said abruptly, surprising her again. "I do care about the miners, about Hoarsbreath. It's because I care that I want to challenge that ice-dragon with all the skill I possess. Is it better to let you live surrounded by danger, in bitter cold, carving half-lives out of snow and stone, so that you can come fully alive for one month of the year?"

"You could have asked us."

"I did ask you."

She sighed. "Where will it live, if you drive it away from Hoarsbreath?"

He didn't answer for a few paces. In the still day, he loosed no colors, though Peka thought she saw shadows of them around his pack. His head was bowed; his eyes were burning back at a memory. "It will find some strange, remote place where there is no gold, only rock; it can ring itself around emptiness and dream of its past. I came across an ice-dragon unexpectedly once, in a land of ice. The bones of its wings seemed almost translucent. I could have sworn it cast a white shadow."

"Did you want to kill it?"

"No. I loved it."

"Then why do you—"

But he turned at her suddenly, almost angrily, waking out of a dream. "I came here because you've built your lives on top of a terrible danger, and I asked for a guide, not a gadfly."

"You wanted me," she said flatly. "And you don't care

about Hoarsbreath. All you want is that dragon. Your voice is full of it. What's a gadfly?"

"Go ask a cow. Or a horse. Or anything else that can't live on this forsaken, frostbitten lump of ice."

"Why should you care, anyway? You've got the whole great world to roam in. Why do you care about one dragon wrapped around the tiny island on the top of nowhere?"

"Because it's beautiful and deadly and wrapped around my heartland. And I don't know—I don't know at the end of things which of us will be left on Hoarsbreath." She stared at him. He met her eyes fully. "I'm very skilled. But that is one very powerful dragon."

She whirled, fanning snow. "I'm going back. Find your own way to your harrowing. I hope it swallows you."

His voice stopped her. "You'll always wonder. You'll sit in the dark, drinking wormspoor twelve months out of thirteen, wondering what happened to me. What an ice-dragon looks like, on a winter's day, in full flight."

She hovered between two steps. Then, furiously, she followed him.

They climbed deeper into mist, and then into darkness. They camped at night, ate dried meat and drank wormspoor beside a fire in the snow. The night sky was sullen and starless as the day. They woke to gray mists and traveled on. The cold breathed up around them; walls of ice, yellow as old ivory, loomed over them. They smelled the chill, sweaty smell of the sea. The dead riverbed came to an end over an impassable cliff. They shifted ground, followed a frozen stream downward. The ice walls broke up into great jewels of ice, blue, green, gold, massed about them like a giant's treasure hoard. Peka stopped to stare at them.

Ryd said with soft, bitter satisfaction, "Wormspoor."

She drew breath. "Wormspoor." Her voice sounded small, absorbed by cold. "Ice jewels, fallen stars. Down here you could tell me anything and I might believe it. I feel very strange." She uncorked the wormspoor and took a healthy swig. Ryd reached for it, but he only rinsed his mouth and spat. His face was pale, his eyes red-rimmed, tired.

"How far down do you think we are?"

"Close. There's no dragon. Just mist." She shuddered suddenly at the soundlessness. "The air is dead. Like stone. We should reach the ocean soon."

"We'll reach the dragon first."

They descended hillocks of frozen jewels. The stream they followed fanned into a wide, skeletal filigree of ice and rock. The mist poured around them, so painfully cold it burned their lungs. Peka pushed fur over her mouth, breathed through it. The mist or wormspoor she had drunk was forming shadows around her, flickerings of faces and enormous wings. Her heart felt heavy; her feet dragged like boulders when she lifted them. Ryd was coughing mist; he moved doggedly, as if into a hard wind. The stream fanned again, going very wide before it met the sea. They stumbled down into a bone-searing flow of mist. Ryd disappeared; Peka found him again, bumping into him, for he had stopped. The threads of mist untangled above them, and she saw a strange black sun, hooded with a silvery web. As she blinked at it, puzzled, the web rolled up. The dark sun gazed back at her. She became aware then of her own heartbeat, of a rhythm in the mists, of a faint, echoing pulse all around her: the icy heartbeat of Hoarsbreath.

She drew a hiccup of a breath, stunned. There was a mountain cave ahead of them, from which the mists breathed and eddied. Icicles dropped like bars between its grainy white surfaces. Within it rose stones or teeth as milky white as quartz. A wall of white stretched beyond the mists, vast, earthworm round, solid as stone. She couldn't tell, in the blur and welter of mist, where winter ended and the dragon began.

She made a sound. The vast, silvery eyelid drooped like a parchment unrolled, then lifted again. From the depths of the cave came a faint rumbling, a vague, drowsy waking question: *Who?*

She heard Ryd's breath finally. "Look at the scar under its eye," he said softly. She saw a jagged track beneath the black sun. "I can name the Harrower who put that there three hundred years ago. And the broken eyetooth. It razed a marble fortress with its wings and jaws; I know the word that shattered that tooth, then. Look at its wing scales. Rimed with silver. It's old. Old as the world." He turned, finally, to look at her. His white hair, slick with mists, made him seem old as winter. "You can go back now. You won't be safe here."

"I won't be safe up there, either," she whispered. "Let's both go back. Listen to its heart."

"Its blood is gold. Only one Harrower ever saw that and lived."

"Please." She tugged at him, at his pack. Colors shivered into the air: sulfur, malachite, opal. The deep rumble came again; a shadow quickened in the dragon's eye. Ryd moved quickly, caught her hands. "Let it sleep. It belongs here on Hoarsbreath. Why can't you see that? Why can't you see? It's a thing made of gold, snow, darkness—" But he wasn't seeing her; his eyes, remote and alien as the black sun, were full of memories and calculations. Behind him, a single curved claw lay like a crescent moon half-buried in the snow.

Peka stepped back from the Harrower, envisioning a bloody moon through his heart, and the dragon roused to fury, coiling upward around Hoarsbreath, crushing the life out of it. "Ryd Yarrow," she whispered. "Ryd Yarrow. Please." But he did not hear his name.

He began to speak, startling echoes against the solid ice around them. "Dragon of Hoarsbreath, whose wings are of hoarfrost, whose blood is gold—" The backbone of the hoar-dragon rippled slightly, shaking away snow. "I have followed your path of destruction from your beginnings in a land without time and without seasons. You have slept one night too long on this island. Hoarsbreath is not your dragon's dream; it belongs to the living, and I, trained and titled Dragon-Harrower, challenge you for its freedom." More snow shook away from the dragon, baring a rippling of scale and the glistening of its nostrils. The rhythm of its mist was changing. "I know you," Ryd continued, his voice growing husky, strained against the silence. "You were the white death of the fishing island Klonos, of ten Harrowers in Ynyme, of the winter palace of the ancient lord of Zuirsh. I have harried nine ice-dragons—perhaps your children—out of the known world. I have been searching for you for many years, and I came back to the place where I was born to find you here. I stand before you armed with knowledge, experience, and the dark wisdom of necessity. Leave Hoarsbreath, go back to your birthplace forever, or I will harry you down to the frozen shadow of the world."

The dragon gazed at him motionlessly, an immeasurable ring of ice looped about him. The mist out of its mouth was for a moment suspended. Then its jaws crashed together, spitting splinters of ice. It shuddered, wrenched itself loose from the ice. Its white head reared high, higher, ice booming and cracking around it. Twin black suns stared down at Ryd from the gray mist of the sky. Before it roared, Peka moved.

She found herself on a ledge above Ryd's head without remembering how she got there. Ryd vanished in a flood of mist. The mist turned fiery; Ryd loomed out of it like a red shadow, dispersing it. Seven crescents lifted out of the snow, slashed down at him, scarring the air. A strange voice shouted Ryd's name. He flung back his head and cried a word. Somehow the claw missed him, wedged deep into the ice.

Peka sat back. She was clutching the skin of wormspoor against her heart; she could feel her heartbeat shaking it. Her throat felt raw; the strange voice had been hers. She uncorked the skin, took a deep swallow, and another. Fire licked down her veins. A cloud of ice billowed at Ryd. He said something else, and suddenly he was ten feet away from it, watching a rock where he had stood freeze and snap into pieces.

Peka crouched closer to the wall of ice behind her. From her high point she could see the briny, frozen snarl of the sea. It flickered green, then an eerie orange. Bands of color pinioned the dragon briefly like a rainbow, arching across its wings. A scale caught fire; a small bone the size of Ryd's forearm snapped. Then the cold wind of the dragon's breath froze and shattered the rainbow. A claw slapped at Ryd; he moved a fraction of a moment too slowly. The tip of a talon caught his pack. It burst open with an explosion of glittering colors. The dragon hooded its eyes; Peka hid hers under her hands. She heard Ryd cry out in pain. Then he was beside her instead of in several pieces, prying the wormspoor out of her hands.

He uncorked it, his hands shaking. One of them was seared silver.

"What are they?" she breathed. He poured wormspoor on his burned hand, then thrust it into the snow. The colors were beginning to die down.

"Flame," he panted. "Dragon-flame. I wasn't prepared to handle it."

"You carry it in your pack?"

"Caught in crystals, in fire-leaves. It will be more difficult than I anticipated."

Peka felt language she had never used before clamor in her throat. "It's all right," she said dourly. "I'll wait."

For a moment, as he looked at her, there was a memory of fear in his eyes. "You can walk across the ice to the mainland from here."

"You can walk to the mainland," she retorted. "This is my home. I have to live with or without that dragon. Right now there's no living with it. You woke it out of its sleep. You burnt its wing. You broke its bone. You told it there are people on its island. You are going to destroy Hoarsbreath."

"No. This will be my greatest harrowing." He left her suddenly and appeared flaming like a torch on the dragon's skull, just between its eyes. His hair and his hands spattered silver. Word after word came out of him, smoldering, flashing, melting in the air. The dragon's voice thundered; its skin rippled and shook. Its claw ripped at ice, dug chasms out of it. The air clapped nearby, as if its invisible tail had lifted and slapped at the ground. Then it heaved its head, flung Ryd at the wall of mountain. Peka shut her eyes. But he fell lightly, caught up a crystal as he rose, and sent a shaft of piercing gold light at the upraised scales of its underside, burrowing toward its heart.

Peka got unsteadily to her feet, her throat closing with a sudden whimper. But the dragon's tail, flickering out of the mist behind Ryd, slapped him into a snowdrift twenty feet away. It gave a cold, terrible hiss; mist bubbled over everything, so that for a few minutes Peka could see nothing beyond the lip of the ledge. She drank to stop her shivering. Finally, a green fire blazed within the white swirl. She sat down again slowly, waited.

Night rolled in from the sea. But Ryd's fires shot in raw, dazzling streaks across the darkness, illuminating the hoary, scarred bulk of dragon in front of him. Once, he shouted endless poetry at the dragon, lulling it until its mist-breath was faint and slow from its maw. It nearly put Peka to sleep, but Ryd's imperceptible steps closer and closer to the dragon kept her watching. The tale was evidently an old one to the dragon; it didn't wait for an ending. Its head lunged and snapped unexpectedly, but a moment too soon. Ryd leaped for shelter in the dark, while the dragon's teeth ground painfully on nothingness. Later, Ryd sang to it, a whining, eerie song that showered icicles around Peka's head. One of the dragon's teeth cracked, and it made an odd, high-pitched noise. A vast webbed wing shifted free to fly, unfolding endlessly over the sea. But the dragon stayed, sending mist at Ryd to set him coughing. A foul, ashy-gray miasma followed it, blurring over them. Peka hid her face in her arms. Sounds like the heaving of boulders and the spattering of fire came from beneath her. She heard the dragon's dry roar, like stones dragged against one another. There was a smack, a musical shower of breaking icicles, and a sharp, anguished curse. Ryd appeared out of the turmoil of light and air, sprawled on the ledge beside Peka.

His face was cut, with ice, she supposed, and there was blood in his white hair. He looked at her with vague amazement.

"You're still here."

"Where else would I be? Are you winning or losing?"

He scooped up snow, held it against his face. "I feel as if I've been fighting for a thousand years . . . Sometimes, I think I tangle in its memories, as it thinks of other Harrowers, old dragon-battles, distant places. It doesn't remember what I am, only that I will not let it sleep . . . Did you see its wingspan? I fought a red dragon once with such a span. Its wings turned to flame in the sunlight. You'll see this one in flight by dawn."

She stared at him numbly, huddled against herself. "Are you so sure?"

"It's old and slow. And it can't bear the gold fire." He paused, then dropped the snow in his hand with a sigh and leaned his face against the ice-wall. "I'm tired, too. I have one empty crystal, to capture the essence of its mist, its heart's breath. After that's done, the battle will be short." He lifted his head at her silence, as if he could hear her thoughts. "What?"

"You'll go on to other dragons. But all I've ever had is this one."

"You never knew—"

"It doesn't matter that I never knew it. I know now. It was coiled all around us in the winter, while we lived in warm darkness and firelight. It kept out the world. Is that such a terrible thing? Is there so much wisdom in the flatlands that we can't live without?"

He was silent again, frowning a little, either in pain or faint confusion. "It's a dangerous thing, a destroyer."

"So is winter. So is the mountain, sometimes. But they're also beautiful. You are full of so much knowledge and experience that you forgot how to see simple things. Ryd Yarrow, miner's son. You must have loved Hoarsbreath once."

"I was a child, then."

She sighed. "I'm sorry I brought you down here. I wish I were up there with the miners, in the last peaceful night."

"There will be peace again," he said, but she shook her head wearily.

"I don't feel it." She expected him to smile, but his frown deepened. He touched her face suddenly with his burned hand.

"Sometimes I almost hear what you're trying to tell me. And then it fades against all my knowledge and experience. I'm glad you stayed. If I die, I'll leave you facing one maddened dragon. But still, I'm glad."

A black moon rose high over his shoulder and she jumped. Ryd rolled off the ledge into the mists. Peka hid her face from the peering black flare. Blue light smoldered through the mist, the moon rolled suddenly out of the sky, and she could breathe again.

Streaks of dispersing gold lit the dawn sky like the sunrises she saw one month out of the year. Peka, in a cold daze on the ledge, saw Ryd for the first time in an hour. He was facing the dragon, his silver hand outstretched. In his palm lay a crystal so cold and deathly white that Peka, blinking at it, felt its icy stare into her heart.

She shuddered. Her bones turned to ice; mist seemed to flow into her veins. She breathed bitter, frozen air as heavy as water. She reached for the wormspoor; her arm moved sluggishly, and her fingers unfolded with brittle movements. The dragon was breathing in short, harsh spurts. The silver hoods were over its eyes. Its unfolded wing lay across the ice like a limp sail. Its jaws were open, hissing faintly, but its head was reared back, away from Ryd's hand. Its heartbeat, in the silence, was slow, slow.

Peka dragged herself up, icicle by icicle. In the clear wintry dawn, she saw the beginning and the end of the enormous ring around Hoarsbreath. The dragon's tail lifted wearily behind Ryd, then fell again, barely making a sound. Ryd stood still; his eyes, relentless, spring-blue, were his only color. As Peka watched, swaying on the edge, the world fragmented into simple things: the edges of silver on the dragon's scales, Ryd's silver fingers, his old-man's hair, the pure white of the dragon's hide. They faced one another, two powerful creatures born out of the same winter, harrowing one another. The dragon rippled along its bulk; its head reared farther back, giving Peka a dizzying glimpse of its open jaws. She saw the cracked tooth, crumbled like a jewel she might have battered inadvertently with her pick, and winced. Seeing her, it hissed, a tired, angry sigh.

She stared down at it; her eyes seemed numb, incapable of sorrow. The wing on the ice was beginning to stir. Ryd's head lifted. He looked bone-pale, his face expressionless with exhaustion. But the faint, icy smile of triumph in his eyes struck her as deeply as the stare from the death-eye in his palm.

She drew in mist like the dragon, knowing that Ryd was not harrowing an old, tired ice-dragon, but one out of his memories who never seemed to yield. "You bone-brained dragon," she shouted, "how can you give up Hoarsbreath so easily? And to a Dragon-Harrower whose winter is colder and more terrible than yours." Her heart seemed trapped in the weary, sluggish pace of its heart. She knelt down, wondering if it could understand her words or only feel them. "Think of Hoarsbreath," she pleaded, and searched for words to warm them both. "Fire. Gold. Night. Warm dreams, winter tales, silence—" Mist billowed at her and she coughed until tears froze on her cheeks. She heard Ryd call her name on a curious, inflexible note that panicked her. She uncorked the wormspoor with trembling fingers, took a great gulp, and coughed again as the blood shocked through her. "Don't you have any fire at all in you? Any winter flame?" Then a vision of gold shook her: the gold within the dragon's heart, the warm gold of wormspoor, the bitter gold of dragon's blood. Ryd said her name again, his voice clear as breaking ice. She shut her eyes against him, her hands rising through a chill, dark dream. As he called the third time, she dropped the wormspoor down the dragon's throat.

The hoods over its eyes rose; they grew wide, white-rimmed. She heard a convulsive swallow. Its head snapped down; it made a sound between a bellow and a whimper. Then its jaws opened again and it raked the air with gold flame.

Ryd, his hair and eyebrows scored suddenly with gold, dove into the snow. The dragon hissed at him again. The stream beyond him turned fiery, ran toward the sea. The great tail pounded furiously; dark cracks tore through the ice. The frozen cliffs began to sweat under the fire; pillars of ice sagged down, broke against the ground. The ledge Peka stood on crumbled at a wave of gold. She fell with it in a small avalanche of ice-rubble. The enormous white ring of dragon began to move, blurring endlessly past her eyes as the dragon gathered itself. A wing arched up toward the sky, then another. The dragon hissed at the mountain, then roared desperately, but only flame came out of its bowels, where once it had secreted winter. The chasms and walls of ice began breaking apart. Peka, struggling out of the snow, felt a lurch under her feet. A wind sucked at her hair, pulled at her heavy coat. Then it drove down at her, thundering, and she sat in the snow. The dragon, aloft, its wingspan the span of half the island, breathed fire at the ocean, and its husk of ice began to melt.

Ryd pulled her out of the snow. The ground was breaking up under their feet. He said nothing; she thought he was scowling, though he looked strange with singed eyebrows. He pushed at her, flung her toward the sea. Fire sputtered around them. Ice slid under her; she slipped and clutched at the jagged rim of it. Brine splashed in her face. The ice whirled, as chunks of the mountain fell into the sea around them. The dragon was circling the mountain, melting huge peaks and cliffs. They struck the water hard, heaving the ice-floes farther from the island. The mountain itself began to break up, as ice tore away from it, leaving only a bare peak riddled with mine shafts.

Peka began to cry. "Look what I've done. Look at it." Ryd only grunted. She thought she could see figures high on the top of the peak, staring down at the vanishing island. The ocean, churning, spun the ice-floe toward the mainland. The river was flowing again, a blue-white streak spiraling down from the peak. The dragon was over the mainland now, billowing fire at the harbor, and ships without crews or cargo were floating free.

"Wormspoor," Ryd muttered. A wave ten feet high caught up with them, spilled, and shoved them into the middle of the channel. Peka saw the first of the boats taking the swift, swollen current down from the top of the island. Ryd spat out seawater, and took a firmer grip of the ice. "I lost every crystal, every dragon's fire I possessed. They're at the bottom of the sea. Thanks to you. Do you realize how much work, how many years—"

"Look at the sky." It spun above her, a pale, impossible mass of nothing. "How can I live under that? Where will I ever find dark, quiet places full of gold?"

"I held that dragon. It was just about to leave quietly, without taking half of Hoarsbreath with it."

"How will we live on the island again? All its secrets are gone."

"For fourteen years I studied dragons, their lore, their flights, their fires, the patterns of their lives and their destructions. I had all the knowledge I thought possible for me to acquire. No one—"

"Look at all that dreary flatland."

"No one," he said, his voice rising," ever told me you could harrow a dragon by pouring wormspoor down its throat!"

"Well, no one told me, either!" She slumped beside him, too despondent for anger. She watched more boats carrying miners, young children, her mother, down to the mainland. Then the dragon caught her eye, pale against the winter sky, somehow fragile, beautifully crafted, flying into the wake of its own flame.

It touched her mourning heart with the fire she had given it. Beside her, she felt Ryd grow quiet. His face, tired and battered, held a young, forgotten wonder, as he watched the dragon blaze across the world's cap like a star, searching for its winter. He drew a soft, incredulous breath.

"What did you put into that wormspoor?"

"Everything."

He looked at her, then turned his face toward Hoarsbreath. The sight made him wince. "I don't think we left even my father's bones at peace," he said hollowly, looking for a moment less a Dragon-Harrower than a harrowed miner's son.

"I know," she whispered.

"No, you don't," he sighed. "You feel. The dragon's heart. My heart. It's not a lack of knowledge or experiences that destroyed Hoarsbreath, but something else I lost sight of: you told me that. The dark necessity of wisdom."

She gazed at him, suddenly uneasy, for he was seeing her. "I'm not wise. Just lucky—or unlucky."

"Wisdom is a flatlander's word for your kind of feeling. You put your heart into everything—wormspoor, dragons, gold—and they become a kind of magic."

"I do not. I don't understand what you're talking about, Ryd Yarrow. I'm a miner; I'm going to find another mine—"

"You have a gold mine in your heart. There are other things you can do with yourself. Not harrow dragons, but become a Watcher. You love the same things they love."

"Yes. Peace and quiet and private places—"

"I could show you dragons in their beautiful, private places all over the world. You could speak their language."

"I can't even speak my own. And I hate the flatland." She gripped the ice, watching it come.

"The world is only another tiny island, ringed with a great dragon of stars and night."

She shook her head, not daring to meet his eyes. "No. I'm not listening to you anymore. Look what happened the last time I listened to your tales."

"It's always yourself you are listening to," he said. The gray ocean swirled the ice under them, casting her back to the bewildering shores of the world. She was still trying to argue when the ice moored itself against the scorched pilings of the harbor.

# A Matter of Music

Cresce Dami was the daughter of Yrida Dami, teacher for thirty-nine years at the great Bardic School at Onon. When she was three, Cresce began learning simple, ancient rhymes. When she was five, she was given eight different instruments and seven years to learn how to play them. By the time she was fifteen, she could sing the hundred and one Songs of Changing Fortune of the reclusive hill-people of Jazi. She could tune the strings of her cyrillaya to any of the nine changes passed through centuries from the first Bard of Onon. She knew to play the trihorne for the salute to anyone below the rank of a king; the flute for the funeral of a king's child; the cyrillaya for fanfares of death and victory at the hunt for anyone attached to the king's court at Hekar; the lovely, reedy cothone that looked like a cow's bag with eight teats only when she was asked. Then she was told that the difficult part of her studies was just beginning. When she was twenty-one she was given a new set of instruments made by each of her teachers, and the information that the Lords of Daghian had requested a bard. And that night the heavy rafters of the dark, smoky tavern the students frequented rocked with laughter, songs, and glasses emptied and broken with high-pitched trihorne notes in her honor.

"I am going to become a Bard of Daghian," she said for the fortieth time. Ruld Egemi, who had been her friend since she was eight and her lover since she was nineteen, nodded and laughed. A trihorne note, a wail out of the long brass throats tuned to battle, shattered the glass in his hand, spilling spiced wine over them both. He laughed again, and she stared, swallowing, at the curve of his mouth and the conjunction of bones at his throat. "I'm going to leave you."

He looked too drunk and happy to realize it. "I'll come to Daghian. Maybe in a year," he said. "Maybe they'll hire me to play the trihorne fanfares for death at private hunts, if nothing else."

"If you play the trihorne for that in Daghian," someone said, pulling up a chair with a screech, "you'll wind up in Jazi playing for corn-dances until you're ninety. The Lords of Daghian claim equal rank with the king."

"You play the cyrillaya for no one but the king or his relatives, or anyone acting in his name, at a hunt," Ruld said stubbornly. "Isn't that right, Cresce?"

"The Lords of Daghian are of the king's bloodline; if you use the trihorne that would be a mortal insult. That's right, isn't it, Cresce?"

"They're of a bastard line—"

"They are of an ancient, powerful line, and you sing one version of the Battle of Hekar Pass to them, and another to the king—"

The tavern keeper mopped up the wine on the table and set steaming glasses down with a flourish. People even from beyond the city came to his small, ancient tavern to hear the students sing and play to one another as they drank. The rare nights of the rampant trihorne and shattered wineglasses were a ritual amply paid for. Cresce smiled at him without seeing him; she heard the argument without listening. She leaned back in Ruld's shadow, her mind running over things she had packed. The case of resin, soft cloth, oils, and spare reeds Ruld had given her. Clothes. Blankets and skins, for Daghian was beyond the mountains, and she might not always find lodgings as she traveled. The set of tiny pipes her father had carved for her when she was a child. His cothone, which was the only instrument of his she had not burned when he died. The cothone, with its many haunting voices, was her instrument, tuned to the deepest voices within herself, as the trihorne in Ruld's hands became his own voice. The love of the cothone she had inherited from her father, and his strong, skilled fingers. Her small bones, her straight black hair, her face with its wide-set eyes and wide cheekbones, she had inherited from her mother's hill-blood, the streak of Jazi in her that made their songs throb in her blood as she sang them.

"Cresce—"

The argument was beginning to heat. Slapping her hand down on the table, she said, "Hear me!" Then she whispered, tuned to their silence, "Oh, hear. To the courts of the King at

Hekar nine hundred years ago came the riches and glory of the kingdom. To the vanquished court at Daghian came the first Bard of Onon, possessing nothing but the cyrillaya. To him, not to the king, the Lords of Daghian gave honor. In his memory, the ritual music of the royal instrument, the cyrillaya, honors the Lords of Daghian." She lifted her hand, closed it, gripping their attention. "And if you dare remind the Lords of Daghian with a trihorne that the king outranks them, they will tie you in a knot around it."

Ruld, hovering in her spell with his chair balanced on one leg, brought it upright with a crash. "Play," he said. "Play the cothone." His eyes were suddenly as she loved to see them, dark, intense with desire. Then she heard an echo of her own words in her head, and a chill shot through her, turning her hands icy.

"I am going to Daghian. Bards have left Hekar itself to go to Daghian. Oh, Ruld, how do I dare? They'll laugh at the cothone. I'm so small they won't see me when I stand up to play. My reeds will squeak."

"The Lords of Daghian expect from Onon the best the school has to offer. The musicians chose you," Ruld said. "Play the cothone."

She slid the strap from her shoulder and stood up. She put the pipe to her mouth, drew from the soft, tanned skin full of air deep, haunting phrases, the wordless voices half-heard at twilight, from dark forests, from the far side of still lakes. Then, leaving one soft, low note weaving through the air, she added voices to it from the fourth and seventh pipes, the pipes of longing and of passion. She played her longing; the full, humming notes of the cothone called it out of her bones, out of her heart's marrow. There was not a sound or movement in the tavern. Faces were blurred beyond her, torch fire shivering over them. Their silence played to her song. Then, beside her, Ruld's trihorne began to weave its pure, fiery voice into the voices of the cothone. The long horn slid in her slow rhythm through its changes. It was a stroke of pure gold under the smoky torchlight. Her throat swelled; she played simple, ancient Jazi music while the tears of sorrow and happiness burned down her face.

She rode out of Onon the next morning before sunrise. It was midautumn; she wore a long, heavy coat split down the back for riding, and high boots lined with sheepskin. Her instruments were encased in furs and skins; they made odd, bulky shapes on her shadow as the sun rose. She sang to keep her voice warm. Her song broke in puffs of mist in front of her. The fear in her was gone. She was the daughter of Yrida Dami, who had played at Hekar five years for the king; and the teachers of Onon had chosen her above all the musicians to send to the proud, critical court at Daghian. She got out one of her tiny pipes as the morning warmed and answered back to the birds flying around her.

It took her twelve days to reach Daghian. She sang some nights at wayside inns, earning money for lodgings and supplies. She watched the weary faces of travelers ease as they listened to her. They were simple folk, who knew and loved the cothone, and she felt well paid by their silence. As she neared the mountains, even farmhouses became scarce. The pass through the mountains whistled with wild, empty autumn winds. She camped at night then, sitting close to her fire, singing ballads back at the winds in her deep, sweet voices. She saw the last leaves ripped from the trees as she rode. River water shimmered white with the wind's white breath. The mountains at morning were ghostly with mist. But the loneliness of the pass did not reach her heart. She was Cresce Dami, going to Daghian, and even the winds knew it was bad luck to harm a bard.

On the twelfth day, she reached the other side of the mountains and saw the flatlands veined with rivers, and the courts and cities built among them. Each river had a name; each was the name of a battle site, and each battle had spawned ballads of a dozen variations: one to be sung on a street corner, one at the market square under a mayor's window, one at Hekar, one at Daghian . . . Before she was fourteen, Cresce had learned them all. She headed her horse down the hillside toward a main road.

The court of the Lords of Daghian lay in wild country. Dark pine moaned of winter as she traveled down the winding road to Daghian. But she heard, shimmering across hard, empty fields, the timbreless, haunting notes of the cyrillaya, tuned to the victory of the hunt within the forests. Riders swept across the fields, their rich cloaks of deep green, blood-red, gold, and brown whirling behind them like leaves in the wind. They would feast, Cresce knew, on the kill, and she would be there, silent and anonymous, until the bones were picked, and servants brought washing bowls of scented water, and more wine. Then she would stand, interrupting their hunting stories, drawing their wine-flushed faces toward her, like the faces in the tavern, with a sweep of a hunting phrase across the cyrillaya.

*I am Cresce Dami, Bard of Onon. Lords, hear me! I will tell you a tale of the hunt stranger than any hunt you have ever ridden to the cyrillaya of victory . . .*

Then she saw the court of the Lords of Daghian.

It was a small city within vast double walls of black stone. She counted eight towers and the great Keep, old as any song out of Daghian. Within, a massive, soaring building, half castle, half fortress, sprawled on a rise of land. The flame of Daghian snapped above it in the wind: a blood-red pennant a dozen feet long, bordered with gold. The hunters were riding through the broad gates. They swung shut again ponderously, but Cresce knew that no door in the kingdom would refuse to admit a Bard of Onon.

Twilight was falling when she reached the gates. The guards recognized her odd bundles of instruments, the cothone in its case about her neck. The gates had begun to open even before she spoke. She heard a sound that thrilled her to the marrow: notes of a trihorne splashing across the evening, raised in the ancient salute to a Bard of Onon. The passage between the walls was torchlit. When she rode out of it into the yard, men were waiting to take her horse.

She slung her instrument cases about her and walked into the great hall of the Lords of Daghian.

Firelight, the smell of hot meat, and the voices of close to a thousand people talking and laughing rolled at her as she crossed the threshold. She stopped, her heart thudding at the sheer immensity of the place. There were nine open fire beds scattered through the hall; on each the carcasses of deer and boar turned slowly on their spits. Long tables surrounded them in rough disorder; red light caught at the faces of richly dressed men, women, and children, plates of silver and gold, cups and ewers of dyed glass. Groups of musicians played near each fire bed. They used flutes and harps, pipes and small drums. They were sweating; pitchers of water and wine stood near them, and trays of sliced fruits. Their listeners, at first glance, seemed oblivious to them. But Cresce saw young boys running too close to one group called sharply to order. She watched the great gathering of the court of Daghian. Beneath their laughter and conversation, the men and women seemed sensitive to every change in rhythm and song, and sometimes broke off mid-sentence to applaud an intricate passage of music.

Cresce smiled a little. Then a servant spoke to her, led her to a place at one of the outer tables. She put her instruments down and took off her coat. Relief musicians sat at the table; their own instruments were scattered along the benches. Their eyes flicked to her instruments, her face, in sudden comprehension. She saw the respect in their faces, but they did not speak to her. She would break her silence at the court of Daghian only one way. She sat down, her fingers trembling slightly. She ate the food brought to her without tasting it, her mind tuned to all the nuances of sound around her.

Finally, the intensity of voices seemed to slacken. Charred bones were removed from the fire-beds; servants began to dispense towers of finger bowls, trays full of pitchers of scented water, pitchers of wine, and great platters of sweet-meats and nuts. Musicians around the fire-beds drew their playing to a close. The relief musicians, their eyes on Cresce, began reaching for their instruments. Her throat swelled suddenly, as if she had swallowed air from a cothone. She stood up, drew the cyrillaya from its case. The musicians dropped back into their seats, watching her with a combination of wonder and excitement, as if she had walked out of a legend in front of them.

Their table was half in shadow, and she was hardly taller than the boys who had been scolded for running. So she climbed on top of the table, stood under the flare of torch-light. The cyrillaya flared silver as she lifted it. She plucked the taut strings softly, tuned a couple. Then she pulled the mute out of the silver throat that amplified the taut, pure notes until not even a trihorne's brilliance could overwhelm it. She swept her hand across the strings; even the boys wrestling in the shadows and the servants with piles of dirty plates stopped moving.

Standing on the table, she could see the three Lords of Dahgian, their wives, and an assortment of relatives. The older men were smiling, but there was not a flicker of expression on the faces of the Lords. One, the youngest, turned to another suddenly, opened his mouth. She stopped him with a single phrase: the first notes of the battle cry of Daghian. Then his face blurred into all the others as she drew breath, and said, "I am Cresce Dami, Bard of Onon. Lords of Daghian, the winds of autumn batter your walls; the flame of Daghian burns bright against the cold. Let me tell you a tale . . ." Her fingers skimmed over rhythms of the chase. "A long time ago . . ." Then because somebody was coughing, and a pair of lovers in the far corner had begun to whisper, and because the cyrillaya held pride and beauty, but the cothone held all her soul, she let the bright instrument drop to her side and swung the cothone into her hands. A low, plaintive call, the wind soughing among bog-reeds where stags drank, filled the hall.

She had startled the Lords. She had also startled the musicians, whose mouths dropped with astonishment. The cothone was a herdsman's instrument, an instrument for rough songs and long nights in the open, during battles or hunts. She wondered when it had been last played at an open feast in the hall.

Some of the guests were glancing at the Lords, wondering whether or not they had been insulted. But the Lords had not made up their minds. Cresce, her voice clear, steady in spite of her sudden nervousness, built out of words and sounds the cold winter's day, the crows' crying in the frozen sky, the slow pace of the young Lord Sere as he tracked a great stag who was not a stag through the marshes of Daghian.

Something was pulling at the hem of her skirt. The first faint tug had stopped her throat, but the cothone had droned on without her. The pulling persisted, but all her training forbade moving. She realized that one of the young children, attracted by her forbidden stance on the table, was mutely demanding to be lifted up. She tried to ignore it, hoping one of the musicians would see it. But the hall was shadowy behind her, and the musicians were caught up in her tale. She drew out of the second pipe the quick staccato flash of distant hunting horns, as the hunters that Sere had become separated from called to him. Her long, full skirt began flapping to the rhythm like a sail.

One of the musicians gasped; she heard a ripple of laughter from the closer tables. She stepped forward on two beats, pulling her skirt out of the child's grip. Her foot struck one of the musicians' drums with a hollow thump, knocked it off the table. It thumped again on the bench, and once more on the ground. The musician grabbed at it, but the child pounced on it first and sat on it.

A servant swept the child off the floor, and returned the drum to the musician, but Cresce's throat had dried in the sudden laughter. Some of the women were talking. They quieted quickly as Cresce continued, but the words scratched in her throat. Then the thing too terrible to consider happened:

the reed in the eighth pipe, dry with cold, split as she played a stag's bellow. The deep bellow ran up into a strangled squeal, and dogs napping all over the hall started up howling at the sound.

They were slapped into silence almost instantly. But all through the room, men and women were weeping with laughter. Even one of the Lords had turned his face away, shaking. The older Lord beside him stared carefully down at his hands. The third Lord did not move. His eyes were narrowed slightly and he was not smiling. The musicians seemed transfixed. Cresce dropped the cothone mechanically, shifted the cyrillaya back into her hands almost without losing a beat. But her heart was pounding raggedly, and the cyrillaya sounded too pure, almost colorless, after the rich, plaintive voices of the cothone. She swept the sound of Sere's last arrow soaring above the marshes to strike at the heart of the stag.

She heard a low murmuring from the men. Wine sloshed over the rims of their cups as they turned to one another. Cresce, her voice wavering a little, realized that muted arguments were flaring all over the room. She cast back desperately, wondering what she had done wrong. The cyrillaya was in tune; her voice was still strong and in key. She wondered if there was some ancient custom forbidding the playing of the cyrillaya to follow the cothone. But she would have remembered. Then she saw the agonized faces of the musicians, and the blood swept completely out of her face.

In her nervousness, she had skipped an entire section of the tale. Men who knew it vaguely were trying to remember what was wrong. Old hunters who knew it well were telling them. Some were even singing it softly. Sere's first glimpse of the legendary stag, and his arduous, exhausting chase that lasted for three days and three nights through the marshes — she had jumped over it entirely when she switched instruments.

A whole table of scarred hunters was beginning to take up the passage. Their cups were waving to the melody; as one forgot the lines, another took them up. Cresce, her fingers shaking, picked up their melody on the cyrillaya. She sang with them, trying to coax the song away from them. But their beat was ragged, their lines jumbled, and they were content with their wine and their voices.

The children had begun to talk again. Some of the people were still listening, but Cresce knew it was out of pity, because they could hardly hear her. She had lost their attention. Her hands were trembling badly; she did not dare look at the musicians. Her voice was beginning to stick in her throat; her face was burning, and her lips were dry. A servant collecting wine pitchers let them clatter together on his tray. She knew, even without looking toward the Lords, that the sound was the judgment of Daghian.

She almost stopped. The men singing, holding out their cups for more wine, would scarcely have noticed. The Lords of Daghian would send her back to Onon anyway in the morning. She thought of Ruld, the wine cup shattering between them, signaling the end of her life at Onon, and knew suddenly that she could never go back. Nor would she stay at Daghian, even for a night. She would finish her song and then leave. In the darkness of the autumn night, she would decide what to do.

So she lifted her trihorne, blew a great, discordant blast on it. Singers and servants stopped short; one of the Lords choked on his wine. She said gravely into the sudden silence blasting back at her,

"And so, Lords, in the frail, ice-colored twilight melting across the marshes of Daghian, the Lord Sere first glimpsed the great animal he tracked."

They were outraged. She saw it in their faces. But she gave them no time to tell her what they thought. Pitching the cyrillaya to vibrate the stone walls, she sent the enormous stag running through the hall to vanish again into the winter dusk. Then she used every instrument she possessed as Sere followed it. Her drum beat his horse's hooves; the haunting sixth pipe of the cothone, the pipe of warning, tracked his passage through the dangerous, moonlit marshes. Her small pipes brought the sun up, as marsh birds called to one another across the wastes. Her twelve-stringed harp, unexpectedly gentle after the cyrillaya, played again and again the brief, wondrous glimpses of the stag that lured Sere deeper and deeper into the marshlands. The death of his exhausted horse as it struggled vainly in the deep mud it had stumbled into, she played on the cothone; the drum beat its dirge. The red sun flared to the trihorne's salute across the morning of the third day. The hoarfrost on every tree limb, on every blade of grass, burned in Sere's eyes; the winds ringing in the ice-world she struck on tiny tubular bells. The cothone played Sere's exhaustion, his hunger, his obsession as he broke a path on foot through the lonely, fiery world. Finally, he saw the great stag clearly. The trihorne rang its turning as it stopped and faced him.

His last arrow soared with the cyrillaya, burned into nothingness before it reached the stag. In Sere's world of ice and silence, only the drum beat the slow steps of the white stag as it came toward him. Sere, weaponless, strengthless, lay where he had fallen, watching it come. He looked into its eyes. For two beats, there was no sound in the great hall of Daghian. Then the brass stag's bell of the trihorne faded into the slow, pure voice of the flute as the stag faded into a woman whose eyes were the color of winter nights. She turned again, moved slowly away from Sere into the glittering winds. Flute notes ascended, shaped a great, dark bird, whirled to its flight as it vanished into the light. The cothone brought twilight once again over the world. Horses' hooves snapped over the bog-ice. The hunters found Sere, half-dead of cold and hunger. The spare, comfortless voices of the fourth pipe, the pipe of longing, wept with his weeping as he rode with them back to Daghian.

The cothone stilled in Cresce's hands. She let it fall, stood looking out over the motionless hall. The faces were shadowed by the dying fires. She bowed her head to the Lords of Daghian. But before she could turn to leave, a musician beside one of the fire-beds leaped to his feet. He threw back his head, raised the trihorne to his mouth. The single high, piercing note set wineglasses ringing like ice all over the hall before they shattered.

The youngest Lord of Daghian rose. There was a sudden clamor from the men at the tables. Cresce, her heart thudding in her throat, realized suddenly that they were shouting requests to her for other ballads. Her hands, so steady as she played, began to shake badly. The Lord of Daghian overtook a servant bringing a wine cup to her. He brought it himself, held it up to her as she stood frozen on the tabletop.

"Welcome. I am Sere of Daghian." He had wild, dark hair burnished with red and a lean, proud face like a bird of prey. But his eyes were smiling. He added, "The hunter was my grandfather. Drink."

She took the cup of chilled, spiced wine and drained it. He signaled to the relief musicians; they rose, took their places, while logs thrown on the fire-beds illumined the hall once more. Servants were dispensing cups, sweeping up glass. They were smiling, Cresce noticed, in spite of the extra work. She found herself able to move again, and she sat down abruptly on the edge of the table.

"I was about to leave," she whispered.

"I know." He sat on the table beside her. "I would have followed you. This is Daghian, not Hekar, where you would have been tossed into the autumn winds for playing the cothone at an open feast. I handle matters of music at Daghian, and I have never in my life heard the cothone played like that." He paused a moment, studying her. "You are Jazi."

"My mother was a hill-woman. My father met her when he went to Jazi for a year to learn the Songs of Changing Fortune."

"Have you been there?"

"To Jazi? No. I was born at Onon. My father taught there. I've never been anywhere except Onon."

"Taught? Is he dead?"

She nodded. "They're both dead." She added after a moment, "I burned all his instruments except his cothone when he died."

"I have a cothone," he said, almost abruptly. He was silent a little, frowning at some memory. Then the smile slid back into his eyes. "That was my son, pulling on your skirt. He's three. I'll teach him to show more respect for a Bard of Daghian. But you won't be standing on tabletops after this."

Her hands slid to the table edge, gripped it. "Lord. Do you want me to stay?"

"Do I want you to stay?" He ran both his hands through his hair, and the shadow in his eyes lifted, giving her a glimpse of his wonder. "Look at the high table. The big, dark-haired Lord with the face carved by a blunt knife is my brother Breaugh. The fair-haired, hot-tempered man beside him is my brother Hulme. They have heard that tale of Sere and the stag hunt a hundred times. And yet from the time you blew that sour note on the trihorne, until the musician spilled all our wine with his trihorne, I could have sworn neither one of them breathed. You will honor Daghian. Besides," he added, standing up again, "I want you to teach me to play the cothone."

She played again before the feast was ended. Men sang hunting ballads with her; musicians added their own rich, soft accompaniment. Finally, past midnight, the hall began to empty, and the musicians put away their instruments. They introduced themselves to her, left her head spinning with half a hundred names. Then she met the two older Lords of Daghian.

"Breaugh handles matters of estate," Sere explained, "and Hulme matters of peace and war. I handle matters of music, which is the pride of Daghian." He introduced their wives to her. But of his own wife, he said nothing, and she wondered. As he was leaving the hall with her, to show her where she would live in the great house, he stopped suddenly, as if to tell her something. But he changed his mind. Later, before she fell asleep, she found herself wondering again. Then the appalling memory of her near-disaster washed over her. She flung the bedcovers over her head and curled up in the darkness, listening to her heart pound until she fell asleep.

She sang and played nearly every evening then, either in

the great hall or in the Lords' chambers if they dined privately. She played for the hunt, if there were guests from the king's court. She taught new musicians the ritual music for such occasions as weddings, namings, funerals, and welcoming salutes to various officials and guests. She taught Lord Sere the cothone; she taught Hulme's wife the harp, and Breaugh's oldest daughter the flute. Some nights she was so tired that she played through her dreams and woke exhausted. But there was a happiness in her that flashed out in her music, even on the most sullen autumn evenings.

Sere learned the cothone very quickly. He already played the trihorne and the cyrillaya, but Cresce sensed something in him that woke to the haunting voices of the cothone. He used a very old instrument. Its pipes were pitched differently from Cresce's instrument; they were scrolled all over with delicate carving and bound to the kidskin with gold. The deep pipe, the pipe of mourning, was so low it seemed to breathe through Cresce's bones whenever she played it. She wondered often where he had gotten it. One day he told her.

"It was my wife's."

They were in a room in one of the oldest wings of the house. It was full of instruments: ancient pipes, flutes, drums of painted tree bark that were from Jazi, harps of varying sizes, from a five-stringed harp fashioned to a rough triangle of oak, to a thirty-stringed harp of pure gold that had been played only once, on someone's wedding day. There were trihornes of a hundred battles; there was the cyrillaya that the first Bard had carried into Daghian. There were instruments so old that Cresce had only seen drawings of them. She had been given keys to the various cases, and she loved the room. Sere practiced there because the old walls were three feet thick, and his brothers could not hear the squeals and nasal drones he startled out of the cothone before he began to master it.

He sat down on one of the window ledges, letting the cothone rest on his knee. The thick glass behind his head warped the cloudy landscape into a formless mist. When he did not continue, Cresce asked softly, "Is she dead?"

He shook his head. "I don't know. Like you, she is half-Jazi." He was silent again, frowning down at the cothone. He said abruptly, harshly, to the cothone, "She was so beautiful. Her eyes were true Jazi gray, gray as marsh mist at dusk. Her hair was so black it blinded me sometimes. We had known each other always. But one day she left me and didn't come back. She took only a horse I had raised for her. She left me our son and her cothone."

"It's—" Cresce had to stop to clear her throat. "It's older than anyone living. That cothone."

"I know. It belonged to her great-grandmother. She had been taken forcibly from Jazi by a Lord of Daghian, as the army of Daghian marched through the hills to attack Hekar from the north."

She drew breath suddenly. "Hekar Pass."

"You sing one version in Daghian, and another to the king. The army of Daghian was massacred in the hills by the king's army. Only nine men and one hill-woman survived to come back to Daghian. Men of Jazi betrayed Daghian's position to the king. With some justice." He touched the rings of gold on the cothone. "I think we had stolen their Bard. That was seventy years ago. Since then, no man of Daghian has been permitted in Jazi."

"So you couldn't look for your wife."

"No. The last man of Daghian who went to Jazi was found at our gates wrapped in corn husks. There wasn't a mark on him, but he was dead. I think the hills called her until she went back to them."

Cresce sat down beside him on the window ledge. She said softly, "Bards of Onon are permitted in Jazi, even during their most private rituals. I could take a message to her."

He looked at her. Then he dropped his arm around her shoulders. "Thank you." She realized suddenly how rarely he smiled. "But I think that, like the woman my grandfather followed through the marshes, she doesn't want to be found."

A few days later, men from Hekar on the king's business came to speak to the Lords of Daghian. Cresce sang for them, playing at Sere's request both the cyrillaya and the cothone. Later one of the men spoke privately to her, suggesting that Hekar would be a more suitable place for her great gift, since the king would never ask her to play a herdsman's instrument at his court. She told that to Sere, and he laughed. But he was annoyed. When the Lords took the visitors from Hekar hunting in the waning days of autumn, Cresce rode with them to sound the fanfares of death. But Sere, with a ghost of malice in his eyes, had insisted she bring only her cothone. Breaugh and Hulme had grown so used to hearing the cothone that they scarcely noticed. But the visitors, after she played the fanfare for a stag's death, were insulted. They said little, for they were in the middle of the Daghian marshes and could not have left the hunt without getting lost. But Cresce wished she had disregarded Sere and brought the cyrillaya instead. Its silvery voice would have broken through shreds of mists hanging over the marshes. The cothone seemed to gather mist, to bring it closer around them until the riders that she followed seemed shadowy, and Sere's cloak, striped gold and red, was the one clear point in the world.

She sounded fanfares for a deer, a brace of hare, a wild boar that charged unexpectedly out at them from some trees. The mists deepened in the early afternoon, until she had no idea which direction Daghian lay. She heard Breaugh suggest calmly that in another hour they should start back. The visitors agreed quickly. Someone sighted another deer; there was a short chase, and then Cresce heard Sere ahead of her, calling for a fanfare. She raised the cothone; the deep pipe of mourning sent the announcement of its death across the marshes.

Then the mists closed about her completely. Softly, from the other side of the mists, a cothone began to play.

How long she listened, she never knew. Its voices were deep, melding layer upon layer of fanfares across the marshes. Sitting breathless, motionless on her horse, she heard fanfares for the deaths of men and animals mingling with phrases from the winter rituals of Jazi. Slowly the salutes to death came to an end. Only the seventh pipe, with a rich, husky timbre she had never heard before, still sang through the mists. It troubled her, stirring things in her she felt she should have remembered but could not. She did not remember lifting her own cothone. But suddenly she was playing it in answer to the wild, unfamiliar music, while she guided her horse deeper into the marshes trying to find the other side of the mists.

Something swirled out of the mist; a shadow pulled at her reins. She realized for the first time that she had been moving. She let her cothone fall. At the same time the strange music stopped. She heard only the lonely cry of a marsh bird and the faint trickle of water. She shuddered suddenly. Then she recognized the rider beside her.

Neither of them spoke for a moment. Then Sere, whose face was expressionless, colorless in the mist, said only, "Sometimes the marshes pull you deeper into them when you're trying to get out. Sound the battle-call of Daghian, so that Breaugh and Hulme know I've found you. We'll have to smell our way home through this mist."

Not long afterward, on the first day of winter, the long silence between Daghian and Jazi was broken. One of the porters at the main gates interrupted the Lords as they sat after supper listening to their ancient steward giving his seasonal account of their household, lands, and finances. Hulme was stifling a yawn when the porter murmured to him, and dropped something that looked vaguely like a bird's nest onto the table. Cresce, playing the muted cyrillaya, strained a little to see what the odd jumble was. Her thumb slipped off a string, struck a sour note, and Sere looked at her. She colored hotly. Then she saw the expression in his eyes.

"Please," he said. "Come here."

"Someone nailed this clutter with an arrow to the gate?" Hulme said incredulously. He fingered a dried corn husk. It rustled secretly under his touch. Then he eyed Sere. "What's the matter with you?" he said roughly. Some of the blood came back into Sere's face at his tone. The steward tossed his pen down with a sigh.

Breaugh said, "Let's see the arrow." The porter gave it to him. He touched its tip, then looked at Sere, and then at Hulme. "Bone. It's a hill-arrow. Look at the holes in its tip."

"It whistled," the porter said.

"It's a matter of peace and war," Breaugh said shortly, and turned back to the account book. But his brows were drawn. "Have we offended Jazi lately?"

"How would I know?" Hulme demanded. "We offend Jazi by breathing." He shoved his chair back suddenly, stood up. He added to the porter, "All right. Let us know if you get shot." He stood behind Sere, laid his hands on his brother's shoulders. "Corn husks. That's all I understand of it. Remember the man they left at our doorstep bound from hair to heel in corn husks." He touched a flat, thin tongue of wood. "What is that?"

"A reed." Sere's eyes had not moved from Cresce's face as she gazed down at the odd bundle of items. "A cothone reed. The arrow sings. Hulme, it's a matter of music. A reed like that fits into one of the mouthpieces of the cothone. Which pipe?"

Cresce picked it up. Her voice slid suddenly deep, husky. "The fourth. The pipe of longing."

There was silence. Sere's face was expressionless. Breaugh picked up a strip of leather studded with tiny jewels. "It looks like a piece of bridle. And nine dead leaves . . . But what—"

Sere moved abruptly. He stood up, went to one of the windows to stare out at the night. When no one spoke, he said to Cresce, "Is the singing arrow a part of their rituals?"

She nodded a little jerkily. "In winter and spring." She picked up the hollow arrow, blew into the shaft. The pitch was deep. "In winter, for the rituals of Changing Fortune, they pitch them low, to sing with the pipe of mourning."

"Winter." he turned. Thoughts were breaking into his eyes. "The ritual. When is it?"

"The ninth day of winter."

"And the leaves?"

No one moved. He stepped back to the table. Hulme, breathing something, caught his arm as he reached for them.

"Think," he said flatly. "If you go into Jazi, it is no longer a matter of music. If they kill you, it's a matter of war. If Daghian goes to war against Jazi, the king will be at our throats faster than a mad bog-wolf."

"Take the issue to Hekar," Sere said shortly. "Demand justice from the king."

The blood flared into Hulme's face; he looked for a moment as if Sere had struck him. "If I find you wrapped in corn husks on our doorstep, I'm supposed to crawl to Hekar to beg for justice? For that?"

"Hulme—"

"What kind of justice did Hekar show Daghian at Hekar Pass?"

"That was seventy years ago."

"Jazi went to Hekar for justice then—an entire army slaughtered over one woman. That's the worthless bone of justice Hekar would toss to us. If she wants to see you, why can't she come here? Tell me that. You send her a message: a leaf of black hellebore for every year she's been away, wrapped in bark from the scarred birch trees in Hekar Pass. In nine centuries Daghian hasn't begged so much as a rat-dropping from Hekar. And you expect us to go begging for justice as if—as if we were subject—"

Sere turned. His fists rose and slammed down on the table, spilling ink across the account book. "Will you be reasonable! I'm not even dead, yet!"

The three men glared at one another, while the steward stared in horror at the mess. Then Breaugh growled, "Oh, sit

down." He righted the inkstand. "Oak leaves." He looked at
Sere. "There is no oak in Daghian until you reach the far side
of the marshes. The border hills are covered with it."

"Breaugh—" Hulme said.

"If he wants to go looking for his wife among ten thousand
oak trees, it's his business. If he gets killed, then it's our business. Until then, it's not a matter of war or estate or music—
it's a private affair." He reached across the table suddenly,
stirred the corn husks with one finger. "What's that?"

"Birch bark," said the steward wearily. Sere unrolled the
dry fragment of yellowish bark gently. He gazed down at it a
moment, then looked at Cresce. "I can't read music."

"Read it," Breaugh grunted. "You don't read it, you listen
to it."

"At Onon, they wrote changeless ritual music—salutes,
hunting fanfares, wedding and funeral music—so that we
could memorize it quickly." She studied the square notes
pricked into the bark with red dye. Then the notes came together in her mind and she started.

Sere said, "What is it?"

"The trihorne salute to the Bard of Daghian." There was
another silence. Then Sere crumpled the bark in one hand,
and Cresce said, astonished, "It's an invitation."

"An invitation to what?" Hulme asked sourly. She looked
at him without seeing him, envisioning a land beyond ten
thousand oak, the land whose heart-voice was the cothone.

"To their winter ritual. The Bard of Daghian is welcome . . ." She turned to Sere, her brows slanting upward
perplexedly. "And you, also?"

"Invited," he said. He touched one of the minute blue jewels on the bridle, his face harsh with conflicting memories.

"Not necessarily welcome." She watched him a moment, uneasy, glimpsing his emotions like a complex instrument she had not been trained to play.

Breaugh said softly, "It is a matter of music."

The cothone sang to her deeply, distantly, out of the mists. "May I go?" she asked, drawing Sere abruptly back from his past. She saw herself then as he saw her: small and dark-haired, a Jazi woman in spite of her background and rigorous training, who might vanish forever among the hills she had never seen.

"No." Then he touched her shoulder, his voice gentler. "No. Not when the invitation is pinned to the gate with an arrow. Not this time." And, oddly, she was relieved at his reply.

But he went, quietly and alone, at dawn. He returned twelve days later, with one of the watch parties Hulme had sent after him. He looked weary and bad-tempered; his replies to questions his brothers asked were brief. But, alone with Cresce after supper, he showed her a second bundle of corn husks.

"I found it pinned to an oak on the other side of the mountain."

She drew out the arrow and opened the message carefully. Three reeds dropped out, a ring of white horsehair, a gold ring, and some dried oak leaves. "You didn't see her?"

"She wasn't there." He added, as she fingered the reeds, "The horse I gave her was white."

"But why—"

"I don't know. Yes, I do. The invitation was for you. I didn't bring you." She stared at him, bewildered, and he added, "Will you come with me?"

"But, Lord, I don't understand. Why does she want me?"

"She." He drew breath, closing his eyes. "I don't even know if she's still alive. I only know someone is reaching out of Jazi, luring me with memories, you with music."

"I am Bard of Daghian," Cresce said a little stiffly. She blew into the arrow. Its pitch was high, light. "Spring. Seven oak leaves. The seventh day of spring." Something caught at her throat. "Lord, at one point in the spring rituals, the cothone is played from sunrise to sunrise. At that time, all visiting Bards are permitted to play."

He held up the ring. "Look. It took me an entire morning to recognize that."

She took it, circled it with her thumb and finger. "It's from a cothone . . . a very old one, like the cothone your wife left you . . ."

"I think they want you to bring that cothone."

She closed her fingers over the ring, uneasy again at the tale being spun out of the darkness, within the unknown land, herself being moved skillfully within the tale.

Sere said, "Look at the reeds."

She picked them up. "The fourth again. The pipe of longing. The eighth . . ."

"The pipe of mourning. That one I recognized." She turned the third reed in her hand. When she did not speak, he looked at her. "What is it?"

"The sixth. The pipe of warning."


On the first day of spring, they left Daghian together. At Breaugh's suggestion, Sere wore plain, rough-woven clothes, a cloak and boots of sheepskin, as if he were some herdsman the Bard of Daghian had hired to guide her across the marshes. Hulme suggested only that if Sere found himself dead and buried in corn husks, he should not bother coming home; the men of Daghian would come to Jazi to get him. The frozen marshes were still furrowed with ice. But the wild, violent spring winds, humming every voice of the cothone, had swept the sky clear, and the hills bordering Jazi looked very close. They crossed the marshes in five days. Cresce listened for the strange cothone, but the only sound she heard was the discordant babble of marsh birds returning after winter. She wondered: *Did I dream it?* and knew she had not. Sere was lost in his own dreams. He had spoken very little as they traveled together. At evenings, she pitched her music to ease into the mist of his memories, draw him back into the quiet night, the dark, rich smell of the marshes, the tiny circle of light that enclosed them. Sometimes she would lead him so far out of his mists that he would lift his head to meet her eyes across the fire. Then he would smile, acknowledging her skill, and she would wish they were back in Daghian, where life was complex and exact, and the language of the heart was not spoken in corn husks.

On the afternoon of the fifth day, they rode out of the thinning marsh trees into the ancient, rolling hills of Jazi.

They were covered, as far as Cresce could see, with bare, tangled oak. Nothing, human or animal, seemed to live among the trees. The voice of the wind had changed as they came out of the marshes. It piped with a spare, hollow timbre through the empty curves and shadows of the hills. Cresce wondered what instruments the musicians of Jazi, hearing that wind, had fashioned to match its voice.

"There," said Sere. He was pointing to one gnarled tree. "That's where I found the last message."

The trunk was bare. Cresce glanced vaguely at the endless forests. "My mother lived among these hills," she said surprisedly, as if she had just realized it. "Lord, we have two days to find the place where they hold their rituals."

"I know." But neither of them moved. The oak shadows strained down the faces of the hills, flung back by the westering sun. The air smelled of emptiness.

"Well, what should we do?"

He shook his head a little. Then he said, "You're a bard. They're expecting you. Let them know you're here."

She thought a moment. Then she lifted her cothone and blew on the first pipe, the pipe of joy, the opening phrases of the first Song of Fortune for the spring ritual.

There was a silence. The lovely fragment of song faded away. Sere turned to her, half-smiling, the tenseness wearing away from his face. Before he could speak, the empty oaks themselves sang an answer: every voice of the cothone echoing and overlapping one another in the salute to the Bard of Daghian.

Men on beautiful, long-legged hill horses rode out of the trees. Sere caught at Cresce's reins, but they came too fast. They surrounded Cresce and Sere, their horses weaving in and out of one another in a complex circle. The men carried hawks with fierce golden eyes on their shoulders; around their wrists small pipes dangled from leather thongs. The men were wiry and dark, with wide, high cheekbones and eyes that had taken their color from the winter mists. Only one of them, half a head taller than the others, had hair bright as copper, and eyes as golden as the hawks'. It was he who reached out finally, without speaking, caught Sere by the neck of his cloak, and wrenched him from his horse to the ground.

The men slid off their horses then; the ring of horses melted away. The hawks stirred, crying harshly as the men grappled with Sere. Their arms locked around him so tightly he could not struggle. One of the men gripped his hair, jerked his head back. His mouth opened; hands full of corn-husks pushed down over his face.

Cresce, frozen on her horse, saw his body begin to convulse. She snatched air and her trihorne at the same time. The note she blasted down at the men loosened their hold of both Sere and the corn husks. They looked up at her, pained, incredulous, while Sere, half-conscious, dragged at the wind. She said to the red-haired man, whose eyes were as furious as the hawks' eyes at the sound,

"If you kill him, I will play the winter Songs of Fortune at your spring rituals. Every note backwards."

He straightened, gripped her reins lightly. His head gave a little, frightened shake. But there was no fear either in his face or his voice when he spoke. "No." Behind him, the men shifted, easing their grip on Sere. "You are the Bard of Daghian?"

"Yes."

"You're part Jazi."

She nodded, her throat dry. She realized he was younger than Sere, even younger than she, and Sere's own hair held the same touch of burnished copper. Her eyes widened. "You're part Daghian."

The muscles in his face knotted. "True. Bard. In ancient hill language, the words were interchangeable." He turned, bent over Sere. Cresce could not see what he did, but Sere's body jerked, then sagged in the hill-men's hands. The men lifted him, threw him facedown across Cresce's saddlebow.

She put her hand beneath his throat, but she could not tell, with her own racing pulse, if he were still alive. She stared at the empty hills, the silent men with their eyes of mist, and suddenly she began to cry.

"All he came to do was find his wife!"

Their faces changed. They surrounded her, speaking quickly, worriedly, all at the same time so that she could hardly understand them. She gathered, wiping the tears angrily off her face, that nothing but respect was ever shown to a bard in Jazi, that she should not be afraid, that the people of Jazi showed peace and courtesy toward all strangers except those of Daghian, who were scarcely human anyway, and that a bard's tears would salt the cornfields, and they would be grateful if she would stop crying. At that point Sere's head lifted; he muttered something thickly. The hilt of a knife caught him behind the ear, silencing him again. The red-haired man took Cresce's reins in his hand, flicked the pipes at his wrist to his mouth, and called his horse with three quick notes. The other men were gathering their horses. For a moment the air flurried with light, tangled music. Someone caught Sere's horse, which was headed back toward the marshes. Then, in a long single file, they escorted Cresce into Jazi.

The hills parted on the other side, to join other hills ringing a plain where the people of Jazi farmed. A river, slow and green, wandered through it, sending a veinwork of streams through rougher pastureland where flocks of sheep grazed. Out of the center of the plain something shaped like an enormous black arch rose over a circle of barren ground. Scattered around the arch, among the threads of streams, were houses of oak and stone, sheds, barns, and walled fields. At the edge of the fallow field, in front of the arch, stood a gigantic oak. Its boughs seemed to have stretched out to gather years and centuries. In the oval of earth its vast shadow swept, nothing stood except a great dwelling of black stone.

Its outer walls were open to all light, wind, and weather. The harsh, twisted shadow of the oak probed through the dark archways in its walls. Light from the setting sun rimmed one wall of arches with fire. Cresce remembered something that her father had told her, long ago, about the black house at the edge of Forever where the Bards of Jazi lived.

She broke her long silence, asked the young, red-haired man beside her, who rode his horse and wore the hawk on his shoulder as if they were extensions of him, "Who played the cothone to welcome me?"

He was silent so long she thought he had not heard. But finally he said, "The Bard of Jazi."

"The Bard played a Daghian salute? But how did she know I was from Daghian? How—" The question snagged suddenly in her throat. "Who—What is your name?"

He looked at her with the odd mixture of bitterness and courtesy in his eyes. "Hroi Tuel. And yours, Bard?"

"Cresce Dami. Who is the Bard of Jazi?"

He held her eyes a moment longer. Then he lifted Sere's head by the hair, let it drop again. "His wife."

They reached the black house under the ancient oak at twilight. Someone had sounded a salute at the edge of the village. Women with torches, trays of food and wine, met Cresce as she dismounted, welcomed her, smiling. They wore her face. Some of them had grown up with her mother. They asked questions about her mother's life in Onon, if she had been happy, how she had died. They were oblivious to Sere, as if he were a saddle pack slung across Cresce's horse. But she saw a couple of men bring him into the house. The women took her inside, into one of the inner rooms. A brazier warmed it; oil lamps lit the rough, colorful tapestries on the black walls, the oak chairs and chests covered with sheepskins. The men had left Sere lying among Cresce's possessions on the rugs. The women, assured by Cresce repeatedly that they could do nothing more for her, left finally.

She knelt beside Sere, turned his head gently. Blood had dried in his hair, crusted on the side of his face. She washed it away as well as she could and covered him with sheepskins. Then she sat watching him, her arms tight around her knees. She heard steps in another part of the house, the voices of the women again. Then something that sounded like a horn moaned the salute to the Bard of Hekar across the village, and she closed her eyes, hid her face against her knees.

A quarter of an hour later, the Bard of Hekar himself appeared at her door.

He was twice her age, a richly dressed, fair-haired man with a thin, lined face and a sour expression in his eyes. He said nothing to Cresce; his lean, sensitive musician's hands searched the crusted wound in Sere's hair and the dark bruise on his jaw. Then he sat back on his heels, and demanded, "Why? Why did you bring him into Jazi?"

She slid her wrists over her ears. "Don't shout at me."

"Do you realize what will happen if he dies here? I don't know how you managed to keep him alive this long."

"I cried. They said it would ruin their crops."

He was silent, gazing at her. A corner of his mouth twisted unwillingly. "Cresce Dami. You played the cothone for men of the king's court while they hunted at Daghian last autumn. What would your father have said?"

"Did you know my father?"

"I was a musician at Hekar the five years he was Bard there. I have been at Hekar since I was born." He ran his hands through his hair, jerked his head at Sere. "Why did he come? If he dies here, Daghian will go to war against Jazi, and Hekar will be forced to war against Daghian. You and I will play battle charges on opposite fields."

She said his name softly. "Ytir Agora. The Bard with the throat of gold."

"There is not much chance to sing on a battlefield," he said bitterly. He stood up. "Daghian fool," he muttered to Sere's unresponsive face. Then he whirled at her. "Why?"

"I don't know why! Ask the Bard of Jazi—she sent for him! She's his wife." She stood up under his amazed stare. "Where is she, anyway?"

"In the hills, sounding salutes. There are other bards coming. That makes no sense! Does she want him dead?"

She stared numbly down at Sere. "I don't know."


She met the Bard of Jazi at midnight. Sere had wakened finally; he seemed surprised at being alive. He drank a little wine, then drifted to sleep again. Bards from other courts and cities introduced themselves to Cresce. They seemed, like the people of Jazi, to regard Sere as an embarrassment, of possible concern only if he were dead. When they left, Cresce sat playing the cothone softly, droning slow dark notes out of the eighth pipe. Finally, she heard someone ride to the doors of the house and dismount. There were voices, murmuring, indistinct, and then quick footsteps through the quiet house.

Cresce let her cothone rest. A woman entered breathlessly, sending the still lamp flames flickering all over the room.

She was as beautiful as Sere had said. Her black hair hung in thick braids to her waist, gold thread woven through them. Her eyes were wide-set, a deep, tempestuous, autumn gray. She was taller than Cresce, almost as tall as Sere, which betrayed her mixed heritage, but gave her a grace and suppleness even in the shapeless bulky skirts and tunics the Jazi women wore. Her eyes went to Sere and then to Cresce, sitting mute with the cothone in her hands. She said nothing; she only knelt beside Cresce, held her tightly a moment. Then she turned to Sere, stroked his face until he woke.

He whispered, "Lelia."

Her throat suddenly swollen, as with deep, unsounded cothone notes, Cresce got up quickly then and left them.

She went outside, into the night. The spring winds had blown stars like seed through the sky above the plain. The moon sat like a white bird on the black gate into Forever. The enormous oak tree murmured like a muted cyrillaya under the wind's touch. Cresce walked in its black moon-shadow toward the edge of the barren field.

She stood looking at the hard, silvery earth, the immense archway the winds were blowing through. Something her father had said teased her mind. Something about a great circle of cothone players around that field, trying to coax an answer from the silence within that arch. In the distance, the river burned a path through the dark plain. She turned away from the field, followed the edge of a tiny stream that made a half-circle, tracing the shadow of the oak.

Outside the great wings of the oak, she saw Hroi Tuel,

restless in the moonlight, flicking pebbles into the stream with a great hawk asleep on his shoulder.

She sat down beside him. He said nothing; she watched rings form and flow into one another as the pebbles dropped. She asked him the simplest question first, her voice stilling his hand.

"Would you have killed Sere?"

"Yes."

"Then why did she call him to Jazi?"

He shrugged. "No one questions the Bard of Jazi. She changes fortune."

"What if she leaves with him, goes back to Daghian?"

"She is not free." He swept his arm in an arch across the stars. "She is not free. So they say. I think the Bards of Jazi bind themselves. And I don't believe in fortune."

She bowed her face against her knees, blocking the stars from her vision. Her hands clenched, a rare, untrained movement. She said carefully, "When the army of Daghian passed through Jazi seventy years ago, they did more than abduct one woman. True?"

"Nine men of Daghian," he said harshly, "survived the battle of Hekar Pass. They knew the truth, but that truth was never spoken in Daghian. Even today, seventy years later, there are children born in Jazi with hair pale as cornsilk. Or red, like mine. Hekar Pass was a matter of justice."

She lifted her head again. "I have her cothone—the woman taken by the Lord of Daghian. Was she a bard?"

"They say so. For seven years after she left, the river was burned dry by the sun, and what sheep the army left in Jazi starved because the pastures dried. She wasn't there to change fortune." He was silent. Then he sent a fistful of pebbles spattering into the water, and faced her. "Is it because I'm part Daghian that I don't believe that? When you said today that you would play the winter rituals if we killed the Daghian, the other men were frightened. Maybe they are old enough and wise enough to be afraid."

"I don't know. How would I know?"

"You are half-Jazi and a bard. You should know."

"I know the Songs of Changing Fortune. I don't know anything about fortune." She picked up one of his pebbles suddenly, sent it skimming down the stream. "This much is true: the Bard of Jazi controls Sere's fortune."

"She brought you. She brought you both."

"Are the Bards of Jazi always women?"

"No. The Bards of Jazi are chosen by the dead."

She felt something shiver through her bones. "How?"

He shrugged again, the hawk clinging in its sleep to his shoulder as to a swaying tree. "I don't know." For the first time, his voice seemed free of bitterness, dragged into wonder. "In Jazi, the dead are burned, and their ashes blow through the gates of Forever into that bare ground. You tell me how the dead can play the cothone."

"You've heard it," she whispered.

"Once. When Lelia Daghian played the cothone at the spring rituals. No one even knew her name . . ." His shadowed, eyeless face turned again to Cresce as she shuddered. He reached out, gripped her shoulder with a steady hawk's grip. "She was from Daghian. Chosen by the dead."

She stared at the mask the moon made of his face. "It's a matter of music. No more."

"I try to believe that." His hand loosened until it lay very gently on her shoulder. "Men and women of Jazi killed by that Daghian army were burned and scattered through those gates . . . I don't know what to believe. My father is Overlord of Jazi, and I am his red-haired son. And the part of me born to hate Daghian is also drawn to the world beyond Jazi. I can't sleep at nights; my dreams are torn in two, from not knowing . . . You are half-Jazi, Bard of Daghian, and the dead will listen to you play. What will you do?"

She rose, splashed across the shallow stream. Facing him again, she could see his eyes, bitter, haunted, the huge hawk awake on his broad shoulder.

He said, "Where will you go, Bard? Back to Daghian? You are not free. Neither of us is free."

In the black house again, curled under sheepskin in the darkness, she heard the words again and again, hounding her into sleeplessness.

She woke with a start at midmorning. Sere was up, washing the dried blood out of his hair in a basin of water. He turned at her question.

"She went up into the hills again to welcome the visitors." His face was white, drawn; he looked oddly peaceless.

She said anxiously, "I thought you would be happier."

He frowned down at her, not seeing her. "There are women here with hair as fair as Hulme's." He turned back to the basin, stared at his reflection in the bloody water. "Something stinks in Daghian history, and the smell is blowing out of Hekar Pass. No wonder they hate us."

"She doesn't." Cresce sat up, pushing hair out of her eyes, trying to see. "She doesn't hate you. Why did she put you in so much danger?"

"She wanted me to come to her. She can't go back to Daghian. She is Bard of Jazi—the fortune of Jazi."

Her lips parted on a sudden breath. "You can't. You can't stay here. You are a Lord of Daghian. There's nothing here but sheep. They'll kill you, and your brothers will come—"

"You stop them." He knelt at her side suddenly, raised her cold fingers and kissed them. "Bard of Daghian, sing the truth of Hekar Pass to Daghian."

She stared at his bent head, the strokes of copper in his wet, tangled hair. She said, her voice shaking, "How do I know what the truth is?"

She rode out of the village an hour later to speak to the Bard of Jazi. The music of the Bard's salutes guided Cresce through the plain, then high up into the hills. A horn call rolled through the valleys, bidding welcome to a group of bards traveling down a road cut between the hills. The Bard herself stood on the crest of a hill overlooking them. As Cresce drew nearer, she recognized the twisted, bone-white horn, made of pieces of ram's horn bound together with gold. Its tone was strong, bright; only the fading cadences frayed to a hollowness, like the wind's voice.

The Bard did not seem surprised to see Cresce. She stilled the horn and watched Cresce dismount. Facing her, Cresce saw then what she had seen in Hroi Tuel, and later, in Sere: a confusion, a peacelessness.

She said huskily, "When I came to Daghian, the first ballad I sang was of Sere, and his hunting of the stag that was not a stag. Or maybe it was a stag after all. I never wondered before this. What was Sere really following through the mists? A stag? A woman? A bird? Or something else? When I look at you, I don't understand what I'm seeing. What are you doing? Are you trying to kill Sere?"

"I don't think so." She stood for a moment under Cresce's

incredulous gaze, her hands tight on the ram's horn. Then she took Cresce's arm, led her to a sheepskin rug laid on the bare ground. "Sit down, Cresce Dami. Never, never could I have been Bard of Daghian. But I played my great-grandmother's cothone since I was a child, and in Jazi, that one instrument is enough."

"Why did you leave Daghian?"

"Look at me. Old, old men of Jazi say that I am the bard that the army of Daghian stole, returned at last to Jazi. I am their fortune."

"Are you?"

"Perhaps." She was silent, her thoughts indrawn. "Perhaps. Maybe their only fortune is hope, which I give them. I don't know. I am my own misfortune."

"Why?" she pleaded. "I don't understand you. I don't understand you."

"I am half of Jazi, half of Daghian. If Sere had died yesterday, I would have been free of Daghian." She shook her head again, her face twisting a little at Cresce's expression. "All I can give you is what you asked for. Truth. That was one thought in my mind. But also, I gave Jazi the truth: I didn't want to lie to them about Sere. So I told them what he was. They nearly killed him, and you saved him, as I hoped you could."

"Do you love him?" Cresce whispered. "Or don't you?"

"I don't know. I don't even know if I love the people of Jazi, who demand everything of me—even my freedom. All I know is that I won't ever leave them without a bard."

Cresce was silent. The winds sifted dryly through the oak leaves. She said abruptly, as if the word were surprised out of her, "No."

"In Daghian, I have a son. I have a place in the Lords' house. I have horses, birds, great music. Here, I listen on a windy day to sheep bells. And I wonder what is happening in the great cities of the kingdom. But in Daghian, my face is the face of a woman of Jazi. And the men of Daghian are the sons and grandsons of the army that swept through Jazi seventy years ago, stealing, burning, raping, murdering. Tell me. Where do I belong?"

"Why did you leave Daghian?"

"I followed something one winter through the Daghian marshes. A cothone, played like a promise of passion and wonder beyond the mists, out of the hills of Jazi . . . All I found here were sheep bells." She smiled a little, crooked smile.

"But you didn't leave Jazi."

"No. I became their Bard. How could I have left them? I am their promise of wonder. Of hope." She studied Cresce, the uncertainty in her eyes easing a little. "You are beginning to understand me. I am not terrible. I am just—torn."

"Like Hroi Tuel."

Lelia nodded. "Hroi. Afraid to hope in visions. One day, he'll leave Jazi. But I don't know if he will ever find peace, in or out of Jazi."

"Who played—who played the cothone I heard in the marshes last autumn?"

Lelia was silent. She reached out suddenly, put her hand on Cresce's wrist. "Believe me." Her voice was low, timbreless as a distant horn. "I didn't."

Cresce drew breath soundlessly. She sat with her head bowed, gazing down at the valley below. "If Sere stays with you, the Lords of Daghian will come to get him."

"You stop them."

"Will I be able to? If you—if you leave Jazi—"

"I can't leave."

"If you leave, will you be content in Daghian?"

"I don't know."

"Then why did you call Sere! Why did you give him hope?"

"Sere knows me." She curled the soft wool in her long fingers. "He was very angry with me, last night. I told him exactly what I've told you. The truth."

"Do you love him?"

She sighed. "If I could turn into a bird, fly into a winter twilight . . . I love Sere as I love Jazi. As much as I am able. He knows that. He sees me clearly. And I'm not a woman in a mist. I am his wife, and the mother of his son. I am Bard of Jazi, the good fortune of Jazi. All these things bind me. But only because I choose to be bound."

Cresce was silent. The Bard's face held, she thought suddenly, all the names of the pipes of the cothone. The longing, the mourning, the calling, the passion, the warning . . . She raised her hand suddenly, touched its beauty, and at the touch, remembered its danger.

"I'm free," she whispered.

"Yes."

"Then why," she cried out, rising, "do I have to keep telling myself that?"

Cresce roamed through the hills all day long. At evening, she returned to the Bard's house. Hroi Tuel, escorting the last of the visitors down from the hills, dropped from his horse to her side. She did not speak to him.

He said, "An hour before dawn, the Bard will wake. She'll play the sun's rising at the edge of Forever field. The villagers and guests will gather in a great circle around the field. The cothone will be played from sunrise to sunrise. The Daghian Lord will be killed if he sets one foot out of this house."

She went into the house without looking at him. In her room, she found Sere gazing out through the thin shaft of window at the barren field. She stared helplessly at his back, wondering if he was imprisoning himself out of love for a woman or as a penance for Hekar Pass. She went to his side, stood as close to him as she could without touching him. His eyes met hers; he brushed her cheek gently.

"I'll miss you, Bard."

"You'll die here. You'll hear nothing but sheep bells, and they'll find a reason to kill you."

"No one ever died of listening to sheep bells."

"I would."

"You stop my brothers from coming." His eyes bored into hers harshly. "You can. Make them feel the truth. Or there will be more blood shed between Daghian, Jazi, and Hekar than in all the ballads you learned at Onon."

"Come home."

"No."

She left him. She took sheepskins, crossed the stream, and went to sit at the edge of Forever, facing east, so that she would see the sun rise through the great, dark arch. When the moon set she fell asleep. She woke at the first, dazzling shaft of light sweeping the mouth of the arch, called by the Bard of Jazi on the first pipe of the cothone, the pipe of joy.

Arrows soared through the arch, tuned to the pipe. They turned into minute, hurling splinters of light before they fell earthward again. Women from the village carried great trays of food and wine to the crowd gathering around the field.

They were talking, laughing; some of them sang to the sound of the cothone. Children, herdsmen, farmers, craftsmen, the visiting bards took places around the barren ground, sitting in a great circle while bowmen, to the strains of the ram's horn, sent another blaze of arrows through the arch. Musicians gathered to one side of Cresce. She studied their instruments: painted drums of wood and hollow gourd, copper wind chimes, rows of bells strung on leather, horns, wooden flutes, the small hand pipes the men used to call their horses. The musicians were talking, eating; children surrounded them, tapping on the drums and the bells. Only the Bard ate nothing, and spoke to no one as she brought up the sun.

When she sang the first Song of Changing Fortune, though, there was utter silence.

It was a light, almost dreamlike song, accompanied by the bird-voices of hand-pipes, the wind-stroked chimes, and high, soft bells. The sun had loosed its grip of the hills; the Bard coaxed it higher until it hovered in the center of the archway. Her voice faded into the morning wind. Birds flashed, their wings on fire, across the face of the sun. There was a murmuring from the visitors. Then the Bard lifted the cothone, began to play the second pipe, the pipe of wonder.

Cresce took wine, and some steamed, fruit-filled bread from one of the women. The swelling in her throat made it difficult to swallow at first. Lelia's face seemed remote, peaceful, as if she had left her confusion and pain outside the barren circle. She would not sing again until noon, Cresce remembered. Noon, then twilight, midnight, and sunrise again, the first five of the hundred and one Songs of Changing Fortune. Cresce wondered if Sere could hear her voice. Then she realized someone was sitting beside her.

She turned, wondering how long Hroi Tuel had been with her. He sat as still as the great bird on his shoulder, but she saw his eyes move from face to face around the circle. Once he said, his voice inflectionless, "She has brought up the sun; she will bring up the corn." Then, later, he touched Cresce's wrist. "There's my father."

A big, black-haired man, dressed in a long, wheat-colored ceremonial robe, had seated himself on the other side of the musicians. One of the barefoot children crept up behind him, flung her arms around his neck, and he laughed. But a shadow settled into his eyes a moment later.

Hroi said, regarding him, "He said I should have killed the Daghian Lord." He spat suddenly on the ground. "Men of Daghian are not human. That's what I have been taught. He would have been human enough in my dreams if I had killed him. But now he will stay in Jazi, and no one is permitted to touch him or speak to him. My father says he'll bring misfortune. My father says the Bard brought you here so she could leave Jazi."

"I know."

He looked at her then, angry, tormented. "She is our good fortune. Lelia Daghian." He spat again. Then, at her silence, he asked roughly, "What will you do?"

"I am Bard of Daghian. I have nothing to do with the fortune of Jazi."

"There is no such thing as fortune. There is only a woman playing a cothone who hates Jazi."

"No," Cresce said softly. "She is like you. Listen to her music. She could have walked out of Jazi at any time. But she chose to stay."

"She brought you."

"I won't play. She took that risk."

"Then the man she loves will be a prisoner in Jazi, and the butchers of Daghian will come looking for him. There is no fortune. Only a woman playing a cothone."

"I'll tell the Lords of Daghian the truth. There will be no war."

"What music will you give to Daghian that you refuse to give Jazi? Bard."

She was silent. The Bard changed pipes, began a song on the pipe of laughter.

At noon, Lelia sang to the sun overhead as she walked around the field, her shadow flickering out of its barrenness to touch the new grass pushing toward light on the plain. After her song, the Bard of Hekar began to play. His music was very simple and a little unsure, for he was not used to playing the cothone, but there was a lightness and enthusiasm in it that the Bard had inspired. She smiled across the circle at him, then sat down for the first time in six hours. The women brought her food and wine, but they did not speak to her. Cresce saw her glance once at the black house beneath the oak. The song of the Bard of Hekar ended; another visitor began to play. Cresce realized with surprise that it was one of her teachers from Onon. At mid-afternoon, Lelia began to play again. The musicians beat a wild, raucous dance to her music. The children whirled to it, while some of the old people stretched on the grass and napped. The women serving food disappeared; a little later the smells of roast lamb and wild boar wafted across the field.

The Bard's song at sunset was played on the fourth and fifth pipes: the pipes of longing and of love. Standing on the opposite side of the circle, she eased the brilliant sun into a bed of gold beyond the hills. Its rays touched her face again and again before it withdrew. The oak shadow flung over half the plain faded slowly; the tree loosed the light it had gathered into its boughs. Dusk left the plain in an uncertain, misty light. Then, as the first star appeared, the bowmen shot arrows of flaming pitch high, high toward the arch, trying to send them over it. Only one struck the lower edge of the arch; the others fell through it, sank, burning, into the bare earth. There was laughter, applause. Torches were lit in the grass. Lelia played the measure of a wild dance that was picked up by one of the visiting bards. The musicians shook the crowd awake with the lively beat of drums and flutes. Circles of dancers formed around the torches, whirling and laughing. The full moon began its slow arch above Jazi.

Hroi Tuel, who had appeared and disappeared unexpectedly throughout the day, brought Cresce a plate of food, then vanished again. She sat picking at spiced lamb and pickled vegetables, watching the dancers winding in and out of the torches. Someone dropped down beside her in the shadows. She glanced up expecting Hroi's taut, brooding face. She coughed a little, on a piece of pickled cabbage.

Sere touched her briefly, then shifted back into the shadows. He waited until a woman carrying pitchers of wine had passed them. Then he said softly, "I was going mad in that house, trying to hear. I had to hear. They won't notice me in the dark."

"Have you eaten?" She pushed her plate to him. "They'll kill you if they recognize you."

"They won't." He wrapped lamb in hot bread, chewed it hungrily. "They forgot to feed me. Or maybe they didn't forget. Have you played yet?"

"No. I'm not going to."

He stopped chewing, stared at her. He swallowed. "Why? I want to hear what comes out of you and that cothone."

"I'm not playing."

He held her eyes, his own eyes narrowed, until she looked away. He put her plate down, gripped her wrist. Then a shadow rustled next to Cresce, and Sere seemed to blur into himself, shifting back into his sheepskin cloak. Hroi held out of a cup of wine to Cresce. Then he offered a piece of boar meat to the bird on his shoulder. Cresce, her mouth dry, her hands shaking, sipped wine silently, waiting for the hard, incredulous whip of his voice as he discovered Sere. But Hroi never spoke. Balanced on his haunches, his eyes unwinking, he looked like the hawk on his shoulder, its still eyes drenched with fire.

The dance music began to die. The moon's face hardened into a clear, unbearable beauty, and the Bard of Jazi played a warning on the sixth pipe. Another bard from Onon began playing with her, weaving a restless, minor melody through hers. Other warnings drifted through theirs, the dark music never quite harmonized, never quite chaotic, as if many different voices were trying to describe the same misfortune looming out of the night. Some voices drifted to silence; others took up the warning until it seemed to Cresce that every bard in the circle had played except for her. But there seemed no music in her, as if she had already heeded the Bard's warning.

Finally, all the cothones fell silent, except for Lelia's. She had changed position again; she stood facing west, at the edge of the moon-shadow of the oak. Her face was in shadow; her music drifted into shadow. For a breath the night was soundless. Then, out of moonlight and shadow, came the deep, wild, passionate voice of the seventh pipe.

Cresce felt her heart torn open suddenly, aching. The Bard seemed to know all their languages. She played Hroi's tormented doubt, Sere's anger and love. She played her own confusion of love and restlessness, the pride and beauty she had learned at Daghian, the sorrow and faith of Jazi. And out of all the tangle of their thoughts, she shaped something that ran at the edge of the fiery darkness like a dream: a glimpse of unbearable beauty that existed only to be hunted, never caught. Cresce's hands closed on her own cothone. She kept them still, though the music seemed to gather in her bones. Her silence was a hard, painful knot in her throat. Visions of the great white stag, forever pursued, forever eluded, ran through her heart. She thought of Sere tracking it on foot through the marshes of Daghian; of his grandson at her left pursuing a dream of love; of Hroi Tuel at her right, desperate for an illusion of truth. And she realized then what endless, hopeless visions the Bard herself pursued to create for them their own visions of hope.

She found herself on her feet, in silent salute to the Bard of Jazi. Tears burned in her eyes; her hands seemed frozen on her cothone. Music weltered soundlessly through her, compelled by a heritage of a barren field and a black spring night. But she stood still, forcing herself silent, until she realized slowly the barrenness of her own refusal to pursue the powerful, fleeting vision of her music.

She lifted the eighth pipe to her mouth, understanding at last what it mourned. She waited until the Bard's music died away. Then, with her first low note, she promised Hroi and Sere and the people of Jazi their visions, and the Bard of

Jazi her freedom. She accompanied Lelia through the midnight Song of Fortune. Then she drew the night into her
cothone, sent it out again, note by note, across the barren
field. Pitching her music deep, she sent a slow, dark song into
the arch that seemed to reach out of her bones, out of the
roots beneath her, out of the life beneath the barren field, to
pierce the silence locked within the arch of Forever.

She stopped as abruptly as she had began, when the only
sound left in her was the deep, ragged beat of her heart. She
sat down, dropping the cothone. Slowly, someone else in the
circle took up her song, and she closed her eyes, breathing
deeply in relief, that she had tried and failed, and the silence
surrounding the stars was still unbroken. Then she recognized the rich, husky, unearthly pipes of the cothone answering her.

A wind swept across the plain, carrying echoes of a thousand pipes of joy and mourning. Something seemed to enter
Cresce, touch her bones. She heard Hroi's breath catch, then
catch again. She swallowed dryly, longing suddenly to play
again, to stand with the night to its darkness and end, then
bring the first touch of sunlight into Jazi. Then a voice out of
the shadows cried out harshly, shattering the weave of music
beyond the arch:

"No!"

Hroi was on his feet suddenly, the hawk beating on his
shoulder. He pulled a torch out of the ground, swung it at
the darkness, illuminating Sere as he flung himself back
from the fire.

"You," Hroi breathed. "You." There were tears running
down his face. "You in Daghian were born listening for the
voices of the dead in Jazi."

He hurled the torch at Sere's face. Sere rolled; the torch caught the sheepskin at his back, set it blazing. He threw himself on his back, trying to smother the flames. Hroi, the hawk fluttering off his shoulder, lunged at Sere. Sere's boot slammed into his breastbone, spun him off his feet. Sere straightened, slapping at his cloak. A fist coming out of the darkness cracked across his face and he fell, extinguishing the last of the fire. Cresce, seeing the circle of men closing around him, felt a fury shake her like the bass voices of the cothone.

"Stop it!" Her voice cracked like a reed. "I am the Bard of Jazi! You will not touch him!" She whirled at Hroi, who was starting to rise. "Stop it!" He froze. She looked down at Sere, struggling to his knees. "And you!" His face lifted; her voice cracked again. "Lord of Daghian! Go back to Daghian!"

Lelia, shouldering past the men, went to his side. She tried to help him up; he shook her away, shouted at her, still on his knees, "What are you doing? You called Cresce Dami to take your place—You called us both—You nearly got me killed— You weren't content in Daghian, you aren't content here—"

"I am not made to be content!" She was crying suddenly, still trying to help him, on her knees beside him.

"Then what are you made for?"

"To play the cothone. To know all its voices." She put her arms around him, her voice muffled in charred sheepskin. "I have been faithful to Jazi. I will be that faithful to you. That much I know. That, I chose."

He was silent. His eyes went to Cresce; she saw the look in them that must have been in his grandfather's when the beautiful animal changed shape before his eyes and then changed shape again. Cresce put her hands over her mouth, whispered to Sere, "You. Love her. She will sing the truth in Daghian."

She saw the tears in his own eyes. "I can't let you do this. I can't go back to Daghian leaving you here. You are the pride of Daghian. Your music will die here in the silence. Everything you learned at Onon will be lost."

"I didn't have to play here," she said softly. "I chose to." She swallowed the fire in her throat. "Go home." She looked at the Overlord of Jazi, staring at her in wonder at the edge of the circle of men. "I am Bard of Jazi, chosen by the dead of Jazi. You will permit him to leave in peace. Or I will cry over every cornfield in Jazi."

She turned, walked through the darkness to take Lelia's place at the edge of Forever. Someone had continued to play the cothone through the turmoil and shouting, keeping the ancient ritual of music passed like a flame from bard to bard uninterrupted. She sent him silent gratitude as she took the melody from him. Then she realized, as he lowered his instrument, that it was the Bard of Hekar.

She played through the dark hours of morning until dawn. Then, at the first slow run of fire across the hills, she changed to the first pipe. She did not know where she found the joy to sing the fifth Song of Changing Fortune, but it was in her somehow, as she watched the light wash across the fragile green of the hills, as she looked through the arch and saw the fronds of new leaves on the ancient, twisted oak boughs.

After she sang, she sat for a long time in silence, while the crowd dispersed around her to eat and sleep. The barren field was quiet again. The wind rustled across the plain, bringing her the sound of sheep bells. She drew her knees up, rested her face in her arms, and thought of Daghian. She raised her head again finally. The monotonous, unfamiliar hills still ringed her with their silence.

Hroi Tuel was sitting motionlessly beside her. As she straightened, he put his hand on her shoulder. Then he winced. "That Daghian Lord cracked my ribs." After a moment, he admitted, "There was some justice in that."

Cresce did not answer. But she sensed, through the confusion of despair and faith she had committed herself to, the beginnings of his peace.

# A Troll and Two Roses

Once upon a time there was an old troll who lived under a bridge. He was an ugly, sloppy old troll named Thorn, who liked to flip fish out of the river with his toes and eat them raw, and to leap out at travelers on the road above and collect whatever valuables they dropped before they ran. Like all trolls, he had a weakness for beautiful things. He kept his treasures in an iron chest hidden under tree roots along the bank. When the moon was high and full, he would open the chest and look at them: all the lovely things he had stolen. He had rings and ribbons, lace handkerchiefs, jeweled knives, delicate veils, pouches of gold, silk flowers, feathered hats, and even a stray velvet shoe that a young girl had lost in her terror. He never harmed anyone; he was too lazy, and so ugly he didn't need to. One glimpse of his huge, warty, hairy face peering up over the side of the bridge was enough to make anybody drop whatever they had. "Troll toll!" he would bellow, and collect it, laughing, from the dust.

Almost anybody.

One night he looked over his treasure box and a restless, discontented feeling stirred through him. It was a familiar feeling: it meant that his eyes were tired of all his old things and wanted something new to delight in. He shut his box and hunkered down under the bridge to wait. He didn't expect anyone, for it was late and the gates of the city the road led to were long closed. But he heard in the distance solitary hoofbeats, and he grinned a troll grin, making fish dive out of the reflection of his teeth.

He waited until the hoofbeats thumped and echoed over the center of the bridge. Then he leaped up, all snarled and dank in the moonlight, with his eyes crossed and a frog in his beard. "Troll toll!" he boomed.

An edge of pure silver sliced out of the dark at him so fast it trimmed his hair as he ducked. He yelped. A black horse with yellow eyes bared its teeth and lunged at him. A voice snapped irritably, "Troll toll, indeed! I'll give you troll toll, you frog-eater—" The silver whistled about Thorn's ears again, and he dove into the water and swam away into the night. But not before he had seen what the rider was carrying, and that the moon-shadow in the white dust was crowned.

He was consumed with longing from that moment. He could not eat, he could not sleep. The fish were safe, the travelers were safe. He sat under his bridge, chewing his beard, smoldering with desire, not, as he had done in his youth, for a troll-woman, but for the rose he had glimpsed in the dark rider's hand.

It was white as hoarfrost; it was carved out of winter. Yet it was alive, and the dew clustered on it like diamonds. He knew a little of the world: that kings and princes went on quests for such things, and that they generally gave them away to their true loves, not to untidy trolls. But this prince had been alone, in no great hurry. He had not returned in triumph; he had come back at night, riding slowly, and, even allowing for the unexpected appearance of Thorn, in no good humor. Had his true love not wanted the rose? Well, Thorn did, and finally, at dusk one evening, he dragged himself from under the bridge and went mumbling and thumping through the forest, in no good humor himself, for he hated the world. But there was no other way to possess that rose.

He reached the walls of the city before dawn. He dragged himself up over them and wound through the cobblestone streets, shambling and snorting and giving city folk bad dreams. He found another wall and went over that, and another and went over that. And another—and then he dropped onto a smooth velvety lawn that was covered with rose trees.

A hundred peacock eyes stared at him and folded; the birds went screeching away. He stood in the dawn, smelling of river water, looking, with his little muddy eyes and his clumsy bulk, like something not even a dog would bite. But his thoughts and eyes were full of roses. He walked among the trees, finding roses but never the rose he wanted. Scarlet roses, gold, pink, orange, lavender, blue-white, ivory-white, snow-white, but never crystal-white, ice-white, so white he could have buried his big nose in it and smelled the wintry peaks of his birthplace. He stood beside the last tree, scratching his head and wondering where to go next. He heard a sigh.

It was the prince, standing in the garden gate with the magic rose in his hand.

Thorn studied him a moment, warily. He was a burly young man, unarmed and barefoot, with tousled yellow hair, a morning beard, and black, black eyes. His shirt was loose, his crown was off; he had apparently just gotten out of bed. Thorn ducked behind a row of bushes and crept silently, step by step, up to the prince's back. It hadn't worked the first time, but it might a second. He raised himself on his toes and yelled at the top of his lungs, "Troll toll!"

The prince dropped the rose.

He gave Thorn a furious chase through the rose garden, but Thorn batted at him once with his huge hand, and the prince tumbled among the flowers. Thorn climbed back over the walls faster than he had come. When the sun rose, he was outside the city gates; when the sun set, he was back under his bridge, gazing with utter delight at his rose.

It was whiter than the moon, it was more delicate than an elvish smile. It had no root, but it was alive, caught in some spell that kept it always perfect, with no sign on its tender petals of decay. It smelled of snow and apple blossoms. A diamond of moisture balanced on the very tip of one petal. Thorn touched it with his horny finger and it dropped, dissolving. As he berated himself for his clumsiness, another diamond formed at the heart of the flower and rolled slowly across its crystal petals like a tear.

Then Thorn heard the galloping.

The prince was not alone this time. Thorn winced at the clatter of hooves over his head. He was just wise enough to duck himself down, instead of demanding a toll, and move a little faster than he had ever moved in his life. The dusk enveloped him, blurred his swift bulky form among the river reeds and trees. The prince sighted him, but his army had hard going along the soft, tangled banks. The prince's horse, the black, wicked-eyed mount, seemed to melt like night through brambles and thickets. Thorn, glancing back, could see its yellow eyes burning in the dark long after the shouts and splashes of the prince's army had faded away.

Thorn was fast and tireless. His feet gobbled miles the way he gobbled fish. His leathery soles never felt a sharp stone; they could flatten a wall of brambles without hesitation. The prince's horse followed like a bolt of black lightning. It could never quite catch up with Thorn, but it never fell behind, and all night long its baleful, sulfurous eyes smoldered into Thorn's back. Finally, near morning, Thorn began to tire a little. He wanted to sit down quietly and contemplate the rose in his hand. He wanted breakfast. A dawn wind rose, puffed the last stars out. The sky turned gray as iron. In front of Thorn, massive gray peaks of stones began to separate themselves from the sky.

Thorn ran toward them with relief. He could find an opening, duck inside, and hide himself in the meandering veinwork of caves through which the lifeblood of the mountains flowed. Thorn had been born in a cave; he could see in the dark. He was no more afraid of a mountain than he was of a minnow. So when he bolted into one dark crevice among the boulders, he wasn't prepared to hear the mountain speak with a roar like a thousand cannon. The dark tore away in front of him like a curtain. Light hurt his eyes. He stumbled on wet grass. He stopped, bewildered, blinking. The mountains had vanished.

He was standing on a flat plain, watching the sun rise from the wrong side of the world. There was another thunderclap. The prince and his horse leaped out of a slit in the air into the wrong morning.

The horse snorted and refrained, in its astonishment, from biting Thorn's ear off. The prince slid off its back slowly. The three stood silently, troll, horse, and prince, all with the same expression on their faces. Then, faster than a fish sliding out of Thorn's fingers, the prince's sword was out of its sheath and threatening to burrow into Thorn's troll heart.

"Give me that rose."

There was something in the black eyes more compelling than the meager blade. Visions of an endless chase made Thorn yield the rose. His small eyes blinked; he sighed. The rose passed out of his grasp.

The deadliness faded from the prince's eyes. He held the rose gently to his cheek and said, with a tired, angry sorrow, "It is my wife."

Then Thorn wanted the rose back. The dream-woman entrapped within such a wondrous form made him snort with longing; he took a step toward it, his hand outstretched. The horse's big yellow teeth snapped at his nose. The prince ignored him.

"Look, she's crying. She never cries." He coaxed a tear onto his fingertip and touched it to his lips. Then he became aware of Thorn, his troll chest heaving, his eyes tiny and red with yearning. The prince's hands enfolded the rose, held it closer to his heart.

"She loves me" he said coldly. Then he glanced around the empty, cloud-tossed sky. "Look what you did."

"I didn't!" Thorn protested.

"Where are we?"

Thorn's feet shuffled among the grass. He was hungry, he wanted the rose, he wished the prince with his bad-tempered eyes and tidy, gleaming armor would leave him alone to dangle his feet in a river and nibble toads. He was half again as tall as the prince and twice as burly, and he was bewildered by his own submission. He said pleadingly, "I have a secret treasure box of beautiful things; if you give me the rose—"

"Forget it," the prince said brusquely. "She is a highborn lady, she is not for you. You would make her miserable, and then she would make you even more miserable."

"She could never make me miserable."

"She'd find a way." He looked around the plain again then, and added briskly, "You led us here. Lead us back."

Thorn scowled. "If I knew how to get back to my bridge, prince, I'd be there now." He felt cold and grumpy, for the spell of the rose was aching in his heart. Yet even as he glanced at it again, his throat swelled and his eyes softened. Then at last he thought to ask, "What turned the lady into a rose?"

The prince slid his helm back and scratched his head. "I don't know. An evil spell, but who the sorcerer is, I can't guess. We were up in the mountains alone; she was sitting in my lap, we were dallying among the wildflowers, counting birds, making up riddles—and suddenly she was this rose. I waited, I searched. I shouted, and pleaded, and argued with the wind. She was still a rose. I came back home. Whereupon," he added dourly, "I was assailed by an ugly old troll." Thorn snorted. "And now, I'm here with the troll and the weeping rose in the middle of nowhere." He turned suddenly and mounted. "Well. You can stay here picking at grass with your toes, but I'm going to find the door back." The great black mount whirled.

Thorn cried, "Wait! Wait for me!"

And then the entire plain rumbled. Darkness fell over it, thick and murky, until Thorn could not even see the horse's yellow eyes. The rose began to glow. It was a piercing, ice-white light in the utter black. The plain was shrieking now. Or was it wind? Thorn couldn't tell. He squeezed his eyes shut, put his hands over his ears, and wished with all his heart he were back under his bridge. The wish didn't work. He heard a startled, anguished cry from the prince. Then the plain burned with daylight and Thorn opened his eyes.

He stood staring stupidly, his mind working very slowly. The white rose was now red. The prince was now a princess. The horse was still a horse. The princess was sitting on the ground with the red rose against her cheek. Her brown hair was braided, her cheeks were freckled like apples, she was still crying. It was by her tears that Thorn finally realized who she was.

He fell in love. He forgot his visions of a frosty maiden with diamonds on her smooth, pale skin. He wanted to braid and unbraid the honey-brown hair; he wanted to count all the freckles on the princess's round cheeks. He wanted to catch her tears and carry them in his pocket. His finger moved tentatively toward her face. She noticed him finally.

She scrambled to her feet, staring at him in horror. "Troll," she breathed. "What have you done to my husband?"

He broke grass stems between his toes. "I have a nice bridge," he said shyly, looking hard at the end of his nose. "I can catch fat red salamanders for you to eat. I'll give you a box of beautiful things." He had to wait a little, then, while she shouted and wept and commanded the reluctant horse to consume various parts of Thorn. When she finally ran out of breath, Thorn continued enticingly, "I'll bathe your feet every day myself among the water lilies. I'll bring you little furry bats for pets—" He stopped, for the princess was now on the back of the horse. "Wait! He's nothing more than a rose now; I'll bring you a vase to stick him in. You'll like me—truly. Wait for me!"

He began to run again, only this time it was he in pursuit of the horse.

The horse led him across the plain, up low lumpy hills, into a deep and shining forest. The forest was ancient, dark; the trees were tall and hoary. Their tangled branches linked to net the sun; their trunks were knotted with burls. Occasionally, within a burl, an eye would flick. A thick root would gesture and be still. Spiderwebs gleamed in the shadows as though they were woven of white fire. The shadowy air itself seemed to glint with an eerie brightness. Thorn, preoccupied with catching the horse, didn't notice the forest until the horse slowed. Then he leaped forward, caught the black tail, and yelled, "Ha!"

He picked himself out of a bramble bush a moment later, hearing little sniggers of derision all around him. He scowled, but there was nothing to scowl at. The princess was gazing at him expressionlessly. Her eyes, he saw then, were green as the rose stem.

"Troll," she said, "where are we?"

He looked around. He sighed deeply, for he was very far from his bridge.

"I would think," he said glumly, "in an enchanted forest. Inside a magic land. No place I've ever seen before. Where," he added, "there's enchantment, there's always an enchanter. I don't like them, myself. I prefer being comfortable. Now, take my bridge, that's—" The princess told him what he could do with his bridge. "Oh. Well," he explained, "it's a bit big to stick in my ear."

"Troll," she said loftily, waving the prince like a scepter, "you will lead me to this enchanter."

"I don't know where one is."

"You will find one."

His eyes grew a little smaller. "What will you give me if I do? I'd rather go home and eat breakfast. What will you give me?"

"My embroidered shoes."

"No good."

"The twelve gold ribbons in my hair."

"No."

"My lace petticoat."

"What's that?"

"Never mind," she said crossly. "I'll give you all the jewels I'm wearing. My earrings, my silver swan pin, my gold-and-sapphire chains, my six rings—"

"I count seven."

"All but one."

"That," he said shrewdly, "is the one I want. That, and your hair, and a kiss."

She was silent. She touched her hair, swallowing. "All of it?"

"I want your shiny braids to put into my box."

"You can have that," she said unhappily. "And my wedding ring. But no kiss."

"Yes."

"No."

"Yes."

"All right," she said, while the color ran like wine into her face. "Ouch!" She sucked her thumb, glowering at the rose. Thorn smiled a great yellow smile and nodded happily.

He plodded in front of the horse, tearing down giant luminous spiderwebs and mumbling to himself. "Enchanter . . . where enchanter? Who? Witch? Wizard? Fairy? First princess into rose, then prince into rose. Prince with princess-rose, then princess with prince-rose. Why not both together? Rose, rose. Then I put both in my box." He lifted his head suddenly, scenting the wind like a horse. "Troll? No. Troll magic small, small . . . this is a complicated magic." He stopped mumbling then and listened. Then he bent toward the great old hollow root of a tree and yelled, "Ha!"

"Shut up," a voice hissed.

"Little troll in the tree roots, I see you. Where is the enchanter of this forest?"

"Sh!" The voice in the roots sank to a breath. "Sh . . ."

"Where?" Thorn whispered. "I have a present for you."

"I want that red rose."

"You don't want that. It's an enchanted prince with a bad temper."

"Oh. Then what present?"

"Twelve gold ribbons to weave together into a soft bright hammock for you among the roots."

"H'm," said the voice with interest, and the princess unbound them one by one from her hair. They slid gently through the air, striped Thorn's hand with gold. "H'm," said the little voice. "Bend closer."

Thorn straightened after a few moments. He blinked;

drops of cold sweat rolled into his beard. The princess said uneasily, "What?"

"Um."

"Well, what?"

He shuffled his big feet among the leaves. The horse's head turned very slowly; one eye regarded him evilly. Thorn stared back at it, transfixed. He forgot, suddenly, what he was going to say. He scratched his head. Was it about something to eat? The princess urged the horse forward impatiently.

"Oh, Troll."

Deeper they went into the forest. They crossed a stream as cold and feathery white as moonlight. Ivory-pale frogs croaked on its banks, their staring eyes of various colors full of some strange pleading. Thorn shied away from them. Magic. He had no desire to eat them. A grove of trees with leaves made of pearls and diamonds made the princess stop and stare. Thorn growled deep in his throat and stretched out both hands. Trees trembled; leaves flashed down like tears.

"No," the princess said, as Thorn bent toward them. "No." Her face was pale; he saw the glint of a jewel on her cheek. When she wasn't looking at him, Thorn slipped a pearly leaf into his pocket.

They crossed the grove of weeping trees. Beyond it roared a wild blue river. They stopped on its mossy bank. On the other side of the water rose a great glassy black cliff. Their eyes lifted higher, higher . . . On top of the cliff, so high the birds could scarcely reach it, stood a rose garden.

The princess's eyes fell from it to the rose in her hand. She looked again at the garden, again at the rose. The troll heard her breathing quicken. He was musing . . . Something? Fish in the river . . . twelve gold ribbons . . . the black horse, standing so quietly, still as the black cliff. Yellow ribbons, yellow eyes . . .

"Ah." He remembered what he had been wanting to say. "That's it. You might want to get off that horse."

The princess's face turned as white as the rose she had been. Thorn stopped sidling away from the horse, transfixed again by love. He heaved a sigh. The princess screamed. The black horse laughed, and with a mighty thrust of its haunches, soared into the sparkling, blue-white air, leaping upward toward the roses. Thorn, dangling from the horse's tail, which in an exuberance of love he had clutched, shut his eyes and howled.

He thumped like a bad apple among the rose trees. The horse was no longer a horse, but a sorcerer with terrible yellow eyes. The prince was a prince again. Every time he moved toward the sorcerer, a bramble would snake out of the earth and catch his wrist or his boot. The princess was becoming a whole rose tree. The prince, still struggling, was becoming a bramble man, thorny with anger, with blood-red blooms here and there on his body. The sorcerer was staring into his eyes. Thorn decided it was a good time to go fishing.

He began to sneak away behind the sorcerer's back. But diamonds were showering out of the crystal white rose tree. Scent wafted from it of distant, snowy peaks. Lovely, perfect roses, made for touching, beckoned to him, and he thought of the shiny braids the princess owed him, and the kiss. He hummed silently and waffled. Thorns were sliding through the prince's yellow hair. The sorcerer was enthralled by his spell. Thorn thought again of the kiss.

He thrust his hairy, warty face in front of sorcerer's nose and bellowed, "Troll toll!"

The sorcerer jumped. The spell tangled in his mind. Brambles reached toward him, tangled within his powerful confusion. The prince drew a hand loose, a foot. His sword slashed at the thorns, then at the troll, who was about to pluck a blossom from his lady-love.

"Just one!"

The prince snarled. His sword flashed toward the sorcerer, who was two yellow eyes in a mass of brambles. The flash kindled a fire in the sky, which shouted the instant before it disappeared. The roses, the ensorcelled sorcerer, the cliff, the forest, vanished in a well of darkness. Thorn heard a slow drip of water in the night. He smelled limestone. Then he could see again.

"Where are we?" the princess said. She had a white rose petal in her hair, and rose leaves on her skirt. The prince had lost his sword, and his clothes looked as though birds had been pecking at them. "It's so quiet. Are you here? I can't see . . ."

They were sitting on damp limestone inside a mountain. Thorn crept toward them. The princess started, and her hand went to her cheek.

"Did you do that?"

"What?"

"Never mind . . . Troll. Lead us out, and I will give you everything else I promised."

The troll smiled.

He led them back to his bridge. It was dusk. The quiet river smelled like a good thick stew of frogs, toads, little bulbous-eyed fish. The prince and the princess, entwined, were murmuring peacefully together.

"Is he dead? What became of your true horse? He cast so many spells. Are all the roses and diamond trees and frogs back in their proper shapes?"

"I don't know, I don't know."

"Where was his land?"

"Inside the mountain . . ."

"No, the mountain was inside the land."

"Could you see me when you were a rose?"

The troll sighed. Their voices wove together, made a private tapestry of events that no one else could see in just their way. "Ah, well," he said, and thumped down underneath his bridge. The iron box was safe; bats circled his head; the river-voice welcomed him home.

The princess called, surprised, "Troll, you may have my hair now."

"I don't want it."

"My ring?"

"Keep it."

The princess was silent. Thorn heard her step from stone to stone. She came to him beneath the shadow of the bridge. She leaned over him as he sat glumly. When she left him, he was smiling.

Their footsteps died away. He reached into his pocket for the leaf of pearls he had stolen, to put into his chest. But he only found a thread of fiery hair.

# Baba Yaga and the Sorcerer's Son

Long ago, in a vast and faraway country, there lived a witch named Baba Yaga. She was sometimes very wise and sometimes very wicked, and she was so ugly mules fainted at the sight of her. Most of the time she dwelled in her little house in the deep woods. Occasionally, she dipped down Underearth as easily as if the earth were the sea and the sea were air: down to the World Beneath the Wood.

One morning when she was vacationing Underground, she had an argument with her house, which was turning itself around and around on its chicken legs and wouldn't stop. Baba Yaga, who had stepped outside to find a plump morsel of something for breakfast, couldn't get back in her door. She had given her house chicken legs to cause wonder and consternation in passersby. Nobody was around now but Baba Yaga, her temper simmering like a soup pot, and yet there it was, turning and swaying on its great bony legs in the greeny, underwater light of Underearth, looking for all the world like a demented chicken watching a beetle run circles around it.

"Stop that!" Baba Yaga shouted furiously. "Stop that at once!" Then she made her voice sweet and said the words that you are supposed to say if you come across her house unexpectedly in the forest, and are brave or foolish or desperate enough to want in: "Little house, turn your back to the trees and open your door to me." But the house, bewildered perhaps by being surrounded by trees, continued turning and turning. Baba Yaga scolded it until her voice was hoarse and flapped her apron at it as if it really were a chicken. "You stupid house!" she raged, for she still hadn't had her breakfast, or even her morning tea. And then, if that wasn't bad enough, the roof of the world opened up at that moment and hurled something big and dark down at her that missed her by inches.

She was so startled the warts nearly jumped off her nose. She peered down at it, blinking, fumbling in her apron for her spectacles.

A young man lay at her feet. He had black hair and black eyelashes; he was dressed in a dark robe with little bits of mirrors and stardust and cat hairs all over it. He looked dead, but, as she stared, a little color came back into his waxen face. His eyes fluttered open.

He gave a good yell, for Baba Yaga at her best caused strong windows to crack and fall out of their frames. Baba Yaga lifted her foot and kicked at a huge chicken foot that threatened to step on him, and he yelled again. By then he had air back in his lungs. He rolled and crouched, staring at the witch and trembling.

Then he took a good look at the house. "Oh," he sighed, "it's you, Baba Yaga." He felt himself: neck bone, shinbone. "Am I still alive?"

"Not for long," Baba Yaga said grimly. "You nearly squashed me flat."

He was silent then, huddled in his robe, eyeing her warily. *Baba Yaga,* mothers said to their children in the world above, *will eat you if you don't eat your supper.* He, unimpressed with the warning, had always fed his peas to the dog anyway. And now look. Here she was as promised, payment for thousands of uneaten peas. Baba Yaga's green, prismed glasses glittered at him like a fly's eyes. He bowed his head.

"Oh, well," he said. "If you don't kill me, my father will. I just blew up his house."

Baba Yaga's spectacles slid to the end of her nose. She said grumpily, "Was it spinning?"

"No. It was just sitting there, being a house, with all its cups in the cupboard, and the potatoes growing eyes in the bin, and dust making fuzz balls under the bed, just doing what houses do—"

"Ha!"

"And I was just . . . experimenting a little, with some magic in the cauldron. Baba Yaga, I swear I did exactly what the Book said to do, except we ran out of Dragon root, so I tossed in some Mandragora root instead—I thought it'd be a good substitute—but . . ." His black eyes widened at the memory. "All of a sudden bricks and boards and I went flying, and here I . . . here I . . . Where am I, anyway?"

"Underground."

"Really?" he whispered without sound. "I blew myself that far. Why," he added a breath later, distracted, "is your house doing that?"

"I don't know."

"Well, isn't—doesn't that make it difficult for you to get in the door?"

"Yes."

"Well, then, why are you letting it—When you talk through your teeth like that, does that mean you're angry?"

Baba Yaga shrieked like a hundred boiling teakettles. The young man's head disappeared. The house continued to spin.

The witch caught her breath. She felt a little better, and there was the matter of the Sorcerer's son's missing head to contemplate. She waited. A wind full of pale colors and light voices sighed through the trees. She smelled roses from somewhere, maybe from a dream somebody was having about the Underwood. The head emerged slowly, like a turtle's head, from the neck of the dark robe. The young man looked pale again, uneasy, but his eyes held a familiar, desperate glint.

"Baba Yaga. You must help me. I'll help you."

She snorted. "Do what? Blow my house up?"

"No. Please. You're terrible and capricious, but you know things. You can help me. Down here, rules blur into each other. A dream is real; a word spoken here makes a shape in the world above. If you could just make things go backward, just for a few moments, back to the moment before I reached for the Mandragora root—before I destroyed my father's house—if it could just be whole again—"

"Bosh," Baba Yaga said rudely. "You would blow it up all over again."

"Would I?"

"Besides, what do you think I am? I can't even get my house to stop spinning, and you want me to unspin the world."

He sighed. "Then what am I to do? Baba Yaga, I love my father, and I'm very sorry I blew up his house. Isn't there anything I can do? I just—Everything is gone. All his sorcery books, all his lovely precious jars and bottles, potions and elixirs, his dragon tooth, his giant's thumbnail, his narwhal tusk—even his five-hundred-year-old cauldron blew into bits. Not to mention the cups, the beds, his favorite chair, and his cats—if I landed down here, they probably flew clear to China. Baba Yaga, he loves me, I know, but if I were him I might turn me into a toad or something for a couple of months—Maybe I should just run away to sea. Please?"

Baba Yaga felt momentarily dizzy, as if all his babbling were sailing around her head. She said crossly, "What could you possibly do? I don't want my woodstove and my tea towels blown to China."

"I promise, I promise . . ." The young man got to his feet, stood blinking at the house twirling precariously on its hen legs among the silent, blue-black trees. It was an amazing sight, one he could tell his children and his grandchildren about if he managed to stay alive that long. *When I was a young man, I fell off the world, down, down to the Underneath, where I met the great witch Baba Yaga. She needed help and only I could help her. . . .*

"Little house," he called. "Little house, turn your back to the trees and open your door to me."

The house turned its feet forward, nestled down like a hen over an egg, opened its door, and stopped moving.

Baba Yaga opened her mouth and closed it, opened her mouth and closed it, looking, for a moment, like the ugliest fish in the world. "How did you—how did you—"

The young man shrugged. "It always works in the stories."

Baba Yaga closed her mouth. She shoved her glasses back up her nose and gave the young man, and then the house, an icy, glittering-green glare. She marched into her house without a word and slammed the door.

"Baba Yaga!" the young man cried. "Please!"

A terrible noise rumbled through the trees then. It was thunder; it was an earthquake; it was a voice so loud it made the grass flatten itself and turn silvery, as under a wind. The young man, his robe puffed and tugged every direction, was blown like a leaf against the side of the house.

"Johann!" the voice said. "Johann!"

The young man squeaked.

The wind died. Baba Yaga's head sprang out of her door like a cuckoo in a clock. "NOW WHAT?"

The young man, trembling again, his face white as tallow, gave a whistle of awe. "My father."

Baba Yaga squinted Upward from behind her prisms. She gave a sharp, decisive sniff, took her spectacles off. Then she took her apron off. She disappeared inside once more. When she came out again, she was riding her mortar and pestle.

The young man goggled. Baba Yaga's house slowly turning on its chicken legs among the trees was an astonishing sight indeed. But Baba Yaga whisking through the air in the bowl she used to grind garlic, rapping its side briskly with the pestle as if it were a horse, made the young sorcerer so giddy he couldn't even tell if the mortar had grown huge, or if Baba Yaga had suddenly gotten very small.

"Come!" she shouted, thrusting a broom handle over the side. He caught it; she pulled him up, dumped him on the bottom of the bowl, and yelled to the mortar, "Geeee-ha!"

Off they went.

It was a wondrous ride. The mortar was so fast it left streaks in the air, which the young man swept away, like clouds, with the broom. Each time he swept he saw a different marvel, far below, like another piece of the rich tapestry of the Underwood. He saw twelve white swans light on a stone in the middle of a darkening sea and turn into princes. He saw an old man standing on a cliff, talking to a huge flounder with a crown on its head. He saw two children, lost in a wood, staring hungrily at the sweet gingerbread house of another witch. He saw a princess in a high tower unbraid her hair and shake it loose so that it tumbled down and down the wall like a river of gold to the bottom, where her true love caught it in his hands. He saw a great, silent palace surrounded by brambles thick as a man's wrist, sharp as daggers, and he saw the King's son who rode slowly toward them. He saw rose gardens and deep, dark forests with red dragons lurking in them. He saw hummingbirds made of crystal among trees with leaves of silver and pearls. He saw secret, solitary towers rising out of the middle of lovely lakes, or from the tops of mountain crags. He whispered, enchanted, as every sweep of the broom filled his eyes with wonders, "There is more magic here than in all my father's books . . . I could stay here . . . Maybe I'll stay here . . . I will stay . . ." He saw a small pond with a fish in it, as gold as the sun, that spoke once every hundred years. It rose up to the surface as he passed. Its eyes were blue fire; its mouth was full of delicate bubbles like a precious hoard of words. It broke the surface, leaped into the light. It said—

"Johann!"

The mortar bucked in the air like a boat on a wave. The young man sat down abruptly. Baba Yaga said irritably to the sky, "Stop shouting, he's coming. . . ."

"Baba Yaga," the young sorcerer whispered. "Baba Yaga." Still sprawled at the bottom of the mortar, he gripped the hem of her skirt. "Where are you taking me?"

"Home."

"I stopped—" he whispered, for his voice was gone. "I stopped your house. I helped you."

"Indeed," the witch said. "Indeed you did. But I am Baba Yaga, and no one ever knows from one moment to the next what I will do."

She said nothing more. The young man slumped over himself, not even seeing the Firebird below, with her red beak and diamond eyes, stealing golden apples from the garden of the King. He sighed. Then he sighed again. Then he said, with a magnificent effort, "Oh, well. I suppose I can stand to leave all this behind and be a toad for a few months. It's as much as I deserve. Besides, if I ran away, he'd miss me." He stood up then and held out his arms to the misty, pastel sky of the world within the World. "Father! It's me! I'm coming back. I'm coming . . ."

Baba Yaga turned very quickly. She rapped the young sorcerer smartly on the head with her pestle. His eyes closed. She caught him in her arms as he swayed, and she picked him up and tossed him over the side of the mortar. But instead of falling down, he fell up, up into the gentle, opalescent sky, up until Up was Down below the feet of those who dwelled in the world Above.

"And good riddance," Baba Yaga said rudely. But she lingered in her mortar to listen.

"Oh," the young sorcerer groaned. "My head."

"Johann! You're alive!"

"Barely. That old witch Baba Yaga hit me over the head with her pestle—"

"Hush, don't talk. Rest."

"Father, is that you? Am I here?"

"Yes, yes, my son—"

"I'm sorry I blew up your house."

"House, shmouse, you blew up your head, you stupid boy, how many times have I told you—"

"It was the Mandragora root."

"I know. I've told you and told you—"

"Is this my bed? The house is still standing? Father, your cauldron, the cats, the pictures on the wall—"

"Nothing is broken but your head."

"Then I didn't—But how did I—Father, I blew myself clear to the Underwood—I saw Baba Yaga's house spinning and spinning, and I stopped it for her, and she took me for a ride in her mortar and pestle—I saw such wonders, such magics, such a beautiful country. . . . Someday I'll find my way back . . ."

"Stop talking. Sleep."

"And then she hit me for no reason at all, after I had helped her, and she sent me back here . . . Did you know she wears green spectacles?"

"She does not!"

"Yes, she does."

"You were dreaming."

"Was I? Was I, really? Or am I dreaming now that the house is safe, and you aren't angry. . . . Which is the true dream?"

"You're making my head spin."

"Mine, too."

The voices were fading. Baba Yaga smiled, and three passing crows fell out of the sky in shock. She beat a drumroll on the mortar with her pestle and sailed back to her kitchen.

# The Fellowship of the Dragon

 A great cry rose throughout the land: Queen Celandine had lost her harper. She summoned north, south, east, west; we rode for days through mud and rain to meet, the five of us, at Trillium; from there we rode to Carnelaine. The world had come to her great court, for though we lived too far from her to hear her fabled harper play, we heard the rumor that at each full moon she gave him gloves of cloth of gold and filled his mouth with jewels. As we stood in the hall among her shining company, listening to her pleas for help, Justin, who is the riddler among us, whispered, "What is invisible but everywhere, swift as wind but has no feet, and has as many tongues that speak but never has a face?"

"Easy," I breathed. "Rumor."

"Rumor, that shy beast, says she valued his hands for more than his harping, and she filled his mouth with more than jewels."

I was hardly surprised. Celandine is as beautiful close as she is at a distance; she has been so for years, with the aid of a streak of sorcery she inherited through a bit of murkiness, an imprecise history of the distaff side, and she is not one to waste her gifts. She had married honorably, loved faithfully, raised her heirs well. When her husband died a decade ago, she mourned him with the good-hearted efficiency she had brought to marriage and throne. Her hair showed which way the wind was blowing, and the way that silver, ash, and gold worked among the court was magical. But when we grew close enough to kneel before her, I saw that the harper was no idle indulgence, but had sung his way into her blood.

"You five," she said softly, "I trust more than all my court. I rely on you." Her eyes, green as her name, were grim; I saw the tiny lines of fear and temper beside her mouth. "There are some in this hall who—because I have not been entirely wise or tactful—would sooner see the harper dead than rescue him."

"Do you know where he is?"

She lowered her voice; I could scarcely hear her, though the jealous knights behind me must have stilled their hearts to catch her answer. "I looked in water, in crystal, in mirror: every image is the same. Black Tremptor has him."

"Oh, fine."

She bent to kiss me: we are cousins, though sometimes I have been more a wayward daughter, and more often, she a wayward mother. "Find him, Anne," she said.

We five rose as one and left the court.

"What did she say?" Danica asked as we mounted. "Did she say Black Tremptor?"

"Sh!"

"That's a mountain," Fleur said.

"It's a bloody dragon," Danica said sharply, and I bellowed in a whisper, "Can you refrain from announcing our destination to the entire world?"

Danica wheeled her mount crossly; peacocks, with more haste than grace, swept their fine trains out of her way. Justin looked intrigued by the problem. Christabel, who was nursing a cold, said stoically, "Could be worse." What could be worse than being reduced to a cinder by an irritated dragon, she didn't mention. Fleur, who loved good harping, was moved.

"Then we must hurry. Poor man."

She pulled herself up, cantered after Danica. Riding more sedately through the crowded yard, we found them outside the gate, gazing east and west across the gray, billowing sky as if it had streamed out of a dragon's nostrils.

"Which way?" Fleur asked. Justin, who knew such things, pointed. Christabel blew her nose. We rode.

Of course we circled back through the city and lost the knights who had been following us. We watched them through a tavern window as they galloped purposefully down the wrong crossroad. Danica, whose moods swung between sun and shadow like an autumn day, was being enchanted by Fleur's description of our quest.

"He is a magnificent harper, and we should spare no pains to rescue him, for there is no one like him in all the world, and Queen Celandine might reward us with gold and honor, but he will reward us forever in a song."

Christabel waved the fumes of hot spiced wine at her nose. "Does anyone know this harper's name?"

"Kestral," I said. "Kestral Hunt. He came to court a year ago, at old Thurlow's death."

"And where," Christabel asked sensibly, "is Black Tremptor?"

We all looked at Justin, who for once looked uncomfortable. "North," she said. She is a slender, dark-haired, quiet-voiced woman with eyes like the storm outside. She could lay out facts like an open road, or mortar them into a brick wall. Which she was building for us now, I wasn't sure.

"Justin?"

"Well, north," she said vaguely, as if that alone explained itself. "It's fey, beyond the border. Odd things happen. We must be watchful."

We were silent. The tavern keeper came with our supper. Danica, pouring wine the same pale honey as her hair, looked thoughtful at the warning instead of cross. "What kinds of things?"

"Evidently harpers are stolen by dragons," I said. "Dragons with some taste in music."

"Black Tremptor is not musical," Justin said simply. "But like that, yes. There are so many tales, who knows which of them might be true? And we barely know the harper any better than the northlands."

"His name," I said, "and that he plays well."

"He plays wonderfully," Fleur breathed. "So they say."

"And he caught the queen's eye," Christabel said, biting into a chicken leg. "So he might look passable. Though with good musicians, that hardly matters."

"And he went north," Justin pointed out. "For what?"

"To find a song," Fleur suggested; it seemed, as gifted as he was, not unlikely.

"Or a harp," I guessed. "A magical harp."

Justin nodded. "Guarded by a powerful dragon. It's possible. Such things happen, north."

Fleur pushed her dish aside, sank tableward onto her fists. She is straw-thin, with a blacksmith's appetite; love, I could tell, for this fantasy made her ignore the last of her parsnips. She has pale, curly hair like a sheep, and a wonderful, caressing voice; her eyes are small, her nose big, her teeth crooked, but her passionate, musical voice has proved Christabel right more times than was good for Fleur's husband to know. How robust, practical Christabel, who scarcely seemed to notice men or music, understood such things, I wasn't sure.

"So," I said. "North."

And then we strayed into the country called "Remember-when," for we had known one another as children in the court at Carnelaine and then as members of the queen's company, riding ideals headlong into trouble, and now, as long and trusted friends. We got to bed late, enchanted by our memories, and out of bed far too early, wondering obviously why we had left hearth and home, husband, child, cat, and goose down bed for one another's surly company. Christabel sniffed, Danica snapped, Fleur babbled, I was terse. As always, only Justin was bearable.

We rode north.

The farther we traveled, the wilder the country grew. We moved quickly, slept under trees or in obscure inns, for five armed women riding together are easily remembered, and knights dangerous to the harper as well as solicitous of the queen would have known to track us. Slowly the great, dark crags bordering the queen's marches came closer and closer to meet us, until we reached, one sunny afternoon, their shadow.

"Now what?" Danica asked fretfully. "Do we fly over that?" They were huge, barren thrusts of stone pushing high out of forests like bone out of skin. She looked at Justin; we all did. There was a peculiar expression on her face, as if she recognized something she had only seen before in dreams.

"There will be a road," she said softly. We were in thick forest; old trees marched in front of us, beside us, flanked us. Not even they had found a way to climb the peaks.

"Where, Justin?" I asked.

"We must wait until sunset."

We found a clearing where the road we followed abruptly turned to amble west along a stream. Christabel and Danica went hunting. Fleur checked our supplies and mended a tear in her cloak. I curried the horses. Justin, who had gone to forage, came back with mushrooms, nuts, and a few wild apples. She found another brush and helped me.

"Is it far now?" I asked, worried about finding supplies in the wilderness, about the horses, about Christabel's stubbornly lingering cold, even, a little, about the harper. Justin picked a burr out of her mount's mane. A line ran across her smooth brow.

"Not far beyond those peaks," she answered. "It's just that—"

"Just what?"

"We must be so careful."

"We're always careful. Christabel can put an arrow into anything that moves, Danica can—"

"I don't mean that. I mean: the world shows a different face beyond those peaks." I looked at her puzzledly; she shook her head, gazing at the mountains, somehow wary and entranced at once. "Sometimes real, sometimes unreal—"

"The harper is real, the dragon is real," I said briskly. "And we are real. If I can remember that, we'll be fine."

She touched my shoulder, smiling. "I think you're right, Anne. It's your prosaic turn of mind that will bring us all home again."

But she was wrong.

The sun, setting behind a bank of sullen clouds, left a message: a final shaft of light hit what looked like solid stone ahead of us and parted it. We saw a faint, white road that cut out of the trees and into the base of two great crags: the light seemed to ease one wall of stone aside, like a gate. Then the light faded, and we were left staring at the solid wall, memorizing the landscape.

"It's a woman's profile," Fleur said. "The road runs beneath the bridge of her nose."

"It's a one-eared cat," Christabel suggested.

"The road is west of the higher crag," Danica said impatiently. "We should simply ride toward that."

"The mountains will change and change again before we reach it," I said. "The road comes out of that widow's peak of trees. It's the highest point of the forest. We only need to follow the edge of the trees."

"The widow," Danica murmured, "is upside down."

I shrugged. "The harper found his way. It can't be that difficult."

"Perhaps," Fleur suggested, "he followed a magical path."

"He parted stone with his harping," Christabel said stuffily. "If he's that clever, he can play his way out of the dragon's mouth, and we can all turn around and go sleep in our beds."

"Oh, Christabel," Fleur mourned, her voice like a sweet flute. "Sit down. I'll make you herb tea with wild honey in it; you'll sleep on clouds tonight."

We all had herb tea, with brandy and the honey Fleur had found, but only Fleur slept through the thunderstorm. We gathered ourselves wetly at dawn, slogged through endless dripping forest, until suddenly there were no more trees, there was no more rain, only the unexpected sun illuminating a bone-white road into the great upsweep of stone ahead of us.

We rode beyond the land we knew.

I don't know where we slept that first night: wherever we fell off our horses, I think. In the morning we saw Black Tremptor's mountain, a dragon's palace of cliffs and jagged columns and sheer walls ascending into cloud. As we rode down the slope toward it, the cloud wrapped itself down around the mountain, hid it. The road, wanting nothing to do with dragons, turned at the edge of the forest and ran off in the wrong direction. We pushed into trees. The forest on that side was very old, the trees so high, their green boughs so thick, we could barely see the sky, let alone the dragon's lair. But I have a strong sense of direction, of where the sun rises and sets, that kept us from straying. The place was soundless. Fleur and Christabel kept arrows ready for bird or deer, but we saw nothing on four legs or two: only spiders, looking old as the forest, weaving webs as huge and intricate as tapestry in the trees.

"It's so still," Fleur breathed. "As if it is waiting for music."

Christabel turned a bleary eye at her and sniffed. But Fleur was right: the stillness did seem magical, an intention out of someone's head. As we listened, the rain began again.

We heard it patter from bough to bough a long time before it reached us.

Night fell the same way: sliding slowly down from the invisible sky, catching us without fresh kill, in the rain without a fire. Silent, we rode until we could barely see. We stopped finally, while we could still imagine one another's faces.

"The harper made it through," Danica said softly; what Celandine's troublesome, faceless lover could do, so could we.

"There's herbs and honey and more brandy," Christabel said. Fleur, who suffered most from hunger, having a hummingbird's energy, said nothing. Justin lifted her head sharply.

"I smell smoke."

I saw the light then: two square eyes and one round among the distant trees. I sighed with relief and felt no pity for whoever in that quiet cottage was about to find us on the doorstep.

But the lady of the cottage did not seem discomfited to see five armed, dripping, hungry travelers wanting to invade her house.

"Come in," she said. "Come in." As we filed through the door, I saw all the birds and animals we had missed in the forest circle the room around us: stag and boar and owl, red deer, hare, and mourning dove. I blinked, and they were motionless: things of thread and paint and wood, embroidered onto curtains, carved into the backs of chairs, painted on the rafters. Before I could speak, smells assaulted us, and I felt Fleur stagger against me.

"You poor children." Old as we were, she was old enough to say that. "Wet and weary and hungry." She was a birdlike soul herself: a bit of magpie in her curious eyes, a bit of hawk's beak in her nose. Her hair looked fine and white as spiderweb, her knuckles like swollen tree burls. Her voice was kindly, and so was her warm hearth, and the smells coming out of her kitchen. Even her skirt was hemmed with birds. "Sit down. I've been baking bread, and there's a hot meat pie almost done in the oven." She turned, to give something simmering in a pot over the fire a stir. "Where are you from and where are you bound?"

"We are from the court of Queen Celandine," I said. "We have come searching for her harper. Did he pass this way?"

"Ah," she said, her face brightening. "A tall man with golden hair and a voice to match his harping?"

"Sounds like," Christabel said.

"He played for me, such lovely songs. He said he had to find a certain harp. He ate nothing and was gone before sunrise." She gave the pot another stir. "Is he lost?"

"Black Tremptor has him."

"Oh, terrible." She shook her head. "He is fortunate to have such good friends to rescue him."

"He is the queen's good friend," I said, barely listening to myself as the smell from the pot curled into me, "and we are hers. What is that you are cooking?"

"Just a little something for my bird."

"You found a bird?" Fleur said faintly, trying to be sociable. "We saw none . . . Whatever do you feed it? It smells good enough to eat."

"Oh, no, you must not touch it; it is only bird-fare. I have delicacies for you."

"What kind of a bird is it?" Justin asked. The woman tapped the spoon on the edge of the pot, laid it across the rim.

"Oh, just a little thing. A little, hungry thing I found. You're right: the forest has few birds. That's why I sew and paint my birds and animals, to give me company. There's wine," she added. "I'll get it for you."

She left. Danica paced; Christabel sat close to the fire, indifferent to the smell of the pot bubbling under her stuffy nose. Justin had picked up a small wooden boar and was examining it idly. Fleur drifted, pale as a cloud; I kept an eye on her to see she did not topple into the fire. The old woman had trouble, it seemed, finding cups.

"How strange," Justin breathed. "This looks so real, every tiny bristle."

Fleur had wandered to the hearth to stare down into the pot. I heard it bubble fatly. She gave one pleading glance toward the kitchen, but still there was nothing to eat but promises. She had the spoon in her hand suddenly, I thought to stir.

"It must be a very strange bird to eat mushrooms," she commented. "And what looks like—" Justin put the boar down so sharply I jumped, but Fleur lifted the spoon to her lips. "Lamb," she said happily. And then she vanished: there was only a frantic lark fluttering among the rafters, sending plea after lovely plea for freedom.

The woman reappeared. "My bird," she cried. "My pretty." I was on my feet with my sword drawn before I could even close my mouth. I swung, but the old witch didn't linger to do battle. A hawk caught the lark in its claws; the door swung open, and both birds disappeared into the night.

We ran into the dark, stunned and horrified. The door slammed shut behind us like a mouth. The fire dwindled into two red flames that stared like eyes out of the darkened windows. They gave no light; we could see nothing.

"That bloody web-haired old spider," Danica said furiously. "That horrible, putrid witch." I heard a thump as she hit a tree; she cursed painfully. Someone hammered with solid, methodical blows at the door and windows; I guessed Christabel was laying siege. But nothing gave. She groaned with frustration. I felt a touch and raised my sword; Justin said sharply, "It's me." She put her hand on my shoulder; I felt myself tremble.

"Now what?" I said tersely. I could barely speak; I only wanted action, but we were blind and bumbling in the dark.

"I think she doesn't kill them," Justin said. "She changes them. Listen to me. She'll bring Fleur back into her house eventually. We'll find someone to tell us how to free her from the spell. Someone in this wilderness of magic should know. And not everyone is cruel."

"We'll stay here until the witch returns."

"I doubt she'll return until we're gone. And even if we find some way to kill her, we may be left with an embroidered Fleur."

"We'll stay."

"Anne," she said, and I slumped to the ground, wanting to curse, to weep, wanting at the very least to tear the clinging cobweb dark away from my eyes.

"Poor Fleur," I whispered. "She was only hungry . . . Harper or no, we rescue her when we learn how. She comes first."

"Yes," she agreed, and added thoughtfully, "The harper eluded the witch, it seems, though not the dragon."

"How could he have known?" I asked bitterly. "By what magic?"

"Maybe he had met the witch first in a song."

Morning found us littered across tree roots like the remains of some lost battle. At least we could see again. The house had flown itself away; only a couple of fiery feathers remained. We rose wordlessly, feeling the empty place where Fleur had been, listening for her morning chatter. We fed the horses, ate stone-hard bread with honey, and had a swallow of brandy apiece. Then we left Fleur behind and rode.

The great forest finally thinned, turned to golden oak, which parted now and then around broad meadows where we saw the sky again, and the high dark peak. We passed through a village, a mushroom patch of a place, neither friendly nor surly, nor overly curious. We found an inn, and some supplies, and, beyond the village, a road to the dragon's mountain that had been cleared, we were told, before the mountain had become the dragon's lair. Yes, we were also told, a harper had passed through . . . He seemed to have left little impression on the villagers, but they were a hardheaded lot, living under the dragon's shadow. He, too, had asked directions, as well as questions about Black Tremptor, and certain tales of gold and magic harps and other bits of country lore. But no one else had taken that road for decades, leading, as it did, into the dragon's mouth.

We took it. The mountain grew clearer, looming high above the trees. We watched for dragon wings, dragon fire, but if Black Tremptor flew, it was not by day. The rain had cleared; a scent like dying roses and aged sunlit wood seemed to blow across our path. We camped on one of the broad grass clearings where we watched the full moon rise, turn the meadow milky, and etch the dragon's lair against the stars.

But for Fleur, the night seemed magical. We talked of her and then of home; we talked of her and then of court gossip; we talked of her and of the harper, and what might have lured him away from Celandine into a dragon's claw. And as we

spoke of him, it seemed his music fell around us from the stars
and that the moonlight in the oak wood had turned to gold.

"Sh!" Christabel said sharply, and, drowsy, we quieted to
listen. Danica yawned.

"It's just harping." She had an indifferent ear; Fleur was
more persuasive about the harper's harping than his harping
would have been. "Just a harping from the woods."

"Someone's singing," Christabel said. I raised my brows,
feeling that in the untroubled, sweetly scented night, anything might happen.

"Is it our missing Kestral?"

"Singing in a tree?" Danica guessed. Christabel sat straight.

"Be quiet," she said sharply. Justin, lying on her stomach,
tossing twigs into the fire, glanced at her surprisedly. Danica
and I only laughed at Christabel in a temper.

"You have no hearts," she said, blowing her nose fiercely.
"It's so beautiful, and all you can do is gabble."

"All right," Justin said soothingly. "We'll listen." But,
moonstruck, Danica and I could not keep still. We told raucous tales of old loves, while Christabel strained to hear, and
Justin watched her curiously. She seemed oddly moved, did
Christabel; feverish, I thought, from all the rain.

A man rode out of the trees into the moonlight at the edge
of the meadow. He had milky hair, broad shoulders; a gold
mantle fanned across his horse's back. The crown above his
shadowed face was odd: a circle of uneven gold spikes, like
antlers. He was unarmed; he played the harp.

"Not our harper," Danica commented. "Unless the dragon
turned his hair white."

"He's a king," I said. "Not ours." For a moment, just a moment, I heard his playing, and knew it could have parted

water, made birds speak. I caught my breath; tears swelled behind my eyes. Then Danica said something and I laughed.

Christabel stood up. Her face was unfamiliar in the moon-light. She took off her boots, unbraided her hair, let it fall loosely down her back; all this while we only watched and laughed and glanced now and then, indifferently, at the wait-ing woodland harper.

"You're hopeless boors," Christabel said, sniffing. "I'm go-ing to speak to him, ask him to come and sit with us."

"Go on then," Danica said, chewing a grass blade. "Maybe we can take him home to Celandine instead." I rolled over in helpless laughter. When I wiped my eyes, I saw Christabel walking barefoot across the meadow to the harper.

Justin stood up. A little, nagging wind blew through my thoughts. I stood beside her, still laughing a little, yet poised to hold her if she stepped out of the circle of our firelight. She watched Christabel. Danica watched the fire dreamily, smil-ing. Christabel stood before the harper. He took his hand from his strings and held it out to her.

In the sudden silence, Justin shouted, "Christabel!"

All the golden light in the world frayed away. A dragon's wing of cloud brushed the moon; night washed toward Christabel, as she took his hand and mounted; I saw all her lovely, red-gold hair flowing freely in the last of the light. And then freckled, stolid, courageous, snuffling Christabel caught the harper-king's shoulders and they rode down the fading path of light into a world beyond the night.

We searched for her until dawn.

At sunrise, we stared at one another, haggard, mute. The great oak had swallowed Christabel; she had disappeared into a harper's song.

"We could go to the village for help," Danica said wearily.

"Their eyes are no better than ours," I said.

"The queen's harper passed through here unharmed," Justin mused. "Perhaps he knows something about the country of the woodland king."

"I hope he is worth all this," Danica muttered savagely.

"No man is," Justin said simply. "But all this will be worth nothing if Black Tremptor kills him before we find him. He may be able to lead us safely out of the northlands, if nothing else."

"I will not leave Fleur and Christabel behind," I said sharply. "I will not. You may take the harper back to Celandine. I stay here until I find them."

Justin looked at me; her eyes were reddened with sleeplessness, but they saw as clearly as ever into the mess we had made. "We will not leave you, Anne," she said. "If he cannot help us, he must find his own way back. But if he can help us, we must abandon Christabel now to rescue him."

"Then let's do it," I said shortly and turned my face away from the oak. A little wind shivered like laughter through their golden leaves.

We rode long and hard. The road plunged back into forest, up low foothills, brought us to the flank of the great dark mountain. We pulled up in its shadow. The dragon's eyrie shifted under the eye; stone pillars opened into passages, their granite walls split and hollowed like honeycombs, like some palace of winds, open at every angle yet with every passage leading into shadow, into the hidden dragon's heart.

"In there?" Danica asked. There was no fear in her voice, just her usual impatience to get things done. "Do we knock, or just walk in?" A wind roared through the stones then, bending trees as it blasted at us. We turned our mounts, flattened ourselves against them, while the wild wind rode over us. Recovering, Danica asked more quietly, "Do we go in together?"

"Yes," I said and then, "No. I'll go first."

"Don't be daft, Anne," Danica said crossly. "If we all go together, at least we'll know where we all are."

"And fools we will look, too," I said grimly, "caught along with the harper, waiting for Celandine's knights to rescue us as well." I turned to Justin. "Is there some secret, some riddle for surviving dragons?"

She shook her head helplessly. "It depends on the dragon. I know nothing about Black Tremptor, except that he most likely has not kept the harper for his harping."

"Two will go," I said. "And one wait."

They did not argue; there seemed no foolproof way, except for none of us to go. We tossed coins: two peacocks and one Celandine. Justin, who got the queen, did not look happy, but the coins were adamant. Danica and I left her standing with our horses, shielded within green boughs, watching us. We climbed the bald slope quietly, trying not to scatter stones. We had to watch our feet, pick a careful path to keep from sliding. Danica, staring groundward, stopped suddenly ahead of me to pick up something.

"Look," she breathed. I did, expecting a broken harp string, or an ivory button with Celandine's profile on it.

It was an emerald as big as my thumbnail, shaped and faceted. I stared at it a moment. Then I said, "Dragon-treasure. We came to find a harper."

"But Anne—there's another—" She scrabbled across loose stone to retrieve it. "Topaz. And over there a sapphire—"

"Danica," I pleaded. "You can carry home the entire mountain after you've dispatched the dragon."

"I'm coming," she said breathlessly, but she had scuttled crabwise across the slope toward yet another gleam. "Just one more. They're so beautiful, and just lying here free as rain for anyone to take."

"Danica! They'll be as free when we climb back down."

"I'm coming."

I turned, in resignation to her sudden magpie urge. "I'm going up."

"Just a moment, don't go alone. Oh, Anne, look there, it's a diamond. I've never seen such fire."

I held my breath, gave her that one moment. It had been such a long, hard journey I found it impossible to deny her an unexpected pleasure. She knelt, groping along the side of a boulder for a shining as pure as water in the sunlight. "I'm coming," she assured me, her back to me. "I'm coming."

And then the boulder lifted itself up off the ground. Something forked and nubbled like a tree root, whispering harshly to itself, caught her by her hand and by her honey hair and pulled her down into its hole. The boulder dropped ponderously, earth shifted close around its sides as if it had never moved.

I stared, stunned. I don't remember crossing the slope, only beating on the boulder with my hands and then my sword hilt, crying furiously at it, until all the broken shards underfoot undulated and swept me in a dry, rattling, bruising wave back down the slope into the trees.

Justin ran to help me. I was torn, bleeding, cursing, crying;

I took a while to become coherent. "Of all the stupid, feeble tricks to fall for! A trail of jewels! They're probably not even real, and Danica got herself trapped under a mountain for a pocketful of coal or dragon fewmets—"

"She won't be trapped quietly," Justin said. Her face was waxen. "What took her?"

"A little crooked something—an imp, a mountain troll— Justin, she's down there without us in a darkness full of whispering things—I can't believe we were so stupid!"

"Anne, calm down, we'll find her."

"I can't calm down!" I seized her shoulders, shook her. "Don't you disappear and leave me searching for you, too—"

"I won't, I promise. Anne, listen." She smoothed my hair with both her hands back from my face. "Listen to me We'll find her. We'll find Christabel and Fleur, we will not leave this land until—"

"How?" I shouted. "How? Justin, she's under solid rock!"

"There are ways. There are always ways. This land riddles constantly, but all the riddles have answers. Fleur will turn from a bird into a woman, we will find a path for Christabel out of the wood-king's country, we will rescue Danica from the mountain imps. There are ways to do these things, we only have to find them."

"How?" I cried again, for it seemed the farther we traveled in that land, the more trouble we got into. "Every time we turn around one of us disappears! You'll go next—"

"I will not, I promise—"

"Or I will."

"I know a few riddles," someone said. "Perhaps I can help."

We broke apart, as startled as if a tree had spoken: perhaps one had, in this exasperating land. But it was a woman. She wore a black cloak with silver edging; her ivory hair and iris eyes and her grave, calm face within the hood were very beautiful. She carried an odd staff of gnarled black wood inset with a jewel the same pale violet as her eyes. She spoke gently, unsurprised by us; perhaps nothing in this place surprised her anymore. She added, at our silence, "My name is Yrecros. You are in great danger from the dragon; you must know that."

"We have come to rescue a harper," I said bitterly. "We were five, when we crossed into this land."

"Ah."

"Do you know this dragon?"

She did not answer immediately; beside me, Justin was oddly still. The staff shifted; the jewel glanced here and there, like an eye. The woman whose name was Yrecros said finally, "You may ask me anything."

"I just did," I said bewilderedly. Justin's hand closed on my arm; I looked at her. Her face was very pale; her eyes held a strange, intense light I recognized; she had scented something intangible and was in pursuit. At such times she was impossible.

"Yrecros," she said softly. "My name is Nitsuj."

The woman smiled.

"What are you doing?" I said between my teeth.

"It's a game," Justin breathed. "Question for answer. She'll tell us all we need to know."

"Why must it be a game?" I protested. She and the woman were gazing at one another, improbable fighters about to engage in a delicate battle of wits. They seemed absorbed in one another, curious, stone-deaf. I raised my voice. "Justin!"

"You'll want the harper, I suppose," the woman said. I worked out her name then and closed my eyes.

Justin nodded. "It's what we came for. And if I lose?"

"I want you," the woman said simply, "for my apprentice." She smiled again, without malice or menace. "For seven years."

My breath caught. "No." I could barely speak. I seized Justin's arm, shook her. "Justin. Justin, please!" For just a moment I had, if not her eyes, her attention.

"It's all right, Anne," she said softly. "We'll get the harper without a battle, and rescue Fleur and Christabel and Danica as well."

"Justin!" I shouted. Above us all the pillars and cornices of stone echoed her name; great, barbed-winged birds wheeled out of the trees. But unlike bird and stone, Justin did not hear.

"You are a guest in this land," the woman said graciously. "You may ask first."

"Where is the road to the country of the woodland king?"

"The white stag in the oak forest follows the road to the land of the harper king," Yrecros answered, "if you follow from morning to night, without weapons and without rest. What is the Song of Ducirc, and on what instrument was it first played?"

"The Song of Ducirc was the last song of a murdered poet to his love, and it was played to his lady in her high tower on an instrument of feathers, as all the birds in the forest who heard it sang her his lament," Justin said promptly. I breathed a little then; she had been telling us such things all her life. "What traps the witch in the border woods in her true shape, and how can her power be taken?"

"The border witch may be trapped by a cage of iron; her staff of power is the spoon with which she stirs her magic. What begins with fire and ends with fire and is black and white between?"

"Night," Justin said. Even I knew that one. The woman's face held, for a moment, the waning moon's smile. "Where is the path to the roots of this mountain, and what do those who dwell there fear most?"

"The path is fire, which will open their stones, and what they fear most is light. What is always coming yet never here, has a name but does not exist, is longer than day but shorter than day?"

Justin paused a blink. "Tomorrow," she said, and added, "in autumn." The woman smiled her lovely smile. I loosed breath noiselessly. "What will protect us from the dragon?"

The woman studied Justin, as if she were answering some private riddle of her own. "Courtesy," she said simply. "Where is Black Tremptor's true name hidden?"

Justin was silent; I felt her thoughts flutter like a bird seeing a perch. The silence lengthened; an icy finger slid along my bones.

"I do not know," Justin said at last, and the woman answered, "The dragon's name is hidden within a riddle."

Justin read my thoughts; her hand clamped on my wrist. "Don't fight," she breathed.

"That's not—"

"The answer's fair."

The woman's brows knit thoughtfully. "Is there anything else you need to know?" She put her staff lightly on Justin's shoulder, turned the jewel toward her pale face. The jewel burned a sudden flare of amethyst, as if in recognition. "My name is Sorcery and that is the path I follow. You will come with me for seven years. After that, you may choose to stay."

"Tell me," I pleaded desperately, "how to rescue her. You have told me everything else."

The woman shook her head, smiling her brief moon-smile. Justin looked at me finally; I saw the answer in her eyes.

I stood mute, watching her walk away from me, tears pushing into my eyes, unable to plead or curse because there had been a game within a game, and only I had lost. Justin glanced back at me once, but she did not really see me, she only saw the path she had walked toward all her life.

I turned finally to face the dragon.

I climbed the slope again alone. No jewels caught my eye, no voice whispered my name. Not even the dragon greeted me. As I wandered through columns and caverns and hallways of stone, I heard only the wind moaning through the great bones of the mountain. I went deeper into stone. The passageways glowed butterfly colors with secretions from the dragon's body. Here and there I saw a scale flaked off by stone; some flickered blue-green black, others the colors of fire. Once I saw a chip of claw, hard as horn, longer than my hand. Sometimes I smelled sulfur, sometimes smoke, mostly wind smelling of the stone it scoured endlessly.

I heard harping.

I found the harper finally, sitting ankle deep in jewels and gold, in a shadowy cavern, plucking wearily at his harp with one hand. His other hand was cuffed and chained with gold to a golden rivet in the cavern wall. He stared, speechless, when he saw me. He was, as rumored, tall and golden-haired, also unwashed, unkempt, and sour from captivity. Even so, it was plain to see why Celandine wanted him back.

"Who are you?" he breathed, as I trampled treasure to get to him.

"I am Celandine's cousin Anne. She sent her court to rescue you."

"It took you long enough," he grumbled, and added, "You couldn't have come this far alone."

"You did," I said tersely, examining the chain that held him. Even Fleur would have had it out of the wall in a minute. "It's gold, malleable. Why didn't you—"

"I tried," he said, and showed me his torn hands. "It's dragon magic." He jerked the chain fretfully from my hold. "Don't bother trying. The key's over near that wall." He looked behind me, bewilderedly, for my imaginary companions. "Are you alone? She didn't send her knights to fight this monster?"

"She didn't trust them to remember who they were supposed to kill," I said succinctly. He was silent while I crossed the room to rummage among pins and cups and necklaces for the key. I added, "I didn't ride from Carnelaine alone. I lost four companions in this land as we tracked you."

"Lost?" For a moment, his voice held something besides his own misery. "Dead?"

"I think not."

"How did you lose them?"

"One was lost to the witch in the wood."

"Was she a witch?" he said, astonished. "I played for her, but she never offered me anything to eat, hungry as I was. I could smell food, but she only said that it was burned and unfit for company."

"And one," I said, sifting through coins and wondering at the witch's taste, "to the harper-king in the wood."

"You saw him?" he breathed. "I played all night, hoping to hear his fabled harping, but he never answered with a note."

"Maybe you never stopped to listen," I said, in growing

despair over the blind way he blundered through the land. "And one to the imps under the mountain."

"What imps?"

"And last," I said tightly, "in a riddle-game to the sorceress with the jeweled staff. You were to be the prize."

He shifted, chain and coins rattling. "She only told me where to find what I was searching for, she didn't warn me of the dangers. She could have helped me! She never said she was a sorceress."

"Did she tell you her name?"

"I don't remember—what difference does it make? Hurry with the key before the dragon smells you here. It would have been so much easier for me if your companion had not lost the riddle-game."

I paused in my searching to gaze at him. "Yes," I said finally, "and it would have been easier than that for all of us if you had never come here. Why did you?"

He pointed. "I came for that."

"That" was a harp of bone. Its strings glistened with the same elusive, shimmering colors that stained the passageways. A golden key lay next to it. I am as musical as the next, no more, but when I saw those strange, glowing strings I was filled with wonder at what music they might make and I paused, before I touched the key, to pluck a note.

It seemed the mountain hummed.

"No!" the harper cried, heaving to his feet in a tide of gold. Wind sucked out of the cave, as at the draw of some gigantic wing. "You stupid, blundering—How do you think I got caught? Throw me the key! Quickly!"

I weighed the key in my hand, prickling at his rudeness.

But he was, after all, what I had promised Celandine to find, and I imagined that washed and fed and in the queen's hands, he would assert his charms again. I tossed the key; it fell a little short of his outstretched hand.

"Fool!" he snapped. "You are as clumsy as the queen."

Stone-still, I stared at him, as he strained, groping for the key. I turned abruptly to the harp and ran my hand down all the strings.

What traveled down the passages to find us shed smoke and fire and broken stone behind it. The harper groaned and hid behind his arms. Smoke cleared; great eyes like moons of fire gazed at us near the high ceiling. A single claw as long as my shin dropped within an inch of my foot. Courtesy, I thought frantically. Courtesy, she said. It was like offering idle chatter to the sun.

Before I could speak, the harper cried, "She played it! She came in here searching for it, too, though I tried to stop her—"

Heat whuffed at me; I felt the gold I wore burn my neck. I said, feeling scorched within as well, "I ask your pardon if I have offended you. I came, at my queen's request, to rescue her harper. It seems you do not care for harping. If it pleases you, I will take what must be an annoyance out of your house." I paused. The great eyes sank a little toward me. I added, for such things seemed important in this land, "My name is Anne."

"Anne," the smoke whispered. I heard the harper jerk in his chain. The claw retreated slightly; the immense flat lizard's head lowered, its fiery scales charred dark with smoke, tiny sparks of fire winking between its teeth. "What is his name?"

"Kestral," the harper said quickly. "Kestral Hunt."

"You are right," the hot breath sighed. "He is an annoyance. Are you sure you want him back?"

"No," I said, my eyes blurring in wonder and relief that I had finally found, in this dangerous land, something I did not need to fear. "He is extremely rude, ungrateful, and insensitive. I imagine that my queen loves him for his hair or for his harper's hands; she must not listen to him speak. So I had better take him. I am sorry that he snuck into your house and tried to steal from you."

"It is a harp made of dragon bone and sinew," the dragon said. "It is why I dislike harpers, who make such things and then sing songs of their great cleverness. As this one would have." Its jaws yawned; a tongue of fire shot out, melted gold beside the harper's hand. He scuttled against the wall.

"I beg your pardon," he said hastily. A dark curved dragon's smile hung in the fading smoke; it snorted heat.

"Perhaps I will keep you and make a harp of your bones."

"It would be miserably out of tune," I commented. "Is there something I can do for you in exchange for the harper's freedom?"

An eye dropped close, moon-round, shadows of color constantly disappearing through it. "Tell me my name," the dragon whispered. Slowly I realized it was not a challenge but a plea. "A woman took my name from me long ago, in a riddle-game. I have been trying to remember it for years."

"Yrecros?" I breathed. So did the dragon, nearly singeing my hair.

"You know her."

"She took something from me: my dearest friend. Of you she said: the dragon's name is hidden within a riddle."

"Where is she?"

"Walking paths of sorcery in this land."

Claws flexed across the stones, smooth and beetle-black. "I used to know a little sorcery. Enough to walk as man. Will you help me find my name?"

"Will you help me find my friends?" I pleaded in return. "I lost four, searching for this unbearable harper. One or two may not want my help, but I will never know until I see them."

"Let me think . . ." the dragon said. Smoke billowed around me suddenly, acrid, ash-white. I swallowed smoke, coughed it out. When my stinging eyes could see again, a gold-haired harper stood in front of me. He had the dragon's eyes.

I drew in smoke again, astonished. Through my noise, I could hear Kestral behind me, tugging at his chain and shouting.

"What of me?" he cried furiously. "You were sent to rescue me! What will you tell Celandine? That you found her harper and brought the dragon home instead?" His own face gazed back at him, drained the voice out of him a moment. He tugged at the chain frantically, desperately. "You cannot harp! She'd know you false by that, and by your ancient eyes."

"Perhaps," I said, charmed by his suggestion, "she will not care."

"Her knights will find me. You said they seek to kill me! You will murder me."

"Those that want you dead will likely follow me," I said wearily, "for the gold-haired harper who rides with me. It is for the dragon to free you, not me. If he chooses to, you will have to find your own way back to Celandine, or else promise not to speak except to sing."

I turned away from him. The dragon-harper picked up his

harp of bone. He said in his husky, smoky voice, "I keep my bargains. The key to your freedom lies in a song."

We left the harper chained to his harping, listening puzzledly with his deaf ear and untuned brain, for the one song, of all he had ever played and never heard, that would bring him back to Celandine. Outside, in the light, I led dragon-fire to the stone that had swallowed Danica, and began my backwards journey toward Yrecros.

# Lady of the Skulls

The Lady saw them ride across the plain: a company of six. Putting down her watering can, which was the bronze helm of some unfortunate knight, she leaned over the parapet, chin on her hand. They were all armed, their warhorses caparisoned; they glittered under the noon sun with silver-edged shields, jeweled bridles and sword hilts. What, she wondered as always in simple astonishment, did they imagine they had come to fight? She picked up the helm, poured water into a skull containing a miniature rosebush. The water came from within the tower, the only source on the entire barren, sun-cracked plain. The knights would ride around in the hot sun for hours, looking for entry. At sunset, she would greet them, carrying water.

She sighed noiselessly, troweling around the little rose-bush with a dragon's claw. If they were too blind to find the tower door, why did they think they could see clearly within it? They, she thought in sudden impatience. They, they, they . . . they fed the plain with their bleached bones, they never learned. . . .

A carrion bird circled above her, counting heads. She scowled at it; it cried back at her, mocking. *You,* its black eye said, *never die. But you bring the dead to me.*

"They never listen to me," she said, looking over the plain again, her eyes prickling dryly. In the distance, lightning cracked apart the sky; purple clouds rumbled. But there was no rain in them, never any rain; the sky was as tearless as she. She moved from skull to skull along the parapet wall, watering things she had grown stubbornly from seeds that blew from distant, placid gardens in peaceful kingdoms. Some were grasses, weeds, or wildflowers. She did not care; she watered anything that grew.

The men below began their circling. Their mounts kicked up dust, snorting; she heard cursing, bewildered questions, then silence as they paused to rest. Sometimes they called her, pleading. But she could do nothing for them. They churned around the tower, bright, powerful, richly armed. She read the devices on their shields: three of Grenelief, one of Stoney Head, one of Dulcis Isle, one of Carnelaine. After a time, one man dropped out of the circle, stood back. His shield was simple: a red rose on white, Carnelaine, she thought, looking down at him, then realized he was looking up at her.

He would see a puff of airy sleeve, a red geranium in an upside-down skull. Lady of the Skulls, they called her, clamoring to enter. Sometimes they were more courteous, sometimes less. She watered, waiting for this one to call her. He did not; he guided his horse into the tower's shadow and dismounted. He took his helm off, sat down to wait, burrowing idly in the ground and flicking stones as he watched her sleeve sometimes, and sometimes the distant storm.

Drawn to his calm, the others joined him finally, flinging off pieces of armor. They cursed the hard ground and sat, their voices drifting up to her in the windless air as she continued her watering.

Like others before them, they spoke of what the most precious thing of the legendary treasure might be, besides elusive. They had made a pact, she gathered: If one obtained the treasure, he would divide it among those left living. She raised a brow. The one of Dulcis Isle, a dark-haired man wearing red jewels in his ears, said, "Anything of the dragon for me. They say it was a dragon's hoard once. They say that dragon bones are wormholed with magic, and if you move one bone the rest will follow. The bones will bring the treasure with them."

"I heard," said the man from Stoney Head, "there is a well and a fountain rising from it, and when the drops of the fountain touch ground they turn to diamonds."

"Don't talk of water," one of the three thick-necked, nut-haired men of Grenelief pleaded. "I drank all mine."

"All we must do is find the door. There's water within."

"What are you going to do?" the man of Carnelaine asked. "Hoist the water on your shoulder and carry it out?"

The straw-haired man from Stoney Head tugged at his long moustaches. He had a plain, blunt, energetic voice devoid of any humor. "I'll carry it out in my mouth. When I come back alive for the rest of it, there'll be plenty to carry it

in. Skulls, if nothing else. I heard there's a sorceress's cauldron, looks like a rusty old pot —"

"May be that," another of Grenelief said.

"May be, but I'm going for the water. What else could be
most precious in this heat-blasted place?"

"That's a point," the man of Dulcis Isle said. Then: "But,
no, it's dragon-bone for me."

"More to the point," the third of Grenelief said, aggrieved,
"how do we get in the cursed place?"

"There's a lady up there watering plants," the man of Carnelaine said, and there were all their faces staring upward;
she could have tossed jewels into their open mouths. "She
knows we're here."

"It's the Lady," they murmured, hushed.

"Lady of the Skulls."

"Does she have hair, I wonder."

"She's old as the tower. She must be a skull."

"She's beautiful," the man of Stoney Head said shortly.
"They always are, the ones who lure, the ones who guard, the
ones who give death."

"Is it her tower?" the one of Carnelaine asked. "Or is she
trapped?"

"What's the difference? When the spell is gone, so will she
be. She's nothing real, just a piece of the tower's magic."

They shifted themselves as the tower's shadow shifted.
The Lady took a sip of water out of the helm, then dipped her
hand in it and ran it over her face. She wanted to lean over
the edge and shout at them all: Go home, you silly, brainless
fools. If you know so much, what are you doing here sitting
on bare ground in front of a tower without a door waiting for
a woman to kill you? They moved to one side of the tower,

she to the other, as the sun climbed down the sky. She watched the sun set. Still the men refused to leave, though they had not a stick of wood to burn against the dark. She sighed her noiseless sigh and went down to greet them.

The fountain sparkled in the midst of a treasure she had long ceased to notice. She stepped around gold armor, black, gold-rimmed dragon bones, the white bones of princes. She took the plain silver goblet beside the rim of the well, and dipped it into the water, feeling the cooling mist from the little fountain. The man of Dulcis Isle was right about the dragon bones. The doorway was the dragon's open yawning maw, and it was invisible by day.

The last ray of sunlight touched the bone, limned a black, toothed opening that welcomed the men. Mute, they entered, and she spoke.

"You may drink the water, you may wander throughout the tower. If you make no choice, you may leave freely. Having left, you may never return. If you choose, you must make your choice by sunset tomorrow. If you choose the most precious thing in the tower, you may keep all that you see. If you choose wrongly, you will die before you leave the plain."

Their mouths were open again, their eyes stunned at what hung like vines from the old dragon's bones, what lay heaped upon the floor. Flicking, flicking, their eyes came across her finally, as she stood patiently holding the cup. Their eyes stopped at her: a tall, broad-shouldered, barefoot woman in a coarse white linen smock, her red hair bundled untidily on top of her head, her long skirt still splashed with the wine she had spilled in the tavern so long ago. In the torchlight it looked like blood.

They chose to sleep, as they always did, tired by the long

journey, dazed by too much rich, vague color in the shadows. She sat on the steps and watched them for a little. One cried in his sleep. She went to the top of the tower after a while, where she could watch the stars. Under the moon, the flowers turned odd, secret colors, as if their true colors blossomed in another land's daylight, and they had left their pale shadows behind by night. She fell asleep naming the moon's colors.

In the morning, she went down to see who had had sense enough to leave.

They were all still there, searching, picking, discarding among the treasures on the floor, scattered along the spiraling stairs. Shafts of light from the narrow windows sparked fiery colors that constantly caught their eyes, made them drop what they had, reach out again. Seeing her, the one from Dulcis Isle said, trembling, his eyes stuffed with riches, "May we ask questions? What is this?"

"Don't ask her, Marlebane," the one from Stoney Head said brusquely. "She'll lie. They all do."

She stared at him. "I will only lie to you," she promised. She took the small treasure from the hand of the man from Dulcis Isle. "This is an acorn made of gold. If you swallow it, you will speak all the languages of humans and animals."

"And this?" one of Grenelief said eagerly, pushing next to her, holding something of silver and smoke.

"That is a bracelet made of a dragon's nostril bone. The jewel in it is its petrified eye. It watches for danger when you wear it."

The man of Carnelaine was playing a flute made from a wizard's thighbone. His eyes, the odd gray-green of the dragon's eye, looked dream-drugged with the music. The man of Stoney Head shook him roughly.

"Is that your choice, Ran?"

"No." He lowered the flute, smiling. "No, Corbeil."

"Then drop it before it seizes hold of you and you choose it. Have you seen yet what you might take?"

"No. Have you changed your mind?"

"No." He looked at the fountain, but, prudent, did not speak.

"Bram, look at this," said one brother of Grenelief to another. "Look!"

"I am looking, Yew."

"Look at it! Look at it, Ustor! Have you ever seen such a thing? Feel it! And watch: It vanishes, in light."

He held a sword; its hilt was solid emerald, its blade like water falling in clear light over stone. The Lady left them, went back up the stairs, her bare feet sending gold coins and jewels spinning down through the crosshatched shafts of light. She stared at the place on the horizon where the flat dusty gold of the plain met the parched dusty sky. Go, she thought dully. Leave all this and go back to the places where things grow. Go, she willed them, go, go, go, with the beat of her heart's blood. But no one came out the door beneath her. Someone, instead, came up the stairs.

"I have a question," said Ran of Carnelaine.

"Ask."

"What is your name?"

She had all but forgotten; it came to her again, after a beat of surprise. "Amaranth." He was holding a black rose in one hand, a silver lily in the other. If he chose one, the thorns would kill him; the other, flashing its pure light, would sear through his eyes into his brain.

"Amaranth. Another flower."

"So it is," she said indifferently. He laid the magic flowers on the parapet, picked a dying geranium leaf, smelled the miniature rose. "It has no smell," she said. He picked another dead leaf. He seemed always on the verge of smiling. It made him look sometimes wise and sometimes foolish. He drank out of the bronze watering helm; it was the color of his hair.

"This water is too cool and sweet to come out of such a barren plain," he commented. He seated himself on the wall, watching her. "Corbeil says you are not real. You look real enough to me." She was silent, picking dead clover out of the clover pot. "Tell me where you came from."

She shrugged. "A tavern."

"And how did you come here?"

She gazed at him. "How did you come here, Ran of Carnelaine?"

He did smile then, wryly. "Carnelaine is poor; I came to replenish its coffers."

"There must be less chancy ways."

"Maybe I wanted to see the most precious thing there is to be found. Will the plain bloom again, if it is found? Will you have a garden instead of skull-pots?"

"Maybe," she said levelly. "Or maybe I will disappear. Die when the magic dies. If you choose wisely, you'll have answers to your questions."

He shrugged. "Maybe I will not choose. There are too many precious things."

She glanced at him. He was trifling, wanting hints from her, answers couched in riddles. Shall I take rose or lily? Or wizard's thighbone? Tell me. Sword or water or dragon's eye? Some had questioned her so before.

She said simply, "I cannot tell you what to take. I do not

know myself. As far as I have seen, everything kills." It was as close as she could come, as plain as she could make it: Leave.

But he said only, his smile gone, "Is that why you never left?" She stared at him again. "Walked out the door, crossed the plain on some dead king's horse and left?"

She said, "I cannot." She moved away from him, tending some wildflowers she called wind-bells, for she imagined their music as the night air tumbled down from the mountains to race across the plain. After a while, she heard his steps again, going down.

A voice summoned her: "Lady of the Skulls!" It was the man of Stoney Head. She went down, blinking in the thick, dusty light. He stood stiffly, his face hard. They all stood still, watching.

"I will leave now," he said. "I may take anything?"

"Anything," she said, making her heart stone against him, a ghost's heart, so that she would not pity him. He went to the fountain, took a mouthful of water. He looked at her, and she moved to show him the hidden lines of the dragon's mouth. He vanished through the stones.

They heard him scream a moment later. The three of Grenelief stared toward the sound. They each wore pieces of a suit of armor that made the wearer invisible: one lacked an arm, another a thigh, the other his hands. Subtly their expressions changed, from shock and terror into something more complex. Five, she saw them thinking. Only five ways to divide it now.

"Anyone else?" she asked coldly. The man of Dulcis Isle slumped down onto the stairs, swallowing. He stared at her, his face gold-green in the light. He swallowed again. Then he shouted at her.

She had heard every name they could think of to shout before she had ever come to the tower. She walked up the stairs past him; he did not have the courage to touch her. She went to stand among her plants. Corbeil of Stoney Head lay where he had fallen, a little brown patch of wet earth beside his open mouth. As she looked, the sun dried it, and the first of the carrion birds landed.

She threw bones at the bird, cursing, though it looked unlikely that anyone would be left to take his body back. She hit the bird a couple of times, then another came. Then someone took the bone out of her hand, drew her back from the wall.

"He's dead," Ran said simply. "It doesn't matter to him whether you throw bones at the birds or at him."

"I have to watch," she said shortly. She added, her eyes on the jagged line the parapet made against the sky, like blunt, worn dragon's teeth, "You keep coming, and dying. Why do you all keep coming? Is treasure worth being breakfast for the carrion crows?"

"It's worth many different things. To the brothers of Grenelief it means adventure, challenge, adulation if they succeed. To Corbeil it was something to be won, something he could have that no one else could get. He would have sat on top of the pile and let men look up to him, hating and envying."

"He was a cold man. Cold men feed on a cold fire. Still," she added, sighing, "I would have preferred to see him leave on his feet. What does the treasure mean to you?"

"Money." He smiled his vague smile. "It's not in me to lose my life over money. I'd sooner walk empty-handed out the door. But there's something else."

"What?"

"The riddle itself. That draws us all, at heart. What is the most precious thing? To see it, to hold it, above all to recognize it and choose it—that's what keeps us coming and traps you here." She stared at him, saw, in his eyes, the wonder that he felt might be worth his life.

She turned away; her back to him, she watered bleeding heart and columbine, stonily ignoring what the crows were doing below. "If you find the thing itself," she asked dryly, "what will you have left to wonder about?"

"There's always life."

"Not if you are killed by wonder."

He laughed softly, an unexpected sound, she thought, in that place. "Wouldn't you ride across the plain if you heard tales of this tower, to try to find the most precious thing in it?"

"Nothing's precious to me," she said, heaving a cauldron of dandelions into shadow. "Not down there, anyway. If I took one thing away with me, it would not be sword or gold or dragon bone. It would be whatever is alive."

He touched the tiny rose. "You mean, like this? Corbeil would never have died for this."

"He died for a mouthful of water."

"He thought it was a mouthful of jewels." He sat beside the rose, his back to the air, watching her pull pots into shadow against the noon light. "Which makes him twice a fool, I suppose. Three times a fool: for being wrong, for being deluded, and for dying. What a terrible place this is. It strips you of all delusions, and then it strips your bones."

"It is terrible," she said somberly. "Yet those who leave without choosing never seem to get the story straight. They must always talk of the treasure they didn't take, not of the bones they didn't leave."

"It's true. Always, they take wonder with them out of this

tower and they pass it on to every passing fool." He was silent a little, still watching her. "Amaranth," he said slowly. "That's the flower in poetry that never dies. It's apt."

"Yes."

"And there is another kind of Amaranth, that's fiery and beautiful and it dies. . . ." Her hands stilled, her eyes widened, but she did not speak. He leaned against the hot, crumbling stones, his dragon's eyes following her like a sunflower following the sun. "What were you," he asked, "when you were the Amaranth that could die?"

"I was one of those faceless women who brought you wine in a tavern. Those you shout at, and jest about, and maybe give a coin to and maybe not, depending how we smile."

He was silent, so silent she thought he had gone, but when she turned, he was still there; only his smile had gone. "Then I've seen you," he said softly, "many times, in many places. But never in a place like this."

"The man from Stoney Head expected someone else, too."

"He expected a dream."

"He saw what he expected: Lady of the Skulls." She pulled wild mint into a shady spot under some worn tapestry. "And so he found her. That's all I am now. You were better off when all I served was wine."

"You didn't build this tower."

"How do you know? Maybe I got tired of the laughter and the coins and I made a place for myself where I could offer coins and give nothing."

"Who built this tower?"

She was silent, crumbling a mint leaf between her fingers. "I did," she said at last. "The Amaranth who never dies."

"Did you?" He was oddly pale; his eyes glittered in the

light as if at the shadow of danger. "You grow roses out of thin air in this blistered plain; you try to beat back death for us with our own bones. You curse our stupidity and our fate, not us. Who built this tower for you?" She turned her face away, mute. He said softly, "The other Amaranth, the one that dies, is also called Love-lies-bleeding."

"It was the last man," she said abruptly, her voice husky, shaken with sudden pain, "who offered me a coin for love. I was so tired of being touched and then forgotten, of hearing my name spoken and then not, as if I were only real when I was looked at and just something to forget after that, like you never remember the flowers you toss away. So I said to him: No, and no, and no. And then I saw his eyes. They were amber with thorns of dark in them: sorcerer's eyes. He said, 'Tell me your name.' And I said, 'Amaranth,' and he laughed and laughed and I could only stand there, with the wine I had brought him overturned on my tray, spilling down my skirt. He said, 'Then you shall make a tower of your name, for the tower is already built in your heart.'"

"Love-lies-bleeding," he whispered.

"He recognized that Amaranth."

"Of course he did. It was what died in his own heart."

She turned then, wordless, to look at him. He was smiling again, though his face was still blanched under the hard, pounding light, and the sweat shone in his hair. She said, "How do you know him?"

"Because I have seen this tower before and I have seen in it the woman we all expected, the only woman some men ever know . . . And every time we come expecting her, the woman who lures us with what's most precious to us and kills us with it, we build the tower around her again and again and again. . . ."

She gazed at him. A tear slid down her cheek and then another. "I thought it was my tower," she whispered. "The Amaranth that never dies but only lives forever to watch men die."

"It's all of us," he sighed. In the distance, thunder rumbled. "We all build towers, then dare each other to enter. . . ." He picked up the little rose in its skull-pot and stood abruptly; she followed him to the stairs.

"Where are you going with my rose?"

"Out."

She followed him down, protesting, "But it's mine!"

"You said we could choose anything."

"It's just a worthless thing I grew, it's nothing of the tower's treasure. If you must take after all, choose something worth your life!"

He glanced back at her, as they rounded the tower stairs to the bottom. His face was bone-white, but he could still smile. "I will give you back your rose," he said, "if you will let me take the Amaranth."

"But I am the only Amaranth."

He strode past his startled companions, whose hands were heaped with *this, no this,* and *maybe this.* As if the dragon's magical eye had opened in his own eye, he led her himself into the dragon's mouth.

# The Snow Queen

**Kay**

They stood together without touching, watching the snow fall. The sudden storm prolonging winter had surprised the city; little moved in the broad streets below them. Ancient filigreed lamps left from another century threw patterned wheels of light into the darkness, illumining the deep white silence crusting the world. Gerda, not hearing the silence, spoke.

"They look like white rose petals endlessly falling."

Kay said nothing. He glanced at his watch, then at the mirror across the room. The torchières gilded them: a lovely couple, the mirror said. In the gentle light Gerda's sunny hair looked like polished bronze; his own, shades paler, seemed almost white. Some trick of shadow flattened Gerda's face, erased its familiar hollows. Her petal-filled eyes were summer blue. His own face, with sharp bones at cheek and jaw, dark eyes beneath pale brows, looked, he thought, wild and austere: a monk's face, a wizard's face. He searched for some subtlety in Gerda's, but it would not yield to shadow. She wore a short black dress; on her it seemed incongruous, like black in a flower.

He commented finally, "Every time you speak, flowers fall from your mouth."

She looked at him, startled. Her face regained contours; they were graceful but uncomplex. She said, "What do you mean?" Was he complaining? Was he fanciful? She blinked, trying to see what he meant.

"You talk so much of flowers," he explained patiently. "Do you want a garden? Should we move to the country?"

"No," she said, horrified, then amended: "Only if—Do you want to? If we were in the country, there would be nothing to do but watch the snow fall. There would be no reason to wear this dress. Or these shoes. But do you want—"

"No," he said shortly. His eyes moved away from her; he jangled coins in his pocket. She folded her arms. The dress had short puffed sleeves, like a little girl's dress. Her arms looked chilled, but she made no move away from the cold, white scene beyond the glass. After a moment he mused, "There's a word I've been trying all day to think of. A word in a puzzle. Four letters, the clue is: the first word schoolboys conjugate."

"Schoolboys what?"

"Conjugate. Most likely Latin."

"I don't know any Latin," she said absently.

"I studied some . . . but I can't remember the first word I was taught. How could anyone remember?"

"Did you feed the angelfish?"

"This morning."

"They eat each other if they're not fed."

"Not angelfish."

"Fish do."

"Not all fish are cannibals."

"How do you know not angelfish in particular? We never let them go hungry; how do we really know?"

He glanced at her, surprised. Her hands tightened on her arms; she looked worried again. By fish? he wondered. Or was it a school of fish swimming through deep, busy waters? He touched her arm; it felt cold as marble. She smiled quickly; she loved being touched. The school of fish darted away; the deep waters were empty.

"What word," he wondered, "would you learn first in a language? What word would people need first? Or have needed, in the beginning of the world? Fire, maybe. Food, most likely. Or the name of a weapon?"

"Love," she said, gazing at the snow, and he shook his head impatiently.

"No, no—cold is more imperative than love; hunger overwhelms it. If I were naked in the snow down there, cold would override everything; my first thought would be to warm myself before I died. Even if I saw you walking naked toward me, life would take precedence over love."

"Then cold," she said. Her profile was like marble, flawless, unblinking. "Four letters, the first word in the world."

He wanted suddenly to feel her smooth marble cheek under his lips, kiss it into life. He said instead, "I can't remember the Latin word for cold." She looked at him, smiling again, as if she had felt his impulse in the air between them.

His thoughts veered off-balance, tugged toward her fine, flushed skin and delicate bones, something nameless, blind and hungry in him reaching toward another nameless thing. She said,

"There's the cab."

It was a horse-drawn sleigh; the snow was too deep for ordinary means. Had she been smiling, he wondered, because she had seen the cab? He kissed her anyway, lightly on the cheek, before she turned to get her coat, thinking how long he had known her and how little he knew her and how little he knew of how much or little there was in her to know.

**Gerda**

They arrived at Selene's party fashionably late. She had a vast flat with an old-fashioned ballroom. Half the city was crushed into it, despite the snow. Prisms of ice dazzled in the chandeliers; not even the hundred candles in them could melt their glittering, frozen jewels. On long tables, swans carved of ice held hothouse berries, caviar, sherbet between their wings. A business acquaintance attached himself to Kay; Gerda, drifting toward champagne, was found by Selene.

"Gerda!" She kissed air enthusiastically around Gerda's face. "How are you, angel? Such a dress. So innocent. How do you get away with it?"

"With what?"

"And such a sense of humor. Have you met Maurice? Gerda, Maurice Crow."

"Call me Bob," said Maurice Crow to Gerda, as Selene flung her fruity voice into the throng and hurried after it.

"Why?"

Maurice Crow chuckled. "Good question." He had a kindly smile, Gerda thought; it gentled his thin, aging, beaky face. "If you were named Maurice, wouldn't you rather be called Bob?"

"I don't think so," Gerda said doubtfully. "I think I would rather be called my name."

"That's because you're beautiful. A beautiful woman makes any name beautiful."

"I don't like my name. It sounds like something to hold stockings up with. Or a five-letter word from a Biblical phrase." She glanced around the room for Kay. He stood in a ring of brightly dressed women; he had just made them laugh. She sighed without realizing it. "And I'm not really beautiful. This is just a disguise."

Maurice Crow peered at her more closely out of his black, shiny eyes. He offered her his arm; after a moment she figured out what to do with it. "You need a glass of champagne." He patted her hand gently. "Come with me."

"You see, I hate parties."

"Ah."

"And Kay loves them."

"And you," he said, threading a sure path among satin and silk and clouds of tulle, "love Kay."

"I have always loved Kay."

"And now you feel he might stop loving you? So you come here to please him."

"How quickly you understand things. But I'm not sure if he is pleased that I came. We used to know each other so well. Now I feel stupid around him, and slow, and plain, even when he tells me I'm not. It used to be different between us."

"When?"

She shrugged. "Before. Before the city began taking little pieces of him away from me. He used to bring me wildflowers he had picked in the park. Now he gives me blood-red roses once a year. Some days his eyes never see me, not even in bed. I see contracts in his eyes, and the names of restaurants, expensive shoes, train schedules. A train schedule is more interesting to him than I am."

"To become interesting, you must be interested."

"In Kay? Or in trains?"

"If," he said, "you can no longer tell the difference, perhaps it is Kay who has grown uninteresting."

"Oh, no," she said quickly. "Never to me." She had flushed. With the quick, warm color in her face and the light spilling from the icy prisms onto her hair, into her eyes, she caused Maurice Crow to hold her glass too long under the champagne fountain. "He is beautiful and brilliant, and we have loved each other since we were children. But it seems that, having grown up, we no longer recognize one another." She took the overflowing glass from Maurice Crow's hand and drained it. Liquid from the dripping glass fell beneath her chaste neckline, rolled down her breast like icy tears. "We are both in disguise."

**The Snow Queen**

Neva entered late. She wore white satin that clung to her body like white clings to the calla lily. White peacock feathers sparkling with faux diamonds trailed down her long ivory hair. Her eyes were black as the night sky between the winter constellations. They swept the room, picked out a face here: Gerda's—How sweet, Neva thought, to have kept that expression, like one's first kiss treasured in tissue paper—and there: Kay's. Her eyes were wide, very still. The young man with her said something witty. She did not hear. He tried again, his eyes growing anxious. She watched Kay tell another story; the women around him—doves, warblers, a couple of trumpeting swans—laughed again. He laughed with them, reluctant but irresistibly amused by himself. He lifted champagne to his lips; light leaped from the cut crystal. His pale hair shone like the silk of Neva's dress; his lips were shaped cleanly as the swan's wing. She waited, perfectly still. Lowering his glass, the amused smile tugging again at his lips, he saw her standing in the archway across the room.

To his eye she was alone; the importunate young lapdog beside her did not exist. So his look told her, as she drew at it with the immense and immeasurable pull of a wayward planet wandering too close to someone's cold, bright, inconstant moon. The instant he would have moved, she did, crossing the room to join him before his brilliant, fluttering circle could scatter. Like him, she preferred an audience. She waited in her outer orbit, composed, mysterious, while he told another story. This one had a woman in it—Gerda—and something about angels or fish.

"And then," he said, "we had an argument about the first word in the world."

"Coffee," guessed one woman, and he smiled appreciatively.

"No," suggested another.

"It was for a crossword puzzle. The first word you learn to conjugate in Latin."

"But we always speak French in bed," a woman murmured. "My husband and I."

Kay's eyes slid to Neva. Her expression remained changeless; she offered no word. He said lightly, "No, no, *ma chère*, one conjugates a verb; one has conjugal relations with one's spouse. Or not, as the case may be."

"Do people still?" someone wondered. "How boring."

"To conjugate," Neva said suddenly in her dark, languid voice, "means to inflect a verb in an orderly fashion through all its tenses. As in: *amo, amas, amat.* I love, you love—"

"But that's it!" Kay cried. "The answer to the puzzle. How could I have forgotten?"

"Love?" someone said perplexedly. Neva touched her brow delicately.

"I cannot," she said, "remember the Latin word for dance."

"You do it so well," Kay said a moment later, as they glided onto the floor. So polished it was that the flames from the chandeliers seemed frozen underfoot, as if they danced on stars. "And no one studies Latin anymore."

"I never tire of learning," Neva said. Her gloved hand lay lightly on his shoulder, close to his neck. Even in winter his skin looked warm, burnished by tropical skies, endless sun. She wanted to cover that warmth with her body, draw it into her own white-marble skin. Her eyes flicked constantly around the room over his shoulder, studying women's faces. "Who is Gerda?" she asked, then knew her: the tall, beautiful, childlike woman who watched Kay with a hopeless, forlorn expression, as if she had already lost him.

"She is my wife," Kay said, with a studied balance of

lightness and indifference in his voice. Neva lifted her hand off his shoulder, settled it again closer to his skin.

"Ah."

"We have known each other all our lives."

"She loves you still."

"How do you know?" he said, surprised. She guided him into a half turn, so that for a moment he faced his abandoned Gerda, with her sad eyes and downturned mouth, standing in her naive black dress, her champagne tilted and nearly spilling, with only a cadaverous, beaky man trying to get her attention. Neva turned him again; he looked at her, blinking, as if he had been lightly, unexpectedly struck. She shifted her hand, crooked her fingers around his bare neck.

"She is very beautiful."

"Yes."

"It is her air of childlike innocence that is so appealing."

"And so exasperating," he exclaimed suddenly, as if, like the Apostle, he had been illumined by lightning and stunned with truth.

"Innocence can be," Neva said.

"Gerda knows so little of life. We have lived for years in this city and still she seems so helpless. Scattered. She doesn't know what she wants from life; she wouldn't know how to take it if she did."

"Some women never learn."

"You have. You are so elegant, so sophisticated. So sure." He paused; she saw the word trembling on his lips. She held his gaze, pulled him deeper, deeper into her winter darkness. "But," he breathed, "you must have men telling you this all the time."

"Only if I want them to. And there are not many I choose to listen to."

"You are so beautiful," he said wildly, as if the word had been tormented out of him.

She smiled, slid her other hand up his arm to link her fingers behind his neck. She whispered, "And so are you."

**The Thief**

Briony watched Gerda walk blindly through the falling snow. It caught on her lashes, melted in the hot, wet tears on her cheeks. Her long coat swung carelessly open to the bitter cold, revealing pearls, gold, a hidden pocket in the lining in which Briony envisioned cash, cards, earrings taken off and forgotten. She gave little thought to Gerda's tears: some party, some man, it was a familiar tale.

She shadowed Gerda, walking silently on the fresh-crushed snow of her footprints, which was futile, she realized, since they were nothing more than a wedge of toe and a rapier stab of stiletto heel. Still, in her tumultuous state of mind, the woman probably would not have noticed a traveling circus behind her.

She slid, shadow-like, to Gerda's side.

"Spare change?"

Gerda glanced at her; her eyes flooded again; she shook her head helplessly. "I have nothing."

Briony's knife snicked open, flashing silver in a rectangle of window light. "You have a triple strand of pearls, a sapphire dinner ring, a gold wedding ring, a pair of earrings either diamond or cubic zirconium, on, I would guess, fourteen-karat posts."

"I never got my ears pierced," Gerda said wearily. Briony missed a step, caught up with her.

"Everyone has pierced ears!"

"Diamond, and twenty-two-karat gold." She pulled at them, and at her rings. "They were all gifts from Kay. You might as well have them. Take my coat, too." She shrugged it off, let it fall. "That was also a gift." She tugged the pearls at her throat; they scattered like luminous, tiny moons around her in the snow. "Oh, sorry."

"What are you doing? Briony breathed. The woman, wearing nothing more than a short and rather silly dress, turned to the icy darkness beyond the window light. She had actually taken a step into it when Briony caught her arm. "Stop!" Briony hauled her coat out of the snow. "Put this back on. You'll freeze!"

"I don't care. Why should you?"

"Nobody is worth freezing for."

"Kay is."

"Is he?" She flung the coat over Gerda's shoulders, pulled it closed. "God, woman, what Neanderthal age are you from?"

"I love him."

"So?"

"He doesn't love me."

"So?"

"If he doesn't love me, I don't want to live."

Briony stared at her, speechless, having learned from various friends *in extremis* that there was no arguing with such crazed and muddled thinking. Look, she might have said, whirling the woman around to shock her. See that snowdrift beside the wall? Earlier tonight that was an old woman who could have used your coat. Or: Men have notoriously bad taste, why should you let one decide whether you live or die? Or: Love is an obsolete emotion, ranking in usefulness somewhere between earwigs and toe mold.

She lied instead. She said, "I felt like that once."

She caught a flicker of life in the still, remote eyes. "Did you? Did you want to die?"

"Why don't we go for hot chocolate and I'll tell you about it?"

They sat at the counter of an all-night diner, sipping hot chocolate liberally laced with brandy from Briony's flask. Briony had short, dark, curly hair and sparkling sapphire eyes. She wore lace stockings under several skirts, an antique vest of peacock feathers over a shirt of simulated snakeskin, thigh-high boots, and a dark, hooded cape with many hidden pockets. The waitress behind the counter watched her with a sardonic eye and snapped her gum as she poured Briony's chocolate. Drawn to Gerda's beauty and tragic pallor, she kept refilling Gerda's cup. So did Briony. Briony, improvising wildly, invented a rich, beautiful, upper-class young man whose rejection of her plunged her into despair.

"He loved me," she said, "for the longest night the world has ever known. Then he dumped me like soggy cereal. I was just another pretty face and recycled bod to him. Three days after he offered me marriage, children, cars as big as luxury liners, trips to the family graveyard in Europe, he couldn't even remember my name. Susie, he called me. Hello, Susie, how are you, what can I do for you? I was so miserable I wanted to eat mothballs. I wanted to lie on the sidewalk and sunburn myself to death. The worms wouldn't have touched me, I thought. Not even they could be interested."

"What did you do?" Gerda asked. Briony, reveling in despair, lost her thread of invention. The waitress refilled Gerda's cup.

"I knew a guy like that," the waitress said. "I danced on his car in spiked heels. Then I slashed his tires. Then I found out it wasn't his car."

"What did I do?" Briony said. "What did I do?" She paused dramatically. The waitress had stopped chewing her gum, waiting for an answer. "Well—I mean, of course I did what I had to. What else could I do, but what women like me do when men dropkick their hearts out of the field. Women like me. Of course women like you are different."

"What did you do?" Gerda asked again. Her eyes were wide and very dark; the brandy had flushed her cheeks. Drops of melted snow glittered like jewels in her disheveled hair. Briony gazed at her, musing.

"With money, you'd think you'd have more choices, wouldn't you? But money or love never taught you how to live. You don't know how to take care of yourself. So if Kay doesn't love you, you have to wander into the snow and freeze. But women like me, and Brenda here—"

"Jennifer," the waitress muttered.

"Jennifer, here, we're so used to fending for ourselves every day that it gets to be a habit. You're not used to fending, so you don't have the habit. So what you have to do is start pretending you have something to live for."

Gerda's eyes filled; a tear dropped into her chocolate. "I haven't."

"Of course you haven't, that's what I've been saying. That's why you have to pretend—"

"Why? It's easier just to walk back out into the snow."

"But if you keep pretending and pretending, one day you'll stumble onto something you care enough to live for, and if you turn yourself into an icicle now because of Kay, you won't be able to change your mind later. The only thing you're seeing in the entire world is Kay. Kay is in both your eyes, Kay is your mind. Which means you're only really seeing one tiny flyspeck of the world, one little puzzle piece. You have to learn to see around Kay. It's like staring at one star all the time and never seeing the moon or planets or constellations—"

"I don't know how to pretend," Gerda said softly. "Kay has always been the sky."

Jennifer swiped her cloth at a crumb, looking thoughtful. "What she says," she pointed out, tossing her head at Briony, "you only have to do it one day at a time. Always just today. That's all any of us do."

Gerda took a swallow of chocolate. Jennifer poured her more; Briony added brandy.

"After all," Briony said, "you could have told me to piss off and mind my own business. But you didn't. You put your coat back on and followed me here. So there must have been something—your next breath, a star you glimpsed—you care enough about."

"That's true," Gerda said, surprised. "But I don't remember what."

"Just keep pretending you remember."

Kay

Kay sat at breakfast with Neva, eating clouds and sunlight. Actually, it was hot biscuits and honey that dripped down his hand. Neva, discoursing on the likelihood of life on other planets, leaned across the table now and then and slipped her tongue between his fingers to catch the honey. Her face and her white negligee, a lacy tumble of roses, would slide like light past his groping fingers; she would be back in her chair, talking, before he could put his biscuit down.

"The likelihood of life on other planets is very, very great," she said. She had a crumb of Kay's breakfast on her cheek. He reached across the table to brush it away; she caught his forefinger in her mouth and sucked at it until he started to melt off the chair onto his knees. She loosed his finger then and asked, "Have you read Piquelle on the subject?"

"What?"

"Piquelle," she said patiently, "on the subject of life on other planets."

He swallowed. "No."

"Have another biscuit, darling. No, don't move, I'll get it."

"It's no—"

"No, I insist you stay where you are. Don't move." She took his plate and stood up. He could see the outline of her pale, slender body under the lace. "Did you say something, Kay?"

"I groaned."

"There are billions of galaxies. And in each galaxy, billions of stars, each of which might well have its courtiers orbiting it." She reached into the dainty cloth in which the biscuits were wrapped. Through the window above the sideboard, snow fell endlessly; her hothouse daffodils shone like artificial light among the bone china, the crystal butter dish, the honey pot, the napkins patterned with an exotic flock of startled birds trying to escape beyond the hems. Kay caught a fold of her negligee between his teeth as she put his biscuit down. She laughed indulgently, pushed against his face and let him trace the circle of her navel through the lace with his tongue. Then she glided out of reach, sat back in her chair.

"Think of it!"

"I am."

"Billions of stars, billions of galaxies! And life around each star, eating, conversing, dreaming, perhaps indulging in startling alien sexual practices—Allow me, darling." She thrust her finger deep into the honey, brought it out trailing a fine strand of gold that beaded into drops on the dark wood. As her finger rolled across his broken biscuit, she bent her head, licked delicately at the trail of honey on the table. Kay, trying to catch her finger in his mouth, knocked over his coffee. It splashed onto her hand.

"Oh, my darling," he exclaimed, horrified. "Did I burn you? Let me see!"

"It's nothing," she said coolly, retrieving her hand and wiping it on her napkin. "I do not burn easily. Where were we?"

"Your finger was in my biscuit," he said huskily.

"The point he makes, of course, is that with so many potential suns and an incredibly vast number of systems perhaps orbiting them, the chances are not remote for life—perhaps sophisticated, intelligent, technologically advanced—life, in essence, as we know it, circling one of those distant stars. Imagine!" she exclaimed, rapt, absently pulling apart a daffodil and dropping pieces of its golden horn down her negligee. The petal pieces seemed to Kay to burn here and there on her body beneath a frail web of white. "On some planet circling some distant, unnamed star, Kay and Neva are seated in a snowbound city, breakfasting and discussing the possibility of life on other planets. Is that not strange and marvelous?"

He cleared his throat. "Do you think you might like me to remove some of those petals for you?"

"What petals?"

"The one, perhaps, caught between your breasts."

She smiled. "Of course, my darling." As he leaped precipitously to his feet, scattering silverware, she added, "Oh, darling, hand me the newspaper."

"I beg your pardon?"

"I always do the crossword puzzle after breakfast. Don't you? I like to time myself. Eighteen minutes and thirty-two seconds was my fastest. What was yours?"

She pulled the paper out of his limp hand, and watched, smiling faintly, as he flung himself groaning in despair across the table. His face lay in her biscuit crumbs; the spilled honey began to undulate slowly out of its pot toward his mouth; coffee spread darkly across the wood from beneath his belly. Neva leaned over his prone body, delicately sipped coffee. Then she opened her mouth against his ear and breathed a hot, moist sigh throughout his bones.

"You have broken my coffee pot," she murmured. "You must kneel at my feet while I work this puzzle. You will speculate, as I work, on the strange and wonderful sexual practices of aliens on various planets."

He slid off the table onto his knees in front of her. She propped the folded paper on his head. "Nine fifty-seven and fourteen seconds exactly. Begin, my darling."

"On the planet Debula, where people communicate not by

voice but by a complex written arrangement whereby words are linked in seemingly arbitrary fashion by a similar letter in each word, and whose lawyers make vast sums of money interpreting and arguing over the meanings of the linked words, the men, being quite short, are fixated peculiarly on kneecaps. When faced with a pair, they are seized with indescribable longing and behave in frenzied fashion, first uncovering them and gazing raptly at them, then consuming whatever daffodil petal happens to be adhering to them, then moistening them all over in hope of eventually coaxing them apart . . ."

"What is a four-letter synonym for the title of a novel by the Russian author Dostoyevsky?"

"Idiot," he sighed against her knees.

"Ah. Fool. Thank you, my darling. Forgive me if I am somewhat inattentive, but your voice, like the falling snow, is wonderfully calming. I could listen to it all day. I know that, as you roam from planet to planet, you will come across some strange practice that will be irresistible to me, and I will begin to listen to you." She crossed her legs abruptly, banging his nose with her knee. "Please continue with your tale, my darling. You may be as leisurely and detailed as you like. We have all winter."

### Gerda

Gerda heaved a fifty-pound sack of potting soil off the stack beside the greenhouse door and dropped it on her workbench. She slit it open with the sharp end of a trowel and began to scoop soil into three-inch pots sitting on a tray. The phone rang in the shop; she heard Briony say,

"Four dozen roses? Two dozen each of Peach Belle and Firebird, billed to Selene Pray? You would like them delivered this afternoon?"

Gerda began dropping pansy seeds into the pots. Beyond the tinted greenhouse walls it was still snowing: a long winter, they said, the longest on record. Gerda's greenhouse— half a dozen long glass rooms, each temperature controlled for varied environments, lying side by side and connected by glass archways—stood on the roof of one of the highest buildings in the city. Gerda could see across the ghostly white city to the frozen ports where great freighters were locked in the ice. She had sold nearly all of her jewelry to have the nursery built and stocked in such a merciless season, but, once open, her business was brisk. People yearned for color and perfume, for there seemed no color in the world but white and no scent but the pure, blanched, icy air. It was rumored that the climatic change had begun, and the glaciers were beginning to move down from the north. Eventually, they would be seen pushing blindly through the streets, encasing the city in a cocoon of solid ice for a millennium or two. Some people, in anticipation of the future, were making arrangements to have themselves frozen. Others simply ordered flowers to replicate the truant season.

"I'm taking a delivery," Briony said in the doorway. "Jennifer isn't back yet from hers." She had cut her hair and dyed it white. It sprang wildly from her head in petals of various lengths, reminding Gerda of a chrysanthemum. Jennifer loved driving the truck and delivering flowers, but Briony pined in captivity. She compensated for it by wearing rich antique velvets and tapestries and collecting different kinds of switchblades. Gerda had persuaded her to work until spring; by then, she thought, Briony might be coaxed through another season. Meanwhile, spring dallied; Briony drooped.

"All right," Gerda said. "I'll listen for the phone. Look, Briony, the lavender seedlings are coming up."

"Of course they're coming up," Briony said. "Everything you touch grows. If you dropped violets from the rooftop, they would take root in the snow. If you planted a shoe, it would grow into a shoetree."

"I want you to sell something for me."

Briony brightened. She kept her old business acquaintances by means of Gerda's jewels, reassuring them that she had only temporarily abandoned crime to help a friend.

"What?"

"A sapphire necklace. I want more stock; I want to grow orchids. Stop by the flat. The necklace is in the safe beneath the still life. Do you know anyone who sells paintings?"

"I'll find someone."

"Good," she said briskly, but she avoided Briony's sharp eyes, for the dismantling of her great love was confined, as yet, only to odds and ends of property. The structure itself was inviolate. She turned away, began to water seedlings. The front bell jangled. She said, "I'll see to it. You wrap the roses."

The man entering the shop made her heart stop. It was Kay. It was not Kay. It might have been Kay once: tall, fair, with the same sweet smile, the same extravagance of spirit.

"I want," he said, "every flower in the shop."

Gerda touched hair out of her eyes, leaving a streak of potting soil on her brow. She smiled suddenly, at a memory, and the stranger's eyes, vague with his own thoughts, saw beneath the potting soil and widened.

"I know," Gerda said. "You are in love."

"I thought I was," he said confusedly.

"You want all the flowers in the world."

"Yes."

He was oddly silent, then; Gerda asked, "Do you want me to help you choose which?"

"I have just chosen." He stepped forward. His eyes were lighter than Kay's, a warm gold-brown. He laughed at himself, still gazing at her. "I mean yes. Of course. You choose. I want to take a woman to dinner tonight, and I want to give her the most beautiful flower in the world and ask her to marry me. What is your favorite flower?"

"Perhaps," Gerda suggested, "you might start with her favorite color, if you are unsure of her favorite flower."

"Well. Right now it appears to be denim."

"Denim. Blue?"

"It's hardly passionate, is it? Neither is the color of potting soil."

"I beg—"

"Gold. The occasion begs for gold."

"Yellow roses?"

"Do you like roses?"

"Of course?"

"But yellow for a proposal?"

"Perhaps a winey red. Or a brilliant streaked orange."

"But what is your favorite flower?"

"Fuchsias," Gerda said, smiling. "You can hardly present her with a potted plant."

"And your favorite color?"

"Black."

"Then," he said, "I want a black fuchsia."

Gerda was silent. The stranger stepped close to her, touched her hand. She was on the other side of the counter suddenly, hearing herself babble.

"I carry no black fuchsias. I'm a married woman, I have a husband—"

"Where is your wedding ring?"

"At home. Under my pillow. I sleep with it."

"Instead of your husband?" he said, so shrewdly her breath caught. He smiled. "Have dinner with me."

"But you love someone else!"

"I stopped, the moment I saw you. I had a fever, the fever passed. Your eyes are so clear, like a spring day. Your lips. There must be a rose the color of your lips. Take me and your lips to the roses, let me match them."

"I can't," she said breathlessly. "I love my husband."

"Loving one's spouse is quite old-fashioned. When was the last time he brought you a rose? Or touched your hand, like this? Or your lips. Like. This." He drew back, looked into her eyes again. "What is your name?"

She swallowed. "Why do you look so much like Kay? It's unfair."

"But I'm so much nicer."

"Are you?"

"Much," he said, and slid his hand around her head to spring the clip on the pin that held her hair so that it tumbled down around her face. He drew her close, repeated the word against her lips. "Much."

"Much," she breathed, and they passed the word back and forth a little.

"I'm off," Briony said, coming through the shop with her arms full of roses. Gerda, jumping, caught a glimpse of her blue, merry eyes before the door slammed. She gathered her hair in her hands, clipped it back.

"No. No, no, no. I'm married to Kay."

"I'll come for you at eight."

"No."

"Oh, and may I take you to a party after dinner?"

"No."

"You might as well get used to me."

"No."

He kissed her. "At eight, then." At the door, he turned. "By the way, do you have a name?"

"No."

"I thought not. My name is Foxx. Two x's. I'll pick you up here, since I'm sure you don't have a home, either." He blew her a kiss. "Au revoir, my last love."

"I won't be here."

"Of course not. Do you like sapphires?"

"I hate them."

"I thought so. They'll have to do until you are free to receive diamonds for your wedding."

"I am married to Kay."

"Sapphires, fuchsias, and denim. You see how much I know about you already. Chocolate?"

"No!"

"Champagne?"

"Go away!"

He smiled his light, brilliant smile. "After tonight, Kay will be only a dream, the way winter snow is a pale dream in spring. Tomorrow, the glaciers will recede, and the hard buds will appear on the trees. Tomorrow, we will smell the earth again, and the roiling, briny sea will crack the ice and the great ships will set sail to foreign countries and so shall you and I, my last love, set sail to distant and marvelous ports of call whose names we will never quite be able to pronounce, though we will remember them vividly all of our lives."

"No," she whispered.

"At eight. I shall bring you a black fuchsia."

**Spring**

"Dear Gerda," Selene said. "Darling Foxx. How wonderful of you to come to my party. How original you look, Gerda. You must help me plan my great swan song, the final, definitive party ending all seasons. As the ice closes around us and traps us for history like butterflies in amber, the violinists will be lifting their bows, the guests swirling in the arms of their lovers, rebuffed spouses lifting their champagne glasses — it will be a splendid moment in time sealed and unchanged until the anthropologists come and chip us out of the ice. Do you suppose their excavations will be accompanied by the faint pop of champagne bubbles escaping the ice? Ah! There is Pilar O'Malley with her ninth husband. Darling Pilar is looking tired. It must be so exhausting hunting fortunes."

"Tomorrow," said Foxx.

"No," said Gerda. She was wearing her short black dress in hope that Foxx would be discouraged by its primness. Her only jewels were a pair of large blue very faux pearls that Briony had pinched from Woolworth's.

"You came with me tonight. You will come with me tomorrow. You will flee this frozen city, your flowerpots, your patched denim —" He guided her toward the champagne, which poured like a waterfall through a cascade of Gerda's roses. "And your defunct marriage, which has about as much life to it as a house empty of everything but memory." He had been speaking so all evening, through champagne and quail, chocolates and port, endlessly patient, endlessly assured. The black silk fuchsia, a sapphire ring, a pair of satin heels, gloves with diamond cuffs were scattered in the back of his sleigh. Gerda, wearied and confused with too many words, too much champagne, felt as if the world were growing unfamiliar around her. There was no winter in Foxx's words, no Kay, no flower shop. The world was becoming a place of exotic, sunlit ports where she must go as a stranger, and as another stranger's wife. What of Briony, whom she had coaxed out of the streets? What of her lavender seedlings? Who would water her pansies? Who would order potting soil? She saw herself suddenly, standing among Selene's rich, glittering guests and worrying about potting soil. She laughed. The world and winter returned; the inventions of the insubstantial stranger Foxx turned into dreams and air, and she laughed again, knowing that the potting soil would be there tomorrow and the ports would not.

Across the room, Kay saw her laugh.

For a moment he did not recognize her; he had never seen her laugh like that. Then he thought, Gerda. The man beside her had taught her how to laugh.

"My darling," Neva said to him. "Will you get me champagne?" She did not wait for him to reply, but turned her back to him and continued her discussion with a beautiful and eager young man about the eternal truths in alchemy. Kay had no energy even for a disillusioned smile; he might have been made of ice for all the expression his face held. His heart, he felt, had withered into something so tiny that when the anthropologists came to excavate Selene's final party, his shrunken heart would be held a miracle of science, perhaps a foreshadowing of the physical advancement of future *homo*.

He stood beside Gerda to fill the champagne glasses, but he did not look at her or greet her. Not even she could reach him, as far as he had gone into the cold, empty wastes of winter's heart. Gerda, feeling a chill brush her, as of a ghost's presence, turned. For a moment, she did not recognize Kay. She saw only a man grown so pale and weary she thought he must have lost the one thing in the world he had ever loved.

Then she knew what he had lost. She whispered, "Kay."

He looked at her. Her eyes were the color of the summer skies none of them would see again: blue and full of light. He said, "Hello, Gerda. You look well."

"You look so sad." She put her hand to her breast, a gesture he remembered. "You aren't happy."

He shrugged slightly. "We make our lives." His champagne glasses were full, but he lingered a moment in the warmth of her eyes. "You look happy. You look beautiful. Do I know that dress? Is it new?"

She smiled. "No." Foxx was beside her suddenly, his hand on her elbow.

"Gerda?"

"It's old," Gerda said, holding Kay's eyes. "I no longer have much use for such clothes. I sold all the jewels you gave me to open a nursery. I grew all the roses you see here, and those tulips and the peonies."

"A nursery? In midwinter? What a brilliant and challenging idea. That explains the dirt under your thumbnail."

"Kay, my darling," said Neva's deep, languid voice behind

them, "you forgot my champagne. Ah. It is little Gerda in her sweet frock."

"Yes," Kay said. "She has grown beautiful."

"Have I?"

"Gerda and I," Foxx said, "are leaving the city tomorrow. Perhaps that explains her unusual beauty."

"You are going away with Foxx?" Kay said, recognizing him. "What a peculiar thing to do. You'll fare better with your peonies."

"Congratulations, my sweets, I'm sure you'll both be so happy. Kay, there is someone I want you to—"

"Why are you going with Foxx?" Kay persisted. "He scatters hearts behind him like other people scatter bad checks."

"Don't be bitter, Kay," Foxx said genially. "We all find our last loves, as you have. Gerda, there is someone—"

"Tomorrow," Gerda said calmly, "I am going to make nine arrangements: two funerals, a birthday, three weddings, two hospital, and one anniversary. I am also going to find an orchid supplier and do the monthly accounts."

"You're not going with Foxx."

"Of course she is," Foxx said.

Gerda took her eyes briefly from Kay to look at him. "I prefer my plants," she said simply.

An odd sound cut through the noise of the party, as if in the distance something immense had groaned and cracked in two. Kay turned suddenly, pushed the champagne glasses into Neva's hands.

"May I come—" His voice trembled so badly he stopped, began again. "May I come to your shop tomorrow and buy a flower?"

She worked a strand of hair loose from behind her ear and

twirled it around one finger, another gesture he remembered. "Perhaps," she said coolly. He saw the tears in her eyes, like the sheen on melting, sunlit ice. He did not know if they were tears of love or pain; perhaps, he thought, he might never know, for she had walked through light and shadow while he had encased himself in ice. "What flower?"

"I read once there is a language of flowers. Given by people to one another, they turn into words like love, anger, forgiveness. I will have to study the language to know what flower I need to ask for."

"Perhaps," she said tremulously, "you should try looking some place other than language for what you want."

He was silent, looking into her eyes. The icy air outside cracked again, a lightning-whip of sound that split through the entire city. Around them, people held one another and laughed, even those perhaps somewhat disappointed that life had lost the imminence of danger, and that the world would continue its ancient, predictable ways. Neva handed the mute and grumpy Foxx one of the champagne glasses she held. She drained the other and, smiling her faint, private smile, passed on in search of colder climes.

# Ash, Wood, Fire

Black, her eye said. Cinder black. And smooth.
Black moved under her eye. She moved, too,
pulling her face out of the crook of her elbow, into
dawn. Gray light spilled over everything: gray stones, gray
hearth, gray ashes on her hands. The black moved, bumping
against her arm. She sat up quickly, making a grating morning sound in her throat. Black beetle, slow, and long as her
thumb. The stones had grown cold under her. She flicked the
beetle onto its back, watched it wave its legs, crawl on air.
Then she blew it upright. It lumped away towards the hearth,
where it would blaze like a coal in her fire. She straightened,
yawning, pushing matted ribbons of hair into her cap. The
beetle disappeared under the grate.

She blew embers alive, piled chips and sticks, and blew, piled more sticks and bark, and blew, and then the wood. Something tiny wailed and snapped, sap bubbled. She burned hearts, bones, black beetles. The warmth touched her face; she closed her eyes. The warmth seeped into her; she was the warmth, warm. Warm, she thought; warm, she breathed. Almost warm enough to come alive. Sap in the wood, seed in the earth, warming . . .

A beetle lumbered, loud and black, grumbling behind her. She hadn't burned it. Or she had, and in the fire it had grown enormous.

"—at her, dreaming, with fires to be . . . fires . . ."

Fires.

She moved to other hearths in the vast kitchen, blowing, coaxing, growing fire in the stone ovens, under great kettles of icy water that ham-hands, red with cold, hung to sway in front of her face. The kitchen filled with the sound. A kettle heaved in front of her, splashing water onto her flame. Ash hissed, smoked. A word licked at her ear; a hand, wet and hard, felt for something under her apron. She made a noise, twisting, picking a smoldering stick out of the fire. A haunch nudged her; she sprawled on stones.

"Nothing but bone; dogs wouldn't sniff at you, they wouldn't bother. Kitchen scraps have more on them."

"Leave her alone," the Beetle said in her flat, harsh, rasping voice. "Leave her to work, then, or I'll toss you to the hounds, you pale horny toad. Slug. Get those kettles hissing. You. Girl. What is her name?" she asked, exasperated, of the hanging sausages. "Does she have one?"

Every morning, every morning.

"Anastasia."

"Rosamunda."

"She never said."

"She can't speak."

"She can."

"Isolde."

"I can talk," she said, her back to them all. "Talk," said the fire. "Talk," said the dripping, hissing kettle. A face, in its shiny, battered side, looked back at her, distorted in the dents. The nose dipped sideways, the chin veered, melted into a pool.

"Talk, then," someone said. "Tell us your name."

The face had no name. She sniffed instead, swiped her nose against her shoulder. Pots laughed, knives snickered in the bacon; an oven door screeched, clanged shut.

"My name is Ash," she said. "My name is Wood. My name is Fire."

"Her name is Patch," someone said, high and grating, through his nose. "Patch, from Thickum Spinney. Salt. Salt, over here."

Salt ran behind her, little light steps on the stones.

"No," argued a furiously stirred pot. "That was the last fire we had. This one's new."

"Naawoh," a spattering pan said derisively. "This one's been here forever. You're new."

"Five years," Pot huffed.

"That's new. Fire's been here forever."

"Fire!" the Beetle snapped. "Over here!"

She made, she made, until the kitchen grew thick, sultry with smoke and steam and smells. Perfumed maids, black flowers, scented the steam as they picked up copper water cans; black stalks of gentlemen appeared and disappeared into the mists, then came back again, for vast silver trays upon which Flower, mute and stunted man, laid a single rose, a white carnation. The argument flared intermittently, little flames here, there, springing to life, sinking.

"The other was shorter."

"This is the other. She grew."

"That high? Overnight?"

"You don't notice," the Beetle said abruptly. "In here. Faces always coming and going. Chopper! Apples, apples, keep them coming. You. Onions. A mountain of onions. A swimming sea of onions. Chop them small as babies' teeth."

"The other's hair was light."

"How could you tell? She's ash, head to foot. She drifts, hearth-creature. Puff at her and she'd waft apart."

"This one's too tall . . ."

"Pepper!"

She tried to think back. Had she been smaller? Or had that been someone else? Fires content, for the moment, she took fresh hot bread from a basket, wedged herself out of the way in a corner of wall and hearth, pushed close to the warmth, and tore at the bread. Stone and fire, stone and fire, nothing else but that, no matter where she looked. Grate and ash, wood, armloads of wood, winter wood, summer wood, each with its smell of snow or sun. Nothing more. Fire never counted years, neither did she. Still, dusted with bread crumbs, warm, nodding a little against the hard warm stones, she saw her hands, fingers gray and black with ash and char, nails broken, knuckles split with dryness and cold, an old mark or two where the fire had tried to eat her. Her hands belonged to fire. Had they ever done anything else? Had they been born smelling of char and sap?

They were what hands looked like that belonged to fire.

She had no other hands. None that had peeled an apple, placed a flower on a tray. She was Fire. What did years matter to fire?

"Fire!"

She moved, dodging around elbows, across floor slick with apple peel, her eyes searching, finding the discontented flame under a vast pan hung on a triple chain, heaped with butter and onion. Eyes stinging with smoke and onion, she heaved wood, built it up with her bare hands, angled this log on that, until the fire itself—billowing, snapping tree-bones, boiling tree-blood—drove her away with its hot breath.

Fire. Wood. Ash.

The black flowers began to return the silver trays, littered now with crusts and cold bacon fat, crumpled napkins, flowers withering in brown pools of tea and chocolate. A hillock of scraps began to grow in a great bowl for the Kitchen Dogs, the Beetle said, though there were no Kitchen Dogs, only Kennel Dogs, fed as carefully as princesses. Salt and Pepper and Choppers, Stirrers and Scrubbers passed and repassed the bowl; dipping into it, swift as birds, pecking away at the mound, a dart of hand, a suddenly rounded cheek. Fire ate only bread, finding tastes—the flood of salt, the sweet tang of orange peel—confusing, disturbing. They brought words into her head; they made her want to speak, though the words that pushed into her mouth were all in some peculiar language—the language that silk spoke, or perfume—and she could neither shape nor understand them.

"Fire!"

In a breath, between meals—the plates scrubbed from one, the quail braising for the next, onions and apples browning in butter, Pins rolling out piecrusts all down a long table, bread out and cooling—the argument flared again.

"She was a little bit of a girl, with no front teeth. This one has teeth." This from a Sauce so lovingly stirred it might have held the last cream, the last sugar, the last rosewater in the world.

"Teeth grow." This from the Kitchen-Beetle herself, huge circle of hips, round and black from behind, a circle of back, a small circle of black head, hair pulled into yet another circle at her neck, so fiercely and unshakably round it might have been carved of stone. Her heavy cheeks were cream threaded with veins of strawberry, her brows as pale as the marble pestles, her eyes shiny black insect eyes that saw everything and had no expression.

"Not as quickly as all that."

"How often does anyone look?" Pastry, pressing rings of beaten egg whites out of a funnel, flung up his arms. Egg white squirted high; Salt watched, open-mouthed. Falling, it just missed the Sauce. "No one would look unless she wasn't there making fires. She didn't have teeth. She has teeth. Who has time to look?" His free hand pounced under the table, drew out a Chopper, small and dark, cheek full of something, his eyes and mouth clenched tightly shut, his body frozen by the hand at his neck. "Look at this one. Does he have front teeth or not?" The Sauce shrugged. Pantry pushed the Chopper back under the table. "Who knows? Who cares? None of them have names."

"I have teeth," said the table. "I have a name. All of us have names."

"What's hers, then, rat?"

"Fire."

Pantry stamped under the table. "Cockroach. Get to work."

"She's too tall," muttered Sauce. Steam enveloped his face; he inhaled rapture, and forgot Fire.

Then the nut pies went in, and the quails stuffed with apples and onions; the kitchen rats reeled, drunk with smells. She hauled wood constantly; going out to the snowy yard, piling it in her arms, taking deep breaths—not of the wild, golden spicy air, but of pitch and wet bark, the inner smells of trees, as varied to her as their names. She had no names for trees, only the pictures in her head that each wood scent conjured: some were dark and bristled, green all year; others stood pale and slender, wore leaves like lace and rustled with secrets at every breeze. The ovens set within the stones ate wood, ate forests. Pitch boiled and wailed, trees gave her their fragrances, their memories, clear to her even in the riot of kitchen smells, so that, kneeling at the grates, sweating, balancing logs, dodging smoke, brushing burning cinders back into the fire with her hands while the kitchen clattered and chopped and roared behind her, a green wood grew around her, the ghosts of trees.

"Fire! Where's that girl?" the Kitchen-Beetle snapped. "She might as well be a block of wood, for all she hears you. Where did she go? She was just there—"

"I'm here," she said from the heart of the wood, and the trees faded away.

"Fire!"

They descended from the upper world, the stately bearers of silver and copper, flowers and food. They bore away entire woods full of quail, whole vegetable gardens of salads, and came back for the nut orchard, and the cream from the milk of a hundred cows. They returned carrying bones, crusts, herbs trapped like green wings in hardening sauce. Scrubbers and Pluckers and Choppers snatched cold leftovers; Cooks, Bakers, Sauces, and the Beetle herself ate hot seasoned quail dripping with sauce, nut pies crusted with brown sugar and butter. Fire, dreamy with heat, ate bits of bread charred with ash, chopped apples that had hung on trees, food going gray in her fingers until it seemed she ate ash. The Kitchen-Beetle's eye, bright and thoughtless as she gnawed birds, swiveled aimlessly and fell on Fire. As always, other eyes followed.

"The other spoke more."

"This one is the other. She's turning."

"Turning?"

"Becoming," the Beetle said impatiently. "They do. They all do. They put out leaves. They begin to dream."

"Her?" Sauce snickered. "She's disappearing, more like it. She's growing ash on her thick as bark. She can't think much, she's put together like twigs. Twigs for bones, wooden thoughts."

The Beetle looked at Fire, great white teeth tearing at quail, her eyes black as the underside of a pot, and as flat. She made a sound, between a snort and an inquiry, and tossed the bones.

"It's in the air," the Beetle said. "She smells it. In the wood." She heaved to her feet; Scraps ran among all their feet, collecting what they had let fall. She raised her voice. "Pluckers!"

Geese, this time, their long white necks lolling across the thighs of Pluckers, trembling at every touch. Their feathers blew everywhere; fire scorched them, Sauce cursed them. Scraps leaped after them, snatching them as they floated. A snowdrift rose between the Pluckers; flurries of down, the last winter storm, swirled around Fire when she opened the door to bring in wood. The kitchen snow confused her; outside, in the melting snow, she smelled gold, she smelled water running slow and warm through still, secret woods. Inside was fire and snow still flying, through the tender green smells of wood.

Mushrooms simmered in butter and rosemary over the flames; geese, headless, impaled, turned slowly on spits—the fires hissed and spattered with their fat. Cauldrons of potatoes and leeks boiled, spilling frothy water into the flames. She made, she made, coaxing drenched fire alive here, there, building and rebuilding next to ovens full of bread shaped into swans, of airy towers spun of egg white and sugar hardening in the heat. Chocolate, and raspberries frozen all winter, and hazelnuts pounded fine as dust, melted together under a flame, never high, never too low, teased with tidbits like a child. The world turned fire under her eyes, her busy fingers; she shaped potato flames, raspberry flames, geese flames, as if she were remaking everything out of fire, while pots were stirred, whisked away, others hung, and the voice of the Kitchen-Beetle wove the clutter and chaos around her into supper.

Then she found herself dreaming in a darkening kitchen, a piece of potato half-eaten in her grimy hand. She leaned against a cooling oven. A solitary Scrubber splashed among the last of the pots. All around her, fires were burying themselves deep into heartwood, in the darkening hearths. A coal fell, a heart snapped—sang. The Kitchen-Beetle sat in the shadows, still and silent, watching, listening to the small noises. Fire watched her: the circles of her knees, her breasts, her darkened face. Cinders fumed. A pot settled on the rack. A flame sprang up, hid itself again. They sat, Fire against the oven stones, Kitchen-Beetle in her chair, in the heart of the fire, listening to the kitchen speak.

The Beetle dwindled, went small, small, a moving bit of dark in the darkness. Fire dreamed of fire. An eye opened among the coals. It was green as leaves: her eye. Another opened. Another. The ring of hearths watched her out of her eyes. A flame danced, spoke. Her voice, her word. She stirred against the stones, murmuring. Her cap brushed off; hair tumbled down, dark as wood. All her eyes watched the beetle crawl toward the hearth. It spoke as it passed her: a sudden gleam across its dark, polished back.

"Fire," it said, and she breathed the word, felt it dance across her heart, light as leaves, whispering, whispering. She rose finally, brought in wood, and water, and began to make.

Morning found cold grates everywhere. Cooks, Sauces, Bakers milled bewilderedly, betrayed, calling, "Fire! Fire!" and never seeing her, while beside the door a young woman stood watching, tall and sapling-slender, her eyes as green as new leaves, her hair shiny as the beetle's back, perfumed with wood. The lowly Scrubbers saw her first, and the Choppers, and Scraps and Stirrers; they flashed their teeth, or lack of them, grinning in wonder, as she opened the door to light.

"Fire!" the Kitchen-Beetle called peremptorily to no one, to anyone, as if a ghost of ashes might rise out of a hearth, a little, smudged, graceless bundle of twigs, and begin to kindle herself alive, while Fire passed out of the kitchen into Spring.

# The Stranger

Syl saw the stranger at ebb tide, standing among the tide pools, half-hidden by great hoary rocks slick with weed and moss and the living sea-things that clung to them. He watched the tide; she watched him as she walked along the shore road that ran between the sea and Liel's sheep pastures. Behind him, the sky turned silken with twilight: rose and mauve and a deep, soft purple, colors she wanted to spin out of the air into thread for tapestries of no more substance than light. Everything in them would be nameless, she decided, her eyes still on the nameless man, like things in dreams. . . . Then the stranger moved.

He pulled something rectangular off his shoulder; his hands flicked across it, opening, pulling, twisting. Odd angles emerged from it, wings, cylinders, strings. He bent his head to it; his hands moved again. A single, deep note broke with a breaking wave, sighed away. A flurry of notes, flute and reed, spun into a gathering wave, and then more strings and a small drum, a single, flat beat, and the wave broke. Syl stopped, swallowing something like a sharp, sweet note in the back of her throat. Then she saw what he was doing to the sky, and the small notes danced along her bones.

Colors moved to his playing, shaped themselves. A cloudy purple wing stretched; an eye peered, whiter than the moon. A dark cloud rolled like tide across the sky; a graceful neck, a black and craggy profile rose out of it like smoke. Gold, a strand of light pulled from beneath the horizon, limned a claw, opening against the black, then plumed into a brilliant cloak of airy feathers. Syl felt the drum beat in the back of her throat.

He is weaving with the sky, she thought. And then the music stopped.

The sky darkened; he was a shadow against it, folding away his secrets, hanging them at his back. Then he blurred, or the night blurred over him. Still she stood motionless, trying to blink away the dark while all the color faded from the sky, and the tide among the broken shells played the only music.

"I saw," she said later to Liel, as she put a bowl of mutton stew in front of him. But she could not say what.

"What, lass?" he asked absently, chewing; his eyes were full of sheep, shearing, skins, wool, lambs to keep, lambs to slaughter. His eyes cleared slowly at her silence; he was seeing her again, his Syl, moving in and out of the firelight, quick, graceful, methodical, laying the bread to be cut on the oak cutting board, the oak-handled knife beside it, and the butter in its yellow crock. She put the back of her hand to her forehead, as she did when she was trying to remember. He waited. Then her hand lifted, her brows lifted, raising brief furrows in her smooth forehead, and she sighed, meeting his eyes.

"I don't exactly know. I was daydreaming, most likely." She sat, spreading her coarse skirt and coarser apron neatly, liking the feel of the rough blue weave and then the rougher cream. He ate another bite.

"Where?"

"Along the shore. I walked to Greta's, to get some black wool from her, since we have so few black, and she has them thick as blackbirds in a field."

"That's where you were, then."

"That's where I was."

They ate a while. The fire whispered, snapped scents and burning stars into the air, whispered again. Liel finished, leaned back in his chair. Syl, musing over the twilight music, lifted her eyes and found his eyes on her. He smiled a little.

"I was just watching you. The way your hands move in the light."

She smiled back, watching the fire pick out threads of brown and gold in his dark hair. He had gray eyes that always told her every thought. His expressions were uncomplicated and familiar: one for sheep, another for thunder, one for watching her weave, another for drinking beer with his brother, another for telling her his dreams, another for untying the ribbons in her hair, and then at her throat, and then at her breast.

She rose, began to clear the table. He watched her a little longer, then got up to open the cottage door and listen to the night as it wrapped itself around the island. He did that every evening, smelling weather in scents of air and earth blowing across from the mainland, listening for unfamiliar noises among the sheep, for warnings in the distant barkings of farm dogs, listening for the tide, which he only heard on the stillest or the stormiest of nights.

"It's quiet," he said at last, and closed the door. She dried the last dish, placed it on the shelf. Then, as she did every night, she stood at her loom, looking at her weaving in the dying firelight, studying the colors and patterns she had chosen. Liel came to stand beside her.

"Pretty," he said, and touched a pearl-gray strand running through a weave of lilac. Then he touched her arm. She turned and followed him to bed.

The next morning, the sea mist swirled across Gamon Kyle's fields, massed itself into a white, winged shape with blue, burning eyes. The fire that came out of its mouth was blue. As the smoke billowed up from Gamon's hayfields, the farmers and fishers came running with buckets, or riding carts from the village full of barrels sloshing half the water out of them before they reached the fields. The animal shaped itself again above their heads. They stared, frozen with wonder at the sight of cloud furling into feather, sky igniting itself. Then the blue poured down again, and they heard the screams inside Gamon's barn.

By the time they got the fire out, most of Gamon's fields were cinder and his barn was a skeleton of charred timber. He stumbled among the ruins carrying salvage: a rake with a burned handle, some harness, a curry comb.

"What was that?" he kept asking hoarsely. "What was that?"

"It was like nothing I've ever seen," Liel told Syl, coming

in at midday sweating and streaked with char. She had been at her weaving all morning; the wind had swept smoke and fire in the opposite direction. She stared at him over her loom. Cinders had eaten his shirt to shreds, raised blisters on his skin. He wore an expression she had never seen before. "Enormous," he said, as she coaxed the cloth from his body. "White. White mist. Its fire was blue. Like the sky. Like it had breathed in sky and turned it into flame. And then it turned Gamon's farm into flame."

He winced as she peeled shirt from his shoulders, and she said, not even trying to make sense of fire in the sky, "I'll fetch water. Oh, Liel. Did he lose it all?"

"All but a couple of hens."

"His horses?" she breathed in horror. He nodded, still wide-eyed, stunned with wonder.

"It might have been beautiful," he said absurdly, "if it hadn't been so terrible."

She shook her head mutely at his babbling. "Sit down," she said gently. "Let me take your boots off. Then I'll get water."

"Don't bother with it. I'll go sit in the stream a while. Syl, I wish you could have seen it. Fearful and deadly, but like—a great wave, or a mountain exploding. You hate what it does, but it's like nothing you could ever imagine, nothing—" He swallowed, all the words crowding into his eyes. Syl dropped his smoldering boots outside the door. She looked up at the sky suddenly, trying to connect it with fire. It held a cloud and a couple of blackbirds. She went back inside to help Liel with his trousers.

The next day, Greye Hamil's barn and apple orchards burned; the smell of scorched green apples spread clear across the island. The day after that something clawed furrows a foot deep down the length of the village street, and nine fishing boats moored at the dock turned into charred husks. Dogs were chained up, doors were barred, no one ventured out but Syl, who had come into the village with the shawl she had woven, to leave it at the shop that sold her work. The silence, the deep scars in the street amazed her; so did the shop's barred door.

She tapped on a window until the shopkeeper opened the door and pulled her hastily inside.

"Syl Reed," she said, a heavy woman with a plump rosy face and perpetually startled eyes. "What possessed you?"

"I brought this," Syl said bewilderedly, unfolding the shawl. A butterfly opened its green and peacock blue wings against a filigree of cream wool. The shopkeeper folded her hands under her chin and forgot the fire.

"Oh, Syl, it's lovely, so lovely." Then the terror came back into her eyes. She took the shawl and drew Syl toward the back of the shop. "You can't go home now, not alone."

"I must," Syl said, eluding her fingers. "I left stock simmering on the hearth. What has gotten into this village?"

"It's the things."

"What things?"

"The things — Syl, where have you been the past three days?"

"Weaving," Syl said blankly. "You know how I get when I work." She stopped abruptly, her own eyes widening, as she remembered the unfamiliar expression on Liel's face. "Things. Something terrible, he said. Something beautiful. And then — he kept talking about the sky."

"Cloud," the shopkeeper said. "It forms itself out of cloud."

Syl touched her throat, where a word had stuck. She whispered, "Oh."

"And it burns everything with fire the color of the sky." She paused, sniffing. "Something's burning," she wailed, and Syl wrenched open the door.

The smoke came from the little wood between Liel's pastures and the sea. Running, feeling the heat from the billowing flames, she turned off the road, cut a corner through the trees, and climbed the stone wall into the summer pastures. She stopped then, sobbing for breath, transfixed by what hung in the sky.

Its wings, spanning the length of the field, were teal and purple and bronze. They tapered to an angle along an intricate web of bone, then the pelt or glistening scales parted here and there into a loose, trailing weave through which ovals of blue sky hung. The head, secret and proud like a swan's, rose on a graceful swan's neck of gold. Its claws were gold. Its eyes were huge, lucent, gold moons.

Its shadow spread across the upturned faces of farmers and villagers who had abandoned the fire to wield pitchforks and rakes against it. The sheep had pushed into a noisy, terrified huddle against the field wall. As Syl stared, the great head dipped downward, precisely as a bird's, and caught a black lamb in its mouth. It stretched upward again, higher than seemed possible, tossed the lamb into the air, let it fall free to shatter itself against the ground, then caught it, with a flick of claw, at the last moment. Blood sprayed across the sheep, across the upturned faces.

Syl ran again, scarcely realizing she moved, seeing only Liel among the islanders. She pushed into the crowd, heard his soft grunt of dismay as he saw her. She gripped his arm and heard someone say, "For a price."

She saw the stranger among them.

His eyes were cold and dark as night, his hair as white as spume. He might have come out of the sea; his skin had little more color than mist. His rectangular box of secret music hung from his shoulder, revealing nothing, not a string or a singing reed. "For a price," he repeated to the silent crowd. He had a singer's voice, each word precise and modulated. He was tall and lithe and still, Syl sensed, as a stone. A part of him was that hard, that ancient. He seemed to her scarcely more human than the beautiful, deadly thing in the air above him. "I have seen these monsters invade before. They are ruthless. Your island is tiny. They will destroy it day by day, until by summer's end it will be little more than a charred cinder rising out of the sea. And on that, they will live."

The monster loosed a stream of blood-red silk, red wind, out of its mouth. Trees along the field wall flamed; sheep turned black. The din and the smell became sickening.

Syl, still staring at the stranger, felt something crawl along her bones. She turned her face against Liel, but still she saw, behind her closed eyes, the cloudy wings forming above the sea to the stranger's music.

"What price?" a villager asked frantically: Sim Jame, who owned a tavern there. Mel Grower, with acres of nut trees and an oak wood, echoed him hoarsely, "What price?"

The stranger named it.

There was no sound for a moment, but from the sheep, and the silken fire breaking the bones of trees.

"How can you control them?" Aron Avrel said abruptly,

his face white and slick with sweat under his black beard. "Are you mage, or what? Did you follow these monsters or did you bring them? For a price you'll help us. Help us into trouble, then help us out?"

The stranger looked at him, his eyes holding no more expression than stones in a field. "Does it matter?" he asked. "You cannot control them. I have known them all my life."

"Show us," Liel said, his voice grim, exhausted. The stranger looked at him, and then at Syl, standing with her fingers linked around Liel's arm, her long red-gold hair tangled and tumbling around her face from her running, her eyes, golden-green as ripening hazelnuts, wide and stunned with recognition of the stranger's face.

Still his expression did not change. But his eyes did not move away from her as he slid the box off his shoulder. He pushed a lever or a knob, or perhaps he only reshaped air and wood with his fingers. A flute of ebony and gold lay half-cradled in the top of the box, half-extended into air. He bent his head, blew a few soft, breathy notes, and then a clear, wild, tuneless keening that brought tears, hot and stinging with smoke, into Syl's eyes. The sheep stopped their din; the islanders stood motionless. The monster dipped its head dreamily toward the trees. It breathed in fire, or it grazed on fire, pulling strands of flame away from the burning leaves and branches until they stood charred and cold, shaking blackened leaves to the ground. Teal and bronze and flame coiled as the great wings closed around the last of the flames. Colors swirled, began, under the mad, haunting whirlwind of notes, to break apart. Fire turned to light, teal misted into sky. Purple lingered longest, Syl saw, a final streak of smoke or an edge of wing.

The music stopped. The musician lifted his head. The sky was empty. Sun struck his face, traced a line beside his mouth, revealed faint shadows beneath his eyes. It was some time before anyone spoke.

"That much," Aron Avrel said slowly, "we'll have to borrow from the mainland."

The stranger slid the flute back into wood and shadow. "They won't wait for it," he warned them.

"But you'll wait."

"I will."

There was argument, drunken and tumultuous, as the islanders cooled their smoke-dry throats with beer, and ate the bread and cheese and hot peppered lamb Syl set out for them. The stranger was mage, he was monster; they should kill him and steal his box. But no one could play it like he could, and then they'd be left with the monsters, and no telling how many of them there might be. They should send to the mainland for money; they should send to the mainland for help: any help would be cheaper than the stranger. But they knew where they could borrow money, but who knew where to find another mage that fast? Who knew the name of any mage, anywhere, anyway? Money. at least, could be found. Even if they had to borrow it against the price of the entire island. If the monsters didn't turn it into a charred rock, first.

Syl saw them fed, refilled their cups, while Liel and others went to see what could be mended and what must be slaughtered of the sheep. The islanders drifted in and out of the cottage, arguing, and keeping an anxious eye on the sky. Syl wandered among them, fretting over Liel and seeing, now and then, instead of him the white-haired stranger with the burning trees behind him, bending over his flute, or standing at the sea's edge, painting pictures with the sky.

She went to her loom, searched for colors among her dyed wools: that teal, that deep purple. And how could she weave the wings themselves, she wondered, the graceful trailing filigree revealing ovals of sky? She wanted other colors suddenly, colors harder, brighter than wool. Liel made lists on scraps. She found a torn bit of paper and some ink. Salt, Liel had written on the paper. Salve for cow's udder. She turned it over and began to sketch the wings.

Near dawn, they smelled it again: the harsh, acrid smell of burning blown across the island. Liel groaned and dressed. Syl waited until he had gone before she dressed. She went out, saw the red glow on the other side of the village where Sly Granger had his hop fields. She stood a moment, the back of her hand against her brow, and tried to think. Then she didn't think; she just guessed and ran across the pastures to the shore road, and then up it to where she had first seen the stranger.

She found him sitting among the rocks, playing music softly. The tide was high; his back was to her. She watched him for a long time from behind a rock, while he sketched wings and faces, massive bodies that appeared and disappeared in the milky mist above the sea. The sky brightened; the mist turned opal, caught flashes of color he wove into his music. He plucked a string, piped a note; a line of wing appeared, an eye. Cloud separated into bone, scales, teeth. He drew another secret out of the box: thin bands of silver that, struck, sounded like high, sweet bells. The sounds turned into a flock of silver birds that flew into the mist.

The sun rose, burning through the mist. He stopped playing

finally and watched the lines of light flash and melt across the waves. Then he turned his head and looked at her.

He did not move or speak, but he drew her across the sand, something alien, marvelous, incomprehensible that chance or wind had blown adrift onto the island. He watched her come, his eyes no longer expressionless, but masking all expression. She said, looking at the bright, empty sky, and then at him, her voice strained with bewilderment, "They're yours. Those monsters. Those beautiful and terrible things. You make them."

"I am them," he said. He folded away the silver bars and then the strings, into the impossibly shallow box. "We are what we make."

She thought above that, holding her hair out of her eyes with one hand against the strong morning wind. "Then you," she said wearily, "are terrible and beautiful, weaving dreams and nightmares with cloud and fire, burning in a breath what small slow things we make through time. And for nothing. For money."

He was silent; again she felt something ancient, wild, inhuman in his stillness. "What," he said finally, "do you make?"

"I dye wool from the sheep you burned. I weave the colors into shawls, blankets, things to wear, to hang."

"For nothing?"

She blinked, at an edge of cold air, or brine. "For money. It's common pay for making things. But I make. I don't unmake. You—" She drew breath slowly, her eyes straying again to the sky. "If I had your colors to make with. If I had the dreams behind your eyes. I would sit here on this beach and weave sea and sky and light until there was nothing left of me but bone to weave with. And then my bones would float away on all the colors of the sea."

There was a flick of expression, a spark off stone, in his eyes. "Colors. They're everywhere."

"For you, maybe. Not for me. I don't know how to make them. You think them into being. You don't have to destroy for that. And you would be paid all the wealth you want."

"I told you," he said evenly, "they are mine. They are what I am. They exist to destroy. They cease to exist when they cannot use their powers. They are made of light and fire. They must use themselves or die. It is what I make."

She was silent then, staring at him. "Then what of you?" she cried abruptly. "What an impossible fire there is in you."

It was as if she struck worn stone, split it through its heart to reveal the secret, jeweled colors, the solid fires of crystals within. And she saw more, as his face struggled against its own expression: the massive burden that had hardened around the secret fire, kept it raw, untouched by time, burning within its secret dark.

He bowed his head. Wordless, he pushed the drumhead back into the box; she saw his hand shake. Then he met her eyes again, his own eyes ancient, haunted, and weary.

"And what light is in you," he said, so softly she barely heard his voice above the tide, "to see me so clearly." He stopped; still held in his gaze she could not move. He was seeing colors now, her colors, her hair, her eyes. He lifted his hand, let a strand of windblown hair brush across his wrist. "Fire," he whispered. "Gold. And your eyes. Amber flecked with green." Her eyes widened; for a moment longer she could not move, she could only watch his hand reach out to her, swift as running tide, then drop, just before he touched her. She could move then. She took a step back, and then another, while he watched.

"I am driven," he said, just before she turned and ran. "I cannot help myself. Nor can I help you."

Liel had come back; she found his ash-streaked clothing on the floor. He was out in the fields, she guessed. Then, with him safe, she stopped thinking. She wove and did not weave, and when she did not weave, she drew, and made watercolors out of her dyes, and painted what she drew, so that when Liel returned at noon, the cottage was full of scraps of paper and linen, covered with wings, faces, eyes.

He said nothing when he saw them. He ate quietly, she nibbled absently, puzzling over how to get the colors brighter, richer, full of fire, full of light. He said finally, finished with his soup, and leaning back in his chair, "Sly lost all his hops. And his house."

She blinked. She saw what surrounded them, then, on chair and loom, hearthstones, floor. She rose quickly, gathered the fragments. She felt him watch her. She said, picking up one last wing, her back to him, "I talked to the stranger."

"Did you?"

"It did no good."

He grunted softly. "No. But you were brave to try." She turned then, met his eyes, saw them wistful, lonely, because she was straying down some dangerous and bewildering path, and he could not see his way to follow.

She went to him; he put his arms around her, as he sat, and dropped his face against her. "It's just the colors," she said helplessly. "They haunt me."

"The colors."

"Is someone going to the mainland?"

"Aron and Gamon and Sim left this morning in Lin Avrel's

boat, after we got the fire out. The sooner the better we all decided. There's nothing else we can do. Is there?"

"No."

"Then don't try."

She touched his hair; his hold tightened. She did not answer. He loosed her slowly after a time, looked up at her; her eyes had filled with colors again, the stranger's dreams. He rose, left the house without speaking.

She went back to her weaving.

At mid-afternoon, when the light dazzled through the windows and open door, making the warm shadows even darker, impenetrable, she heard a step on her threshold. She raised her eyes absently, still intent on her weaving. The figure at the door, limned with sunlight, was at once too bright and too dark to recognize.

Then she recognized its stillness.

"I came to see," he said, "what you make."

She stood slowly, feeling her heart hammer in her throat. It was as though she had found the tide at her doorstep, or something wild from the wood wanting in. He did not wait for her to welcome him. He stepped in, glancing around him at all her simple things: the painted crockery, the iron pots, the red vase full of buttercups, a moonshell, a piece of lace, the hanging she had woven to hide the bed. Then he looked at the weave on her loom, of cream and white and pale yellow, with a thread, here and there, of salmon.

"What is it?"

"A blanket," she said. "A wedding gift."

And then he saw the little pile of her sketches.

He looked through them, holding them so carefully not even the papers rustled as he drew one from behind another.

In the light that fell from the windows over her loom only his hands were illumined, holding what she had made of his makings. His face was in shadow.

"The colors are too pale," she said finally. Her voice sounded odd, loud and tuneless, in the silence. "I had to use my wool dyes for paint. I don't know any other way."

He looked at her finally; she heard his drawn breath before he spoke. "Why?" he whispered. "Why do you want them? They burned your sheep, your wood—"

"I don't know," she said helplessly. "Fire burns. Yet we take it into our houses, we live with it. Because we can't live without it. Something in my heart wants them. They drive you to make them. You should understand."

"They don't harm me."

"Oh, yes," she said, her voice shaking. "Oh, yes. They have driven you out of the world. But still you make them because they are so beautiful, so powerful—they set fire to your heart long before they burned anything else. They have charred you, made a dead island of you to live on. And you let them. You let them. You make them out of light and set them free with your music to burn and kill. You never ask yourself why. You make because. Because you can."

He moved abruptly into light, so that she could see his face, white as the moonshell, and she thought of something that had been born in the sea, and died, and left its hollow, brittle ghost behind.

"And would you?" he asked tautly. "If you could?"

Her eyes filled with tears, at the thought of the screaming animals, Liel's shirt frayed to a web with sparks, the charred trees, the barns and boats and houses burned. "No," she whispered. "I could not."

"I can."

She didn't answer. He waited, his eyes burning dark, challenging on her face. She did not speak. He dropped the sketches; they scattered like leaves across the floor. A face, half bird, half cloud, stared up at her out of one pale yellow eye. He turned; so did she, dropping down onto the stool at her loom, staring at its soft, pale shades, until she heard him leave.

The next day, Hila Burne's cornfields were swept bare by something, Liel said wearily, red as fire, breathing gold fire, with great amber eyes flecked with green. They saved the house and the barn, he added, as Syl, her eyes wide, burning dry as with smoke, patched the holes in his trousers.

"They're not so beautiful now," she said.

"No." Then he thought, leaning back in his chair, his eyes closed, his feet stretched out toward the cold hearth. "Well. There's always that moment when you first see it. You forget, for just that moment, what it does. All you do is see, and then it's like all the things you thought you'd never see in life. Strange lands, palaces, silver rivers rushing in secret through dark forests, mountains older than the moon. It's part of his magic, I think. That, for that one moment, you forget the past, and each of his makings seems the first one and the most wonderful."

She gazed at him, needle suspended. "I never knew you wanted to see those places."

"I never thought about them until now." He didn't speak again; when she opened her mouth, she heard his slow, exhausted breathing. She put his trousers down then and went quietly to the hearth. She knelt and gathered her sketches off the grate, where they would have been consumed in the morning's fire. She put them on the shelf above her loom.

She woke before dawn and walked to the sea.

She didn't think of Liel finding the bed empty beside her; she didn't think of what the stranger might say or do when he saw her. She stood among the rocks, watching the tide catch each changing hue of dawn, carry it ashore, and spread it out in the sand under her eyes. She heard music. She watched the sun rise; the music seemed to pull the great, hot fiery eye above the world. It pulled her; she drifted, following the beckoning tide. She found him where she had first seen him, standing half-hidden in the shadow of a rock. He did not turn his head; she did not speak, only listened, and watched the sky, to see what he might weave on his vast loom.

His music stopped. He looked at her. He did not speak, but his eyes spoke, making and unmaking her.

She turned her head after a moment, gazed at the tide again. She said softly, "I don't know what you are. Something of you is human, it seems."

"I make trouble, and I am paid, and I leave."

"Yes."

"Nothing more."

"I know."

"I have nothing to do with you."

"No."

"Nothing to do with your small weavings, your painted plates, your paper and dyes, your eyes that see beyond fire into light."

She swallowed. "No."

"This is all I am. All I want."

"Yes."

"To ask me to stop is to ask me to die."

She whispered, "I know."

"It would be like drowning in fire."

"Could you—" She drew breath; her voice trembled. "Could you find another—some other way—"

"How can I know that? This is all I know."

"No one has ever—"

"No one has ever asked. No. No one has ever come to me at dawn to watch me weave with the colors of the rising sun. No. I kill, I burn, I unmake. No one has ever been as inhuman as you."

She felt herself tremble, though the morning wind was gentle. She held herself tightly, felt words, edged, sharp, in her tight, burning throat. "I see what I see. What I can make, I will make. I will never be able to forget you. Because your weavings have come between me and my loom. I will be haunted by your colors until I find ways to make them. You have set fire to my world."

She did not see him again. Two days later, she found, among the rocks, his music open in all its parts, seawater playing the flute and reeds, broken shells playing the small drum. No one came for the money borrowed from the mainland, and on the island, nothing burned except in memory.

# Transmutations

Old Dr. Bezel was amusing himself again; Cerise smelled it outside his door. The shade escaping under the thick, warped oak was blue. A darker shadow crossed it restively: he must have conjured up his apprentice, who had been among the invisible folk for five days. Cerise planted the gold-rimmed spectacles Dr. Bezel had made for her firmly on her nose and opened the door.

As usual, Aubrey Vaughn, slumping into a chair, looked blankly at her, as if she had fallen through the ceiling. She noted, with a sharp and fascinated eye, the yellow-gray pallor of his skin. She slid her notebook and pens and the leather bag with her lunch in it onto a table, then opened the notebook to a blank page.

"I'm sorry I'm late," she said in her low, quiet voice. She added to the velvet curtains over the windows, for Dr. Bezel beamed at anything she said and rarely listened, and Aubrey simply never listened, "At least I'm not five days late."

But this time Aubrey blinked at her. He could never remember her name. She was a slender, colorless wraith of a woman who appeared and disappeared at odd times; for all he knew she was conjured out of candle smoke and had no life beyond the moments he encountered her. But gold teased him: the gold of her spectacles catching firelight and lamplight among laughter, sweat, curses, music . . . He made an incautious movement; his elbow slid off the chair arm. He jerked to catch his balance and felt the mad, gnarled imp in his brain strike with the pick, mining empty furrows for thought.

"You were there," he breathed. "Last night."

Behind her spectacles, her gray eyes widened. "You can see me," she said, amazed. "I've often wondered."

"Of course I can see you."

"How long has this been going on? Dr. Bezel, he sees me. You will have to dispose of one of us."

"Yes, my dear Cerise," Dr. Bezel agreed benignly, peering at his intricate, bubbling skeleton of glass. "Now we will wait until the solution turns from blue to a most delicate green."

"You were there," Aubrey persisted, holding himself rigid to calm the imp. "At Wells Inn."

"You are beginning to see me outside of this room? This is astonishing. What is my name?"

"Ah—"

"You see, I had a theory that not only am I invisible to you, the sound of my voice never reaches you. As if one of us is under a spell. Apparently even my name disappears into some muffled thickness of air before you hear it."

"I can hear you well enough now," he said drily. He applied one hand to his brow and made an effort. "It's a sound. Like silk ripping. Cerise."

She was silent, amused and half-annoyed, for on the whole, if their worlds were to merge, she preferred being invisible to Aubrey Vaughn. He was seeing her clearly now, she realized, as something more than a mass and an arbitrary movement in Dr. Bezel's cluttered study. She watched the expression begin to form in his bleared, wincing eyes, and turned abruptly. His voice pursued.

"But what were you doing there?"

"Now see," Dr. Bezel said delightedly, and Cerise forgot the curious voice in the chair as she watched a green like the first leaves flush through the bones of glass. "That is the exact shade. Look, for it goes quickly."

"The exact shade of what?" Aubrey murmured, and for once was himself unheard and invisible. "Of what?" he asked again, with his stubborn persistence, and, unaccountably, Dr. Bezel answered him.

"Of the leaves there. Translucent, gold-green, they fan into the light."

"What leaves where?"

"No place. A dream." He turned, smiling, sighing a little, as the green faded into clear. "I was only playing. Now we will work."

What leaves? Aubrey thought much later, after he had chased spilled mercury across the floor and nearly scalded himself with molten silver. Dr. Bezel, lecturing absently, let fall the names of references intermittently, like thunderbolts.

Cerise noted them in her meticulous script. What dream? she wondered, and made a private note: Green-gold leaves fanning into light.

"Also there is a well," Dr. Bezel said unexpectedly, at the end of the morning. Aubrey blinked at him, looking pained. Dr. Bezel, distracted from his vision by Aubrey's expression, added kindly, "Aubrey, if you tarnish the gold of enlightenment with the fires and sodden flames of endless nights, how will you recognize it?"

Aubrey answered tiredly, "Even dross may be transmuted. So you said."

"So you do listen to me." He turned, chuckling. "Perhaps you are your father's son."

Cerise saw the blood sweep into Aubrey's face. Prudently, she looked down at her notebook and wrote: Well. She had never met Nicholaus Vaughn, who had enlightened himself out of his existence; he had not, it seemed, misspent his youth at Wells Inn. Aubrey said nothing; the sudden stab of the pickax blinded him. In the wash of red before his eyes, he saw his bright-haired father, tall, serene, hopelessly good. Passionless, Aubrey thought, and his sight cleared; he found himself gazing into a deep vessel, some liquid matter gleaming faintly at the bottom.

"Analysis," Dr. Bezel instructed.

"Now?" Aubrey said hoarsely, bone-dry. "It's noon."

"Then let us lay to rest the noonday devils," Dr. Bezel said cheerfully. The woman, Cerise, was chewing on the end of her pen, deliberately expressionless. Aubrey asked her crossly,

"Have you no devils to bedevil you?"

"None," she answered in her low, humorous voice, "I would call a devil. I am intimate with those I know."

"So am I," he sighed, letting a drop from the vessel fall upon a tiny round of glass. Unexpectedly, it was red.

"Then they are not devils but reflections."

He grunted, suddenly absorbed in the crimson unknown. Blood? Dye? He reached for fire. "What were you doing at Wells Inn?" he asked. He felt her sudden, sharp glance and answered it without looking up, "In one way, I am like my father. I am tenacious."

"You are not concentrating," Dr. Bezel chided gently. They were all silent then, watching fire touch the unknown substance. It flared black. Aubrey risked his red-gold brows, rubbed his eyes. At his elbow, Cerise made the first note of his analysis: Turns obscure under fire. Aubrey reached for a glass beaker, poured a bead of crimson into a solution of salts. It fell as gracefully as a falling world.

Retains integrity in solution, Cerise wrote, and added: Unlike the experimenter.

The puzzle remained perplexing. Aubrey, sweating and finally curious by the end of the hour, requested texts. Dr. Bezel sent him out for sustenance, Cerise to the library. There she gathered scrolls and great dusty tomes, and, having deposited them in the study, retired beneath a tree to eat plums and farmer's cheese and pumpernickel bread, and to write poetry. She was struggling between two indifferent rhymes when a beery presence intruded itself.

"What were you doing at Wells Inn last night?"

She looked up. Aubrey's tawny, bloodshot eyes regarded her with the clinical interest he gave an unknown substance. She said simply, "Working. My father owns the place."

He stared at her; she had transformed under his nose. "You work there?"

"Five nights a week, until midnight."

"I never saw—"

"Precisely."

He backed against the tree, slid down the trunk slowly to sit among its roots. "And you work for Dr. Bezel." She closed her notebook, did not reply. "Why?"

She shrugged lightly. "I have no one to pay for my apprenticeship. This is as close as I can get to studying with him."

He was silent, eyeing the distance, his expression vague, uncertain. The woman beside him, unseen, seemed to disappear. He looked at her again, saw her candle-wax hair, her smoky eyes. It was her calm, he decided, that rendered her invisible to the casual eye. Movement attracted attention: her inner movements did not outwardly express themselves. Except, he amended a trifle sourly, for her humor.

"Why?" he asked again, and remembered her in the hot, dense crush at the inn, hair braided, face obscure behind her spectacles, hoisting a tray of mugs. She wore an apron over a plain black dress; now she wore black with lace at her wrists and throat, and her shoulders were covered. He tried to remember her bare shoulders, could not. "What do you need to transmute? Surely not your soul. It must be as tidy as your handwriting."

She looked mildly annoyed at the charge. "What do you?" she asked. "You seem quite comfortable in your own untidiness."

He shrugged. "I am following drunkenly in my father's footsteps. He transmuted himself out of this world, giving me such a pure and shining example of goodness that it sends me to Wells Inn most nights to contemplate it."

Her annoyance faded; she sat quite still, wondering at his candor. "Are you afraid of goodness?"

He nodded vigorously, keeping his haggard, shadow-smudged face tilted upward for her inspection. "Oh, yes. I prefer storms, fire, elements in the raw, before they are analyzed and named and ranked."

"And yet you—"

"Cannot keep away from my father's one great passion: to render all things into their final, changeless, unimpassioned state." The corner of his mouth slid up: a kind of smile, she realized, the first she had seen. He met her eyes. "Now," he said, "tell me why you study such things. Do you want what my father wanted? Perfection?"

"Of a kind," she admitted after a moment, her hands sliding, open, across the closed notebook. She was silent another moment, choosing words; he waited, motionless himself, exuding fumes and his father's legendary powers of concentration. "I thought—by immersing myself in the process—that perhaps I could transmute language."

A brow went up. "Into gold?"

Her mouth twitched. "In the basest sense. I try to write poetry. My words seem dull as dishwater, which I am quite familiar with. Some people live by their poetry. They sell it for money. The little I earn from Dr. Bezel turns itself into books. I work mostly for the chance to learn. I thought perhaps writing poetry might be a way to make a living that's not carrying trays and dodging hands and stepping in spilled ale and piss and transmuted suppers."

His eyes flicked away from her; he remembered a few of his own drunken offerings. "Poets," he murmured, "need not be perfect."

"No," she agreed, "but they are always chasing the perfect word."

"Let me see your poetry."

"No," she said again swiftly, rising. She brushed crumbs from her skirt, adjusted her cuffs, the notebook clamped firmly under one elbow. "Anyway, the bell has run, Dr. Bezel is waiting, and your unknown substance is still unknown." He groaned softly, a boneless wraith in the tree roots, the shadows of leaves gently stroking his father's red-gold hair. She wondered suddenly at the battle in him, tugged as he was between noon and night, between ale and alchemy. "Do you never sleep?" she asked.

"I am now," he said, struggling to his feet, and groaned again as the hot, pure gold dazzled over him, awakening the headache behind his eyes.

Dr. Bezel, bent over an antique alembic and murmuring to himself, remained unaware of their return for some time. "How clear the light," he said once, gazing into the murky, bubbling alembic. "It reveals even the most subtle hues in water, in common stones, in the very clay of earth." Cerise, flipping a poem away from Aubrey's curious eye, made another note of Dr. Bezel's rambles through his dreamworld: Clarity. Something within the alembic popped; a tarry black smeared the glass. Aubrey winced at the noise and the bleak color. Dr. Bezel, surprised out of his musings, sensed the emanations behind him and turned. "Did you see it?" he asked with joy. "Now, then, to your own mystery, Aubery. Cerise has brought your texts."

Aubrey, sweating pallidly, like a hothouse lily, bent over the scrolls. While he studied, Cerise ventured a question.

"Is there a language, in this lovely place, or are all things mute?"

"They are transmuted," Aubrey murmured.

"Puns," Cerise said gravely, "do not transmute: there are no ambiguities in the perfect world."

"Nor," Dr. Bezel said briskly, "is there language."

"Oh," she said, disconcerted.

"It is unnecessary. All is known, all exists in the same unchanging moment." He poured a drop of the tarry black onto a glass wafer. Aubrey gazed bewilderedly at his back.

"Then why," he wondered, "would anyone choose to go there?"

"You do not choose. You do not go. You are. Study, study to find your father's shining path, and someday you will understand everything." He let fall a tear of liquid onto the black substance. It flared. The smell of roses pervaded the room; they were all dazed a moment, even Dr. Bezel. "It is the scent of childhood," he said wistfully, lost in some private moment. Aubrey, saturated by Wells Inn, forgot the word for what he smelled. Driftwood, his brain decided, it was the smell of driftwood. Or perhaps of caraway. Cerise, trying to imagine a world without a word, thought instantly: roses, and watched them bloom inside her head.

Aubrey, after some reading, requested sulfur. Applying it to his unknown and heating it, he dispersed even the memory of roses. Cerise, noting his test, wrote: Due to extreme contamination of surroundings, does not react to sulfur. Neither does his unknown. She drew the curtains apart, opening a window. Light gilded the experimenter's profile; he winced.

"Must you?"

"It's only air and light."

"I'm not used to either." He shook a drop of mercury into a glass tube, and then a drop of mystery. Nothing happened. He held it over fire, carelessly, his face too near, his hand bare. He shook it impatiently; beads of red and silver spun around the bottom, touched each other without reacting. He sighed, ran his free hand through his hair. "This substance has no name."

"Rest a moment," Dr. Bezel suggested, and Aubrey collapsed into a wing-backed chair patterned with tiny dragons. They looked, Cerise thought with amusement, like a swarm of minute demons around his head. He cast a bleared eye at her.

"Water," he ordered, and in that moment, she wanted to close her notebook and thump his head with poetry.

"We are not," she said coldly, "at Wells Inn."

"Look, look," Dr. Bezel exclaimed, but at what they could not fathom. He was shaking salts into a beaker of water; they took some form, apparently, before they dissolved. "There is light at the bottom of the well. Something shines . . . How exquisite."

"I beg your pardon," Aubrey said. Cerise did not answer. "How can I remember," he pleaded, "which world we are in if you flit constantly between them?"

"You could frequent another inn."

"I've grown accustomed to your father's inn."

"You could learn some manners."

Silent, he considered that curious notion. His eyes slid to her face as she stood listening to Dr. Bezel's verbal fits and starts and writing a word now and then. Limpid as a nun, he thought grumpily of her graceful, calm profile, and then saw that face flushed and sweating, still patent under a barrage of noise, heat, the incessant drunken bellowing of orders, with only the faint tension in her mouth as she hoisted a tray high above heedless roisterers, betraying her weariness. He rubbed his own weary face.

"I could," he admitted, and saw her eyes widen. He got to his feet, picked up a carafe of water from a little ebony table. He went to the window, stuck his head out, and poured the water over his hair. Panting a little at the sudden cold, he pulled his dripping head back in and heard Dr. Bezel say with blank wonder, "But of course, it is the shining of enlightenment."

"Where?" Aubrey demanded, parting plastered hair out of his eyes as if enlightenment might be floating in front of his nose. "Is it my unknown?"

"It is at the bottom of the well," Dr. Bezel answered, beaming at his visions, then blinked at his wet apprentice. "From which you seem to have emerged."

"Perhaps," Aubrey sighed. "I feel I might live after all."

"Good. Then to work again. All we lack now is a path . . ."

Path, Cerise wrote under her private notes for Dr. Bezel's unknown. Or did he speak of a path of Aubrey's unknown? she wondered. Their imponderables were becoming confused. Aubrey buried a drop of his under an avalanche of silvery salts, then added an acid. The acid bubbled the salts into a smoking frenzy, but left the scarlet substance isolated, untouched.

"Sorcery," Aubrey muttered, hauling in his temper. "It's the fire-salamander's tongue, the eye of the risen phoenix." He immersed himself in a frail, moldy book, written in script as scrupulous as Cerise's. Dr. Bezel, silent for the moment, pursued his own visions. Cerise, unneeded, turned surreptitiously to her poem, chewed on the end of her pen. It lacks, she thought, frowning. It lacks . . . It is inert, scribbles on paper, nothing living. I might as well feed it to the salamander. But, patently, she crossed out a phrase, clicked words together and let them fall like dice, chose one and not the other, then chose the other, and then crossed them both out and wrote down a third.

"Yes," she heard Dr. Bezel whisper, and looked up. "There." He gazed into a beaker flushed with a pearl-gray tincture, as if he saw in it the map to some unnamed country. Aubrey, his head ringing with elements, turned toward him.

"What?"

"The unknown . . ."

"In there?" He eyed the misty liquid hopefully. "Is that the catalyst? I'd introduce my unknown into a solution of hops at this point." He reached for it heedlessly, dropped a tear of crimson into the mystery in Dr. Bezel's hand.

It seemed, Cerise thought a second later, as if someone had lifted the roof off the room and poured molten gold into their eyes. She rediscovered herself sitting in a chair, her notebook sprawling at her feet. Aubrey was sitting on the floor. The roof had been replaced.

Of Dr. Bezel there was no trace.

She stared at Aubrey, who was blinking at her. Some moment bound them in a silence too profound for language. Then, a moment or an hour later, she found her voice.

"You have transmuted Dr. Bezel."

He got to his feet, feeling strange, heavy, as if his bones had been replaced with gold. "I can't have."

She picked up her notebook, smoothed the pages, then

held it close, like a shield, her arms around it, her eyes still stunned. "He is gone," she said irrefutably.

"I couldn't transmute a flea." He stared bemusedly at his unknown. "What on earth is this?" He looked around him a little wildly, searching tabletop, tubes, alembic. "His beaker went with him."

"No, you see, it was transformed, like him, like your father—it is nothing now. No thing. Everything." Her voice sounded peculiar; she stood up, trembling. Her face looked odd, too, Aubrey thought, shaken out of its calm, its patient humor, on the verge of an unfamiliar expression, as if she had caught the barest glimpse of something inexpressible. She began to drift.

He asked sharply, "Where are you going?"

"Home."

"Why?"

"I seem to be out of a job."

He began to put his unknown down, did not. He was silent, struggling. Her mind began to fill with leaves, with silence; she shook her head a little, arms tightening around her notebook. "Stay," he said abruptly. "Stay. I can't leave. Not without knowing. What he found. How he found it. And there are unknowns everywhere. Stay and help me." She gazed at him, still expressionless. He added, "Please."

"No." She shook her head again; leaves whirled away on a sudden wind. "I can't. I'm going back to buckets and beer, mops and dishwater and voices—"

"But why?"

She backed a step closer to the door. "I don't want a silent shining path of gold. I need the imperfect world broken up into words."

He said again, barely listening to her, hearing little more than the mute call of the unknown, "Please. Please stay, Cerise."

She smiled. The smile transformed her face; he saw fire in it, shadow, gold and silver, sun and moon, all possibilities of language. "You are too much like your father," she said. "What if you accidentally succeed?"

She tore her notes out and left them with him, and then left him, holding a mystery in his hand and gazing after her while she took the path back into the mutable world.

# The Lion and the Lark

There was once a merchant who lived in an ancient and magical city with his three daughters. They were all very fond of each other, and as happy as those with love and leisure and wealth can afford to be. The eldest, named Pearl, pretended domesticity. She made bread and forgot to let it rise before she baked it; she pricked her fingers sewing black satin garters; she inflicted such oddities as eggplant soup and barley muffins on her long-suffering family. She was very beautiful, though a trifle awkward and absent-minded, and she had suitors who risked their teeth on her hard, flat bread as boldly as knights of old slew dragons for the heart's sake. The second daughter, named Diamond, wore delicate, gold-rimmed spectacles, and was never without a book or a crossword puzzle at hand. She discoursed learnedly on the origins of the phoenix and the conjunctions of various astrological signs. She had an answer for everything and was considered by all her suitors to be wondrously wise.

The youngest daughter, called Lark, sang a great deal but never spoke much. Because her voice was so like her mother's, her father doted on her. She was by no means the fairest of the three daughters; she did not shine with beauty or wit. She was pale and slight, with dark eyes, straight, serious brows, and dark braided hair. She had a loving and sensible heart, and she adored her family, though they worried her with their extravagances and foolishness. She wore Pearl's crooked garters, helped Diamond with her crossword puzzles, and heard odd questions arise from deep in her mind when she sang. *What is life?* she would wonder. *What is love? What is man?* This last gave her a good deal to ponder, as she watched her father shower his daughters with chocolates and taffeta gowns and gold bracelets. The young gentlemen who came calling seemed especially puzzling. They sat in their velvet shirts and their leather boots, nibbling burnt cakes and praising Diamond's mind, and all the while their eyes said other things. *Now,* their eyes said. *Now.* Then: *Patience, patience.* "You are flowers," their mouths said, "You are jewels, you are golden dreams." Their eyes said: *I eat flowers, I burn with dreams, I have a tower without a door in my heart, and I will keep you there . . .*

Her sisters seemed fearless in the face of this power — whether from innocence or design, Lark was uncertain. Since she was wary of men and seldom spoke to them, she felt herself safe. She spoke mostly to her father, who only had a foolish, doting look in his eyes, and who of all men could make her smile.

One day their father left on a long journey to a distant city where he had lucrative business dealings. Before he left, he promised to bring his daughters whatever they asked for. Diamond, in a riddling mood, said merrily, "Bring us our names!"

"Oh, yes," Pearl pleaded, kissing his balding pate. "I do love pearls." She was wearing as many as she had, on her wrists, in her hair, on her shoes. "I always want more."

"But," their father said with an anxious glance at his youngest, who was listening with her grave, slightly perplexed expression, "does Lark love larks?"

Her face changed instantly, growing so bright she looked almost beautiful. "Oh, yes. Bring me my singing name, Father. I would rather have that than all the lifeless, deathless jewels in the world."

Her sisters laughed; they petted her and kissed her, and told her that she was still a child to hunger after worthless presents. Someday she would learn to ask for gifts that would outlast love, for when love had ceased, she would still possess what it had once been worth.

"But what is love?" she asked, confused. "Can it be bought like yardage?" But they only laughed harder and gave her no answers.

She was still puzzling ten days later when their father returned. Pearl was in the kitchen baking spinach tea cakes, and Diamond in the library, dozing over the philosophical writings of Lord Thiggut Moselby. Lark heard a knock at the door, and then the lovely, liquid singing of a lark. Laughing, she ran down the hall before the servants could come and swung open the door to greet their father.

He stared at her. In his hands he held a little silver cage. Within the cage, the lark sang constantly, desperately, each note more beautiful than the last, as if, coaxing the rarest, finest song from itself, it might buy its freedom. As Lark reached for it, she saw the dark blood mount in her father's face, the veins throb in his temples. Before she could touch the cage, he lifted it high over his head, dashed it with all his might to the stone steps.

"No!" he shouted. The lark fluttered within the bent silver; his boot lifted over cage and bird, crushed both into the stones.

"No!" Lark screamed. And then she put both fists to her mouth and said nothing more, retreating as far as she could without moving from the sudden, incomprehensible violence. Dimly she heard her father sobbing. He was on his knees, his face buried in her skirt. She moved finally, unclenched one hand, allowed it to touch his hair.

"What is it, Father?" she whispered. "Why have you killed the lark?"

He made a great, hollow sound, like the groan of a tree split to its heart. "Because I have killed you."

In the kitchen, Pearl arranged burnt tea cakes on a pretty plate. The maid who should have opened the door hummed as she dusted the parlor and thought of the carriage driver's son. Upstairs, Diamond woke herself up mid-snore and stared dazedly at Lord Moselby's famous words and wondered, for just an instant, why they sounded so empty. *That has nothing to do with life,* she protested, and then went back to sleep. Lark sat down on the steps beside the mess of feathers and silver and blood, and listened to her father's broken words.

"On the way back . . . we drove through a wood . . . just today, it was . . . I had not found you a lark. I heard one singing. I sent the post boy looking one way, I searched another. I followed the lark's song, and saw it finally, resting on the head of a great stone lion." His face wrinkled and fought itself; words fell like stones, like the tread of a stone beast. "A long line of lions stretched up the steps of a huge castle. Vines covered it so thickly it seemed no light could pass through the windows. It looked abandoned. I gave it no thought. The lark had all my attention. I took off my hat and crept up to it. I had it, I had it . . . singing in my hat and trying to fly. . . . And then the lion turned its head to look at me."

Lark shuddered; she could not speak. She felt her father shudder too.

"It said, 'You have stolen my lark.' Its tail began to twitch. It opened its stone mouth wide to show me its teeth. 'I will kill you for that.' And it gathered its body into a crouch. I babbled—I made promises—I am not a young man to run from lions. My heart nearly burst with fear. I wish it had . . . I promised—"

"What," she whispered, "did you promise?"

"Anything it wanted."

"And what did it want?"

"The first thing that met me when I arrived home from my journey." He hid his face against her, shaking her with his sobs. "I thought it would be the cat! It always suns itself at the gate! Or Columbine at worst—she always wants an excuse to leave her work. Why did you answer the door? Why?"

Her eyes filled with sudden tears. "Because I heard the lark."

Her father lifted his head. "You shall not go," he said fiercely. "I'll bar the doors. The lion will never find you. If it does, I'll shoot it, burn it—"

"How can you harm a stone lion? It could crash through the door and drag me into the street whenever it chooses."

She stopped abruptly, for an odd, confused violence tangled her thoughts. She wanted to make sounds she had never heard from herself before. *You killed me for a bird!* she wanted to shout. *A father is nothing but a foolish old man!* Then she thought more calmly, *But I always knew that.* She stood up, gently pried his fingers from her skirt. "I'll go now. Perhaps I can make a bargain with this lion. If it's a lark it wants, I'll sing to it. Perhaps I can go and come home so quickly my sisters will not even know."

"They will never forgive me."

"Of course they will." She stepped over the crushed cage, started down the path without looking back. "I have."

But the sun had begun to set before she found the castle deep in the forest beyond the city. Even Pearl, gaily proffering tea cakes, must notice an insufficiency of Lark, and down in the pantry, Columbine would be whispering of the strange, bloody smear she had to clean off the porch. . . . The stone lion, of pale marble, snarling a warning on its pedestal, seemed to leap into her sight between the dark trees. To her horror, she saw behind it a long line of stone lions, one at each broad step leading up to the massive, barred doors of the castle.

"Oh," she breathed, cold with terror, and the first lion turned its ponderous head. A final ray of sunlight gilded its eye. It stared at her until the light faded.

She heard it whisper, "Who are you?"

"I am the lark," she said tremulously, "my father sent to replace the one he stole."

"Can you sing?"

She sang, blind and trembling, while the dark wood rustled around her, grew close. A hand slid over her mouth, a voice spoke into her ear. "Not very well, it seems."

She felt rough stubbled skin against her cheek, arms tense with muscle; the voice, husky and pleasant, murmured against her hair. She turned, amazed, alarmed for different reasons. "Not when I am so frightened," she said to the shadowy face above hers. "I expected to be eaten."

She saw a sudden glint of teeth. "If you wish."

"I would rather not be."

"Then I will leave that open to negotiation. You are very brave. And very honest to come here. I expected your father to send along the family cat or some little yapping powder puff of a dog."

"Why did you terrify him so?"

"He took my lark. Being stone by day, I have so few pleasures."

"Are you bewitched?"

He nodded at the castle. Candles and torches appeared on steps now. A row of men stood where the lions had been, waiting, while a line of pages carrying light trooped down the steps to guide them. "That is my castle. I have been under a spell so long I scarcely remember why. My memory has been turning to stone for some time, now. . . . I am only human at night, and sunlight is dangerous to me." He touched her cheek with his hand; unused to being touched, she started. Then, unused to being touched, she took a step toward him. He was tall and lean, and if the mingling of fire and moonlight did not lie, his face was neither foolish nor cruel. He was unlike her sisters' suitors; there was a certain sadness in his voice, and hesitancy and humor that made her want to hear him speak. He did not touch her again when she drew closer, but she heard the pleased smile in his voice. "Will you have supper with me?" he asked. "And tell me the story of your life?"

"It has no story yet."

"You are here. There is a story in that." He took her hand then and drew it under his arm. He led her past the pages and the armed men, up the stairs to the open doors. His face, she found, was quite easy to look at. He had tawny hair and eyes, and rough, strong, graceful features that were young in expression and happier than their experience.

"Tell me your name," he asked, as she crossed his threshold.

"Lark," she answered, and he laughed.

His name, she discovered over asparagus soup, was Perrin. Over salmon and partridge and salad, she discovered that he was gentle and courteous to his servants, had an ear for his musicians' playing, and had lean, strong hands that moved easily among the jeweled goblets and gold-rimmed plates. Over port and nuts, she discovered that his hands, choosing walnuts and enclosing them to crack them, made her mouth go dry and her heart beat. When he opened her palm to put a nut into it, she felt something melt through her from throat to thigh, and for the first time in her life she wished she were beautiful. Over candlelight, as he led her to her room, she saw herself in his eyes. In his bed, astonished, she thought she discovered how simple life was.

And so they were married, under moonlight, by a priest who was bewitched by day and pontifical by night. Lark slept until dusk and sang until morning. She was, she wrote her sisters and her father, entirely happy. Divinely happy. No one could believe how happy. When wistful questions rose to the surface of her mind, she pushed them under again ruthlessly. Still they came—words bubbling up—stubborn, half-coherent: *Who cast this spell and is my love still in danger? How long can I so blissfully ignore the fact that by day I am married to a stone, and by night to a man who cannot bear the touch of sunlight? Should we not do something to break the spell? Why is even the priest, who preaches endlessly about the light of grace, content to live only in the dark?* "We are used to it," Perrin said lightly, when she ventured these questions, and then he made her laugh, in the ways he had, so that she forgot to ask if living in the dark, and in a paradox, was something men inherently found more comfortable than women.

One day she received letters from both sisters saying that they were to be married in the same ceremony, and she must come, she could not refuse them, they absolutely refused to be married without her; and if their bridegrooms cast themselves disconsolately into a dozen millponds, or hung themselves from a hundred pear trees, not even that would move them to marry without her presence.

"I see I must go," she said with delight. She flung her arms around Perrin's neck. "Please come," she pleaded. "I don't want to leave you. Not for a night, nor for a single hour. You'll like my sisters — they're funny and foolish, and wiser, in their ways, than I am."

"I cannot," he whispered, loath to refuse her anything.

"Please."

"I dare not."

"Please."

"If I am touched by light as fine as thread, you will not see me again for seven years except in the shape of a dove."

"Seven years," she said numbly, terrified. Then she thought of lovely, clumsy Pearl and her burnt tea cakes, and of Diamond and her puzzles and earnest discourses on the similarities between the moon and a dragon's egg. She pushed her face against Perrin, torn between her various loves, gripping him in anguish. "Please," she begged. "I must see them. But I cannot leave you. But I must go to them. I promise: no light will find you, my night-love. No light, ever."

So her father sealed a room in his house so completely that by day it was dark as night, and by night as dark as death. By chance, or perhaps because, deep in the most secret regions of his mind he thought to free Lark from her strange, enchanted husband and bring her back to light and into his life, he used a piece of unseasoned wood to make a shutter. While Lark busied herself hanging pearls on Pearl, diamonds on Diamond, and swathing them both in yards of lace, Sun opened a hair-fine crack in the green wood where Perrin waited.

The wedding was a sumptuous, decadent affair. Both brides were dressed in cloth of gold, and they carried huge languorous bouquets of calla lilies. So many lilies and white irises and white roses crowded the sides of the church that, in their windows and on their pedestals, the faces of the saints were hidden. Even the sun, which had so easily found Perrin in his darkness, had trouble finding its way into the church. But the guests, holding fat candles of beeswax, lit the church with stars instead. The bridegrooms wore suits of white and midnight blue; one wore pearl buttons and studs and buckles, the other diamonds. To Lark they looked very much alike, both tall and handsome, tweaking their mustaches straight, and dutifully assuming a serious expression as they listened to the priest, while their eyes said: *at last, at last, I have waited so long, the trap is closing, the night is coming. . . .* But their faces were at once so vain and tender and foolish that Lark's heart warmed to them. They did not seem to realize that one had been an ingredient in Pearl's recipes that she had stirred into her life, and the other a three-letter solution in

Diamond's crossword puzzle. At the end of the ceremony, when the bridegrooms had searched through cascades of heavy lace to kiss their brides' faces, the guests blew out their candles.

In the sudden darkness a single hair-fine thread of light shone between two rose petals.

Lark dropped her candle. Panicked without knowing why, she stumbled through the church, out into light, where she forced a carriage drive to gallop madly through the streets of the city to her father's house. Not daring to let light through Perrin's door, she pounded on it.

She heard a gentle, mournful word she did not understand.

She pounded again. Again the sad voice spoke a single word.

The third time she pounded, she recognized the voice.

She flung open the door. A white dove sitting in a hair-fine thread of light fluttered into the air, and flew out the door.

"Oh, my love," she whispered, stunned. She felt something warm on her cheek that was not a tear, and touched it: a drop of blood. A small white feather floated out of the air, caught on the lace above her heart. "Oh," she said again, too grieved for tears, staring into the empty room, her empty life, and then down the empty hall, her empty future.

"Oh, why," she cried, wild with sorrow, "have I chosen to love a lion, a dove, an enchantment, instead of a fond foolish man with waxed mustaches whom nothing, neither light nor dark, can ever change? Someone who could never be snatched away by magic? Oh, my sweet dove, will I ever see you? How will I find you?"

Sunlight glittered at the end of the hall in a bright and ominous jewel. She went toward it thoughtlessly, trembling, barely able to walk. A drop of blood had fallen on the floor, and into the blood, a small white feather.

She heard Perrin's voice, as in a dream: *Seven years.* Beyond the open window on the flagstones another crimson jewel gleamed. Another feather fluttered, caught in it. On the garden wall she saw the dove turn to look at her.

*Seven years.*

This, its eyes said. Or your father's house, where you are loved, and where there is no mystery in day or night. Stay. Or follow.

*Seven years.*

By the end of the second year, she had learned to speak to animals and understand the mute, fleeting language of the butterflies. By the end of the third year, she had walked everywhere in the world. She had made herself a gown of soft white feathers stained with blood that grew longer and longer as she followed the dove. By the end of the fifth year, her face had grown familiar to the stars, and the moon kept its eye on her. By the end of the sixth year, the gown of feathers and her hair swept behind her, mingling light and dark, and she had become, to the world's eye, a figure of mystery and enchantment. In her own eyes she was simply Lark, who loved Perrin; all the enchantment lay in him.

At the end of the seventh year she lost him.

The jeweled path of blood, the moon-white feathers stopped. It left her stranded, bewildered, on a mountainside in some lonely part of the world. In disbelief, she searched frantically: stones, tree boughs, earth. Nothing told her which direction to go. One direction was as likely as another, and all, to her despairing heart, went nowhere. She threw herself on the ground finally and wept for the first time since her father had killed the lark.

"So close," she cried, pounding the earth in fury and

sorrow. "So close—another step, another drop of blood— Oh, but perhaps he is dead, my Perrin, after losing so much blood to show me the way. So many years, so much blood, so much silence, so much, too much, too much . . ." She fell silent finally, dazed and exhausted with grief. The wind whispered to her, comforting; the trees sighed for her, weeping leaves that caressed her face. Birds spoke.

*Maybe the dove is not dead,* they said. *We saw none of ours fall dying from the sky. Enchantments do not die, they are transformed. . . . Light sees everything. Ask the sun. Who knows him better than the sun who changed him into a dove?*

"Do you know?" she whispered to the sun, and for an instant saw its face among the clouds.

*No,* it said in words of fire, and with fire, shaped something out of itself. *It's you I have watched, for seven years, as constant and faithful to your love as I am to the world. Take this. Open it when your need is greatest.*

She felt warm light in her hand. The light hardened into a tiny box with jeweled hinges and the sun's face on its lid. She turned her face away disconsolately; a box was not a bird. But she held it, and it kept her warm through dusk and nightfall as she lay unmoving on the cold ground.

She asked the full moon when it rose above the mountain. "Have you seen my white dove? For seven years you showed me each drop of blood, each white feather, even on the darkest night."

*It was you I watched,* the moon said. *More constant than the moon on the darkest night, for I hid then, and you never faltered in your journey. I have not seen your dove.*

"Do you know," she whispered to the wind, and heard it question its four messengers, who blew everywhere in the world. *No,* they said, and *No,* and *No.* And then the sweet South Wind blew against her cheek, smelling of roses and warm seas and endless summers. *Yes.*

She lifted her face from the ground. Twigs and dirt clung to her. Her long hair was full of leaves and spiders and the grandchildren of spiders. Full of webs, it looked as filmy as a bridal veil. Her face was moon pale; moonlight could have traced the bones through it. Her eyes were fiery with tears.

"My dove."

*He has become a lion again. The seven years are over. But the dove changed shape under the eyes of an enchanted dragon, and when the dragon saw lion, battle sparked. He is still fighting.*

Lark sat up. "Where?"

*In a distant land, beside a southern sea. I brought you a nut from one of the trees there. It is no ordinary nut. Now listen. This is what you must do . . .*

So she followed the South Wind to the land beside the southern sea, where the sky flashed red with dragon fire, and its fierce roars blew down trees and tore the sails from every passing ship. The lion, no longer stone by daylight, was golden and as flecked with blood as Lark's gown of feathers. Lark never questioned the wind's advice, for she was desperate beyond the advice of mortals. She went to the seashore and found reeds broken in the battle, each singing a different, haunting note through its hollow throat. She counted. She picked the eleventh reed and waited. When the dragon bent low, curling around itself to roar rage and fire at the lion gnawing at its wing, she ran forward quickly, struck its throat with the reed.

Smoke hissed from its scales, as if the reed had seared it. It tried to roar; no sound came out, no fire. Its great neck sagged; scales darkened with blood and smoke. One eye closed. The lion leaped for its throat.

There was a flash, as if the sun had struck the earth. Lark crouched, covering her face. The world was suddenly very quiet. She heard bullfrogs among the reeds, the warm, slow waves fanning across the sand. She opened her eyes.

The dragon had fallen on its back, with the lion sprawled on top of it. A woman lay on her back, with Perrin on top of her. His eyes were closed, his face bloody; he drew deep, ragged breaths, one hand clutching the woman's shoulder, his open mouth against her neck. The woman's weary face, upturned to the sky above Perrin's shoulder, was also bloodstained; her free hand lifted weakly, fell again across Perrin's back. Her hair was as gold as the sun's little box; her face as pale and perfect as the moon's face. Lark stared. The waves grew full again, spilled with a languorous sigh across the sand. The woman drew a deep breath. Her eyes flickered open; they were as blue as the sky.

She turned her head, looked at Perrin. She lifted her hand from his back, touched her eyes delicately, her brows rising in silent question. Then she looked again at the blood on his face.

She stiffened, began pushing at him and talking at the same time. "I remember. I remember now. You were that monstrous lion that kept nipping at my wings." Her voice was low and sweet, amused as she tugged at Perrin. "You must get up. What if someone should see us? Oh, dear. You must be hurt." She shifted out from under him, made a hasty adjustment to her bodice, and caught sight of Lark. "Oh, my dear," she cried, "it's not what you think."

"I know," Lark whispered, still amazed at the woman's

beauty and at the sight of Perrin, whom she had not seen in seven years, and never in the light, lying golden-haired and slack against another woman's body. The woman bent over Perrin, turned him on his back.

"He is hurt. Is there water?" She glanced around vaguely, as if she expected a bullfrog to emerge in tie and tails, with water on a tray. But Lark had already fetched it in her hands, from a little rill of fresh water.

She moistened Perrin's face with it, let his lips wander over her hands, searching for more. The woman was gazing at Lark.

"You must be an enchantress or a witch," she exclaimed. "That explains your—unusual appearance. And the way we suddenly became ourselves again. I am—we are most grateful to you. My father is King of this desert, and he will reward you richly if you come to his court." She took a tattered piece of her hem, wiped a corner of Perrin's lips, then, in afterthought, her own.

"My name is Lark. This man is—"

"Yes," the princess said, musing. Her eyes were very wide, very blue; she was not listening to Lark. "He is, isn't he? Do you know, I think there was a kind of prophecy when I was born that I would marry a lion. I'm sure there was. Of course they kept it secret all these years, for fear I might actually meet a lion, but—here it is. He. A lion among men. Do you think I should explain to my father what he was, or do you think I should just—not exactly lie, but omit that part of his past? What do you think? Witches know these things."

"I think," Lark said unsteadily, brushing sand out of Perrin's hair, "that you are mistaken. I am—"

"So I should tell my father. Will you help me raise him?

There is a griffin just beyond those rocks. Very nice; in fact we became friends before I had to fight the lion. I had no one else to talk to except bullfrogs. And you know what frogs are like. Very little small talk, and that they repeat incessantly." She hoisted Perrin up, brushing sand off his shoulders, his chest, his thighs. "I don't think my father will mind at all. About the lion part. Do you?" She put her fingers to her lips suddenly and gave a piercing whistle that silenced the frogs and brought the griffin, huge and flaming red, up over the rocks. "Come," she said to it. Lark clung to Perrin's arm.

"Wait," she said desperately, words coming slowly, clumsily, for she had scarcely spoken to mortals in seven years. "You don't understand. Wait until he wakes. I have been following him for seven years."

"Then how wonderful that you have found him. The griffin will fly us to my father's palace. It's the only one for miles, in the desert. You'll find it easily." She laid her hand on Lark's. "Please come. I'd take you with us, but it would tire the griffin —"

"But I have a magic nut for it to rest on, while we cross the sea —"

"But you see we are going across the desert, and, anyway, I think a nut might be a little small." She smiled brightly but very wearily at Lark. "I feel I will never be able to thank you enough." She pushed the upright Perrin against the griffin's back, and he toppled facedown between the bright, uplifted wings.

"Perrin!" Lark cried desperately, and the princess, clinging to the griffin's neck, looked down at her, startled, uncertain. But the thrust of the griffin's great wings tangled wind and sand together and choked Lark's voice. She coughed and spat sand while the princess, cheerful again, waved one hand and held Perrin tightly with the other.

"Good-bye . . ."

"No!" Lark screamed. No one heard her but the frogs.

She sat awake all night, a dove in speckled plumage, mourning with the singing reeds. When the sun rose, it barely recognized her, so pale and wild was her face, so blank with grief her eyes. Light touched her gently. She stirred finally, sighed, watching the glittering net of gold the sun cast across the sea. They should have been waking in a great tree growing out of the sea, she and Perrin and the griffin, a wondrous sight that passing sailors might have spun into tales for their grandchildren. Instead, here she was, abandoned among the bullfrogs, while her true love had flown away with the princess. What would he think when he woke and saw her golden hair, heard her sweet, amused voice telling him that she had been the dragon he had fought, and that at the battle's end, she had awakened in his arm? An enchantress—a strange, startling woman who wore a gown of bloodstained feathers, whose long black hair was bound with cobweb, whose face and eyes seemed more of a wild creature's than a human's—had wandered by at the right moment and freed them from their spells.

And so. And therefore. And of course what all this must mean was, beyond doubt, their destiny: the marriage of the dragon and the lion. And if they were very lucky—wouldn't it be splendid—the enchantress might come to see them married.

"Will he remember me?" Lark murmured to the bullfrogs. "If he saw me now, would he even recognize me?" She tried to see her face reflected in the waves, but of the faces gliding and breaking across the sand, none seemed to belong to her, and she asked desperately, "How will he recognize me if I cannot recognize myself?"

She stood up then, her hands to her mouth, staring at her faceless shadow in the sand. She whispered, her throat aching with grief, "What must I do? Where can I begin? To find my lost love and myself?"

*You know where he is,* the sea murmured. *Go there.*

"But she is so beautiful—and I have become so—"

*He is not here,* the reeds sang in their soft, hollow voices. *Find him. He is again enchanted.*

"Again! First a stone lion, and then a dove, and then a real lion—now what is he?"

*He is enchanted by his human form.*

She was silent, still gazing at her morning shadow. "I never knew him fully human," she said at last. "And he never knew me. If we meet now by daylight, who is to say whether he will recognize Lark, or I will recognize Perrin? Those were names we left behind long ago."

*Love recognizes love,* the reeds murmured.

Her shadow whispered, *I will guide you.*

So she set her back to the sun and followed her shadow across the desert.

By day the sun was a roaring lion, by night the moon a pure white dove. Lion and dove accompanied her, showed her hidden springs of cool water among the barren stones, and trees that shook down dates and figs and nuts into her hands. Finally, climbing a rocky hill, she saw an enormous and beautiful palace, whose immense gates of bronze and gold lay open to welcome the richly dressed people riding horses and dromedaries and elegant palanquins into it.

She hurried to join them before the sun set and the gates

were closed. Her bare feet were scraped and raw; she limped a little. Her feathers had grown frayed; her face was gaunt, streaked with dust and sorrow. She looked like a beggar, she knew, but the people spoke to her kindly and even tossed her a coin or two.

"We have come for the wedding of our princess and the Lion of the Desert, whom it is her destiny to wed."

"Who foretold such a destiny?" Lark asked, her voice trembling.

"Someone," they assured her. "The king's astrologer. A great sorceress disguised as a beggar, not unlike yourself. A bullfrog, who spoke with a human tongue at her birth. Her mother was frightened by a lion just before childbirth, and dreamed it. No one exactly remembers who, but someone did. Destiny or no, they will marry in three days, and never was there a more splendid couple than the princess and her lion."

Lark crept into the shadow of the gate. "Now what shall I do?" she murmured, her eyes wide, dark with urgency. "With his eyes full of her, he will never notice a beggar."

Sun slid a last gleam down the gold edge of the gate. She remembered its gift then and drew the little gold box out of her pocket. She opened it.

A light sprang out of it, swirled around her like a storm of gold dust, glittering, shimmering. It settled on her, turned the feathers into the finest silk and cloth of gold. It turned the cobwebs in her hair into a long, sparkling net of diamonds and pearls. It turned the dust on her feet into soft golden leather and pearls. Light played over her face, hiding shadows of grief and despair. Seeing the wonderful dress, she laughed for the first time in seven years, and, with wonder, she recognized Lark's voice.

As she walked down the streets, people stared at her, marveling. They made way for her. A man offered her his palanquin, a woman her sunshade. She shook her head at both, laughing again. "I will not be shut up in a box, nor will I shut out the sun." So she walked, and all the wedding guests slowed to accompany her to the inner courtyard.

Word of her had passed into the palace long before she did. The princess, dressed in fine, flowing silks the color of her eyes, came out to meet the stranger who rivaled the sun. She saw the dress before she saw Lark's face.

"Oh, my dear," she breathed, hurrying down the steps. "Say this is a wedding gift for me. You cannot possibly wear this to my wedding—no one will look at me! Say you brought it for me. Or tell me what I can give you in return for it." She stepped back, half-laughing, still staring at the sun's creation. "Where are my manners? You came all the way from— from—and here all I can do is—Where are you from, anyway? Who in the world are you?" She looked finally into Lark's eyes. She clapped her hands, laughing again, with a touch of relief in her voice. "Oh, it is the witch! You have come! Perrin will be so pleased to meet you. He is sleeping now; he is still weak from his wounds." She took Lark's hand in hers and led her up the steps. "Now tell me how I can persuade you to let me have that dress. Look how everyone stares at you. It will make me the most beautiful woman in the world on my wedding day. And you're a witch, you don't care how you look. Anyway, it's not necessary for you to look like this. People will think you're only human."

Lark, who had been thinking while the princess chattered, answered, "I will give you the dress for a price."

"Anything!"

Lark stopped short. "No—you must not say that!" she cried fiercely. "Ever! You could pay far more than you ever imagined for something as trivial as this dress!"

"All right," the princess said gently, patting her hand. "I will not give you just anything. Though I'd hardly call this dress trivial. But tell me what you want."

"I want a night alone with your bridegroom."

The princess's brows rose. She glanced around hastily to see if anyone were listening, then she took Lark's other hand. "We must observe a few proprieties," she said softly, smiling. "Not even I have had a whole night in my lion's bed—he has been too ill. I would not grant this to any woman. But you are a witch, and you helped us before, and I know you mean no harm. I assume you wish to tend him during the night with magic arts so that he can heal faster."

"If I can do that, I will. But—"

"Then you may. But I must have that dress first."

Lark was silent. So was the princess, who held her eyes until Lark bowed her head. *Then I have lost,* she thought, *for he will never even look at me without this dress.*

The princess said lightly, "You were gracious to refuse my first impulse to give you anything. I trust you, but in that dress you are very beautiful, and you know how men are. Or perhaps, being a witch, you don't. Anyway, there is no need at all for you to appear to him like this. And how can I surprise him on our wedding day with this dress if he sees you in it first?"

*You are like my sisters,* Lark thought. *Foolish and wiser than I am.* She yielded, knowing she wanted to see Perrin with all her heart, and the princess only wanted what dazzled her eyes. "You are right," she said. "You may tell people that I will stay with Perrin to heal him if I can. And that I brought the dress for you."

The princess kissed her cheek. "Thank you. I will find you something else to wear, and show you his room. I'm not insensitive—I fell in love with him myself the moment I looked at him. So I can hardly blame you for—and of course he is in love with me. But we hardly know each other, and I don't want to confuse him with possibilities at this delicate time. You understand."

"Perfectly."

"Good."

She took Lark to her own sumptuous rooms and had her maid dress Lark in something she called "refreshingly simple" but which Lark called "drab," and knew it belonged not even to the maid, but to someone much farther down the social strata who stayed in shadows and was not allowed to wear lace.

*I am more wren or sparrow than Lark,* she thought sadly, as the princess brought her to Perrin's room.

"Till sunrise," she said; the tone of her voice added, *And not a moment after.*

"Yes," Lark said absently, gazing at her sleeping love. At last the puzzled princess closed the door, left Lark in the twilight.

Lark approached the bed. She saw Perrin's face in the light of a single candle beside the bed. It was bruised and scratched; there was a long weal from a dragon's claw down one bare shoulder. He looked older, weathered, his pale skin burned by the sun, which had scarcely touched it in years. The candlelight picked out a thread of silver here and there among the lion's gold of his hair. She reached out impulsively, touched the silver. "My poor Perrin," she said softly. "At least, as a dove, for seven years, you were faithful to me. You shed blood at every seventh step I took. And I took seven steps for every drop you shed. How strange to find you naked in this bed, waiting for a swan instead of Lark. At least I had you for a little while, and at long last you are unbewitched."

She bent over him, kissed his lips gently. He opened his eyes.

She turned away quickly before the loving expression in them changed to disappointment. But he moved more swiftly, reaching out to catch her hand before she left.

"Lark?" He gave a deep sigh as she turned again, and eased back into the pillows. "I heard your sweet voice in my dream . . . I didn't want to wake and end the dream. But you kissed me awake. You are real, aren't you?" he asked anxiously, as she lingered in the shadows, and he pulled her out of darkness into light.

He looked at her for a long time, silently, until her eyes filled with tears.

"I've changed," she said.

"Yes," he said. "You have been enchanted, too."

"And so have you, once again."

He shook his head. "You have set me free."

"And I will set you free again," she said softly, "to marry whom you choose."

He moved again, too abruptly, and winced. His hold tightened on her hand. "Have I lost all enchantment?" he asked sadly. "Did you love the spellbound man more than you can love the ordinary mortal? Is that why you left me?"

She stared at him. "I never left you—"

"You disappeared," he said wearily. "After seven long

years of flying around in the shape of a dove, due to your father's appalling carelessness, I finally turned back into a lion, and you were gone. I thought you could not bear to stay with me through yet another enchantment. I didn't blame you. But it grieved me badly—I was glad when the dragon attacked me, because I thought it might kill me. Then I woke up in my own body, in a strange bed, with a princess beside me explaining that we were destined to be married."

"Did you tell her you were married?"

He sighed. "I thought it was just another way of being enchanted. A lion, a dove, marriage to a beautiful princess I don't love—What difference did anything make? You were gone. I didn't care any longer what happened to me." She swallowed, but could not speak. "Are you about to leave me again?" he asked painfully. "Is that why you'll come no closer?"

"No," she whispered. "I thought—I didn't think you still remembered me."

He closed his eyes. "For seven years I left you my heart's blood to follow . . ."

"And for seven years I followed. And then on the last day of the seventh year, you disappeared. I couldn't find you anywhere. I asked the sun, the moon, the wind. I followed the South Wind to find you. It told me how to break the spell over you. So I did—"

His eyes opened again. "You. You are the enchantress the princess talks about. You rescued both of us. And then—"

"She took you away from me before I could tell her—I tried—"

His face was growing peaceful in the candlelight. "She doesn't listen very well. But why did you think I had forgotten you?"

"I thought—she was so beautiful, I thought—and I have grown so worn, so strange—"

For the first time in seven years, she saw him smile. "You have walked the world, and spoken to the sun and wind . . . I have only been enchanted. You have become the enchantress." He pulled her closer, kissed her hand and then her wrist. He added, as she began to smile, "What a poor opinion you must have of my human shape to think that after all these years I would prefer the peacock to the Lark."

He pulled her closer, kissed the crook of her elbow and then her breast. And then she caught his lips and kissed him, one hand in his hair, the other in his hand.

And thus the princess found them, as she opened the door, speaking softly, "My dear, I forgot, if he wakes you must give him this potion—I mean, this tea of mild herbs to ease his pain a little—" She kicked the door shut and saw their surprised faces. "Well," she said frostily. "Really."

"This is my wife," Perrin said.

"Well, really." She flung the sleeping potion out the window, and folded her arms. "You might have told me."

"I never thought I would see her again."

"How extraordinarily careless of you both." She tapped her foot furiously for a moment and then said slowly, her face clearing a little, "That's why you were there to rescue us! Now I understand. And I snatched him away from you without even thinking—and after you had searched for him so long, I made you search—oh, my dear." She clasped her hands tightly. "What I said. About not spending a full night here. You must not think—"

"I understand."

"No, but really—tell her, Perrin."

"It doesn't matter," Perrin said gently. "You were kind to me. That's what Lark will remember."

But she remembered everything, as they flew on the griffin's back across the sea: her father's foolish bargain, the fearsome stone lion, the seven years when she followed a white dove beyond any human life, the battle between dragon and lion, and then the hopeless loss of him again. She turned the nut in her palm, and questions rose in her head: *Can I truly stand more mysteries, the possibilities of more hardships, more enchanting princesses between us? Would it be better just to crack the nut and eat it? Then we would all fall into the sea, in this moment when our love is finally intact. He seems to live from spell to spell. Is it better to die now, before something worse can happen to him? How much can love stand?*

Perrin caught her eyes and smiled at her. She heard the griffin's labored breathing, felt the weary catch in its mighty wings. She tossed the nut high into the air and watched it fall a long, long way before it hit the water. And then the great tree grew out of the sea, to the astonishment of passing sailors, who remembered it all their lives, and told their incredulous grandchildren of watching a griffin red as fire drop out of the blue to rest among its boughs.

# The Witches of Junket

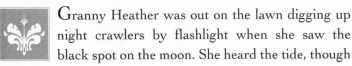Granny Heather was out on the lawn digging up night crawlers by flashlight when she saw the black spot on the moon. She heard the tide, though the sea was twenty miles away, and she saw the massive rock just offshore south of Crane Harbor open vast black eyes and stare at her. Three huge birds flew soundlessly overhead, looking like pterodactyls, glowing bluish white, like ghosts might. She didn't know if she was in the past or future. In the future, the sea might eat its way through the wrinkled old coast mountains, across the pastures where the sheep grazed, to her doorstep. In the past, those dinosaur birds might have flown over Junket, or whatever was there before the town was. She stopped tugging at a night crawler that was tugging

itself back into its hole, and she turned the flashlight off. She made herself as small as possible, hunkering down on her old knees in the damp grass. Her hair felt too bright; she wondered if, under the moonlight, it glowed like the ghost birds. She heard her thin blood singing.

"So," she whispered, "you're awake."

For a moment she felt stared at, as if the full moon were an eye. It could see into her frail bones, find the weakest places where a tap might shatter her. She felt luminous, exposed, her old bones shining like the bones of little fish down in the darkest realms of the sea.

Then it was over, she was disregarded, the moon was no longer interested in her.

She stood up in the dark, tottery, her heart hammering, and made her way back into her house.

The next morning, she took her pole and her night crawlers and her lawn chair down the road to where the old pump house straddled a branch of the Junket River, where the bass liked to feed. She pleated a worm onto her hook and added an afterthought: a green marshmallow. No telling, she thought. She cast her line into the still water.

A trout rose up out of the water, danced on its tail, and said, "Call Storm's children."

It vanished back into the water as she stared, and took the worm clean off the hook, leaving the marshmallow.

She reeled in, sighing. "It's easy," she grumbled to the trout, "for you to say. You don't have to put up with them."

But she had to admit it was right.

Still and all, Storm's children being what they were, she got a second opinion.

She drove her twenty-year-old red VW Beetle over to

Poppy and Cass's house, adding another 3.8 miles to the 32,528.9 she had turned over in twenty years. Cass was in the yard, polishing a great wheel of redwood burl. His work shed, which was a small warehouse left over from when the nearly invisible town of Raventree actually had a dock for river traffic, was cluttered with slabs of redwood and smaller, paler pieces of myrtle. He smiled at Heather, but he didn't speak. He was a shy, untidy giant, with hair that needed pruning and a nicotine-stained mustache. He jerked his head at the house to tell Heather where Poppy was, and Heather, feeling damp in her bones, creaked to the door, stuck her head inside.

"Poppy?"

Poppy came out of the kitchen, wiping her hands on a dish towel. "Why, Heather, you old sweet thing. I didn't hear you drive up. Come on in and sit down. I'll get us some tea." Turning briskly back to the kitchen, she caused whirlwinds: plants moved their faces, table legs clattered, framed photos on the wall slid askew. Heather waited until things quieted, then eased into one of Cass's burl chairs. It had three legs like a stool and a long skinny back with a face, elongated and shy, peering out of the wood grain. A teakettle howled; Poppy came back again carrying mugs of water with mint leaves floating in them. Heather preferred coffee, but she preferred nearly anything to Poppy's coffee. Anyway, she liked chewing on mint leaves.

Poppy settled into a chair with wide arms that had holes for plant pots; delicate strings-of-hearts hung their runners over the sides almost to the floor. Poppy was a tall, big-boned woman who wore her yellow-gray hair in a long braid over one shoulder. Her eyes were wide-set, smoky gray; her brows were still yellow in her smooth forehead. She favored eye-smacking colors and clunky jewelry. Abalone, turquoise, hematite, and coral danced on her fingers. She wore big myrtle wood loops in her ears; a chunk of amber on a chain bounced on her bosom. She was the age Storm would have been, if Storm hadn't skidded into a tree on a rainy night. Heather had looked to Poppy after that, someone for her bewildered eyes to rest on after Storm had vanished, and Poppy had let her, coaxing her along as patiently as if Heather had been one of her ailing plants.

Heather took a sip of tea and spent a moment working a mint leaf out from behind one tooth, while Poppy meandered amiably about her married daughter and her new grandson. "Chance, they named him," she said. "Might as well have named him Luck or Fate or — Still and all, it's kind of catching."

"Poppy," Heather said, having finally swallowed the mint leaf, "I got to send for Storm's children."

Poppy put her mug down on the chair arm. Her brows pinched together suddenly, as if a tooth had jabbed her. "Oh, no."

"I've been told to."

"Who told you?"

"A trout, under Tim Greyson's pump house."

"Well, why, for goodness sake?"

Heather sighed, feeling too old and very frail. "You know what's inside Oyster Rock." Poppy gave a nod, silent. "Well, it's not going to stay there."

Poppy swallowed. She stared at nothing a moment, her sandal tapping — she preferred the cork-soled variety, which lifted her up even taller and slapped her feet as she walked.

"Oh, Lord," she muttered. "Are you sure? It's been down there for eight hundred years, ever since that Klamath woman drove it back into the rock. You'd think it could have stayed there a few more years."

"You'd think so. But—"

"Maybe we don't have to send for Storm's children. Maybe we could handle it ourselves. Still, Annie's up north with her daughter and Tessa has to get her legs worked on, and Olivia's at the mud caves in Montana, rejuvenating her skin—"

"That leaves you and me," Heather said dryly. "Unless you're busy, too."

"Well—"

The point is, that thing's not going to ask us if we have time for it. It's not going to wait around for Annie to get home or Olivia to get the mud off her face. It's coming out. I felt it, Poppy. I saw the warnings. None of us was around eight hundred years ago to know exactly what it does, so if a trout says get help, how're you going to argue with it?"

Poppy drew a breath, held it. "Did you catch the trout?" she asked grimly.

"No."

"Pity. I'd like to deep-fry it." She kicked moodily at the planter again; the ficus in it shivered and dropped a leaf. "Are you sure what's inside the rock isn't the lesser of the two evils?"

"Poppy! Those are my grandchildren you're talking about. Besides," she added, "they're older now. Maybe they've settled down a little."

"Last time they came, they threw a keg party in the church parking lot."

"That was seven years ago, and, anyway, it was at Evan's funeral," Heather said stubbornly. She kicked at the planter herself, feeling the chill at her side where Evan wasn't anymore. "And it was more like a wake. Even I had a sip of beer."

Poppy smiled, patting Heather's hand soothingly, though her brows still tugged together. "Evan would have enjoyed the party," she said. "It's a wonder he didn't shuffle back out of his grave."

"He always was an irreligious old poop. Poppy, I got to do it. I can't ignore what I saw. I can't ignore advice given by water."

"No." Poppy sighed. "You can't. But you can't bring Storm's children back here without explaining why, either. We'd better have a meeting. I'd like to know what we're dealing with. Inside the rock, that is. It had another name, that rock, didn't it? Some older name . . . Then people settling around Crane Harbor renamed it; the old name didn't make any sense to them."

"I don't remember."

"Well, of course it was years before even you were born — Mask. That's what it was. Mask-in-the-Rock."

Heather felt her face wrinkle up, in weariness and perplexity. "Mask. They were right — it doesn't make much sense." Her legs tensed to work herself to her feet. But she didn't move. She wanted to stay in Poppy's house, where the chairs had shy faces and lived in a green forest hidden away from anything called Mask. "Things get old," she said half to herself. "Maybe this Mask-thing got a little tired in eight hundred years."

"More likely," Poppy said, "it had an eight-hundred-year

nap." The door opened; Cass came in, and her face changed quickly. She rose, smiling, flashing amber and mother of pearl, chattering amiably as she picked up Heather's mug. "Heather and I are going to take a little ride, honey. Maybe do a little shopping, go watch some waves, have a bite to eat at Scudder's. Is there anything you want me to pick up for you?"

"I don't think so," Cass said, smoothing his mustache. His hand, broad, solid, muscular, like something he might have carved out of wood, moved with deliberation from his mustache to Poppy's purple shoulder. He smiled at her, seeing her a moment. Then his eyes filled up again with burls, boles, shapes embedded in wood grain. He gave her shoulder an absent pat. "Have fun."

"Fun," Poppy said, grim again, as she fired up Heather's VW and careened onto the two-lane road that ran along the Junket River into Crane Harbor. "Heather, I feel like I'm sitting in a tin can. Is this thing safe?"

"I've had it for twenty years and I never even dinged it," Heather said, clutching the elbow rest nervously. "You be careful with my car, Poppy McCarey. If you land us in the river—"

"Oh, honey, this car would float like a frog egg."

"Maybe," Heather said grumpily. "But you don't got to go so fast—that thing's been in there for eight hundred years."

The road hugged the low, pine-covered mountain on one side and gave them a view of the Junket Valley on the other, with the slow river winding through green fields, the sheep on them white as dandelion seed. Occasionally, they passed small herds of cows, which made Heather remember the old farm back in Nebraska, before the drought boiled the ground dry as a rusty pot.

"There's that Brahma bull," she said as they rounded a curve. She liked looking at it, humpy and gray among the colored cows.

"There's llamas," Poppy said, "over by Port James. Have you seen them?"

"Over by the cranberry bogs?"

"Yeah."

"Yeah."

Poppy weighed down on the gas suddenly to pass a pickup pulling a horse trailer, and Heather closed her eyes. She must have taken a little nap, with the sun flicking in and out of the trees, light and dark chasing each other over her face, for when she opened them again, they were passing the slough, and there were no more hills left in front of them. Then there was no more land left; they had come to the edge of the world. She put her window down to smell the sea.

The air was chilly; the sea, its morning mist rolling away in a dark gray band across the horizon, looked turquoise. The tide heaved against the pilings along the harbor channel; foam exploded like bed ticking into the bright air.

"Tide's in." Poppy turned away from the harbor onto a road that ambled along the cliffs and beaches toward Oyster Rock. Fishers stood at the edge of the tide, casting into the surf.

"Bet the perch are biting now," Heather said wistfully.

Poppy, who hated to fish, said nothing. They passed the Sandpiper hotel, pulled into a viewpoint parking lot behind it. Poppy turned off the engine.

They sat silently. From that angle on the cliff, they could see the grassy knoll on top of Oyster Rock, and the white-spattered ledges where the cormorants nested. The tide boiled around the rock, tried to crawl up it. Gulls circled it, like they circled trawlers and schools of fish, wheedling plaintively. To Heather, their cries seemed suddenly cries of alarm, of warning, at something they had felt stirring beneath their bird feet, inside the massive rock.

"Looks quiet enough," Poppy said after a while.

"Maybe," Heather said, feeling small again, cold. "But it doesn't make me quiet in my bones. Always did before, always whenever we'd drive here to look at it—me and Evan, or me alone after Evan died—in the morning, in the moonlight. You watched the waves, curling around that old rock with the birds on its head, and you feel like as long as that rock stands there, so will the world. Now, it don't feel that way. It just feels—hollow."

Poppy nodded, the myrtle loops rocking in her ears. "The cormorants have all gone," she said suddenly, and Heather blinked. So they had. The dark shadows on the splotched wall where the birds had nested for years were nothing but that—splits in the rock, or maybe shadows of the birds that the birds had left behind, escaping. Poppy's mouth tightened; her ringed hand fiddled nervously with amber. She reached out abruptly and started the engine.

"We've got to make some phone calls."

"Where we going to meet?"

"Your house, of course. Nobody but the cats there to listen in."

"You better get me home then. I got to dust."

Poppy spun to a halt in the gravel. She stared at Heather a second before she laughed. "Listen to you! I swear you wouldn't go to your own funeral unless you cleaned out your refrigerator first."

"I probably won't," Heather retorted. "Now, between this

and that and Storm's children coming, I'll never get my tomatoes planted."

"That's another thing you have to do."

"What?"

"Call Storm's children."

"Oh, fiddle," Heather said crossly. "Damn!"

Sarah Ford came that night, and Tessa, walking with her canes, and Laura Field, who was even older than Heather, from the Victorian mansion across the street, and Dawn Singleton, who was only nineteen, and Rachel Coulter, who always found the thread on the carpet, the stain on the coffee cup, the dust on the whatnot shelf. Heather took oatmeal cookies out of the freezer and jars of Queen Anne cherries from her tree out of the pantry. Olivia Bogg was out of state, Vi Darnelle was down with the flu, and Annie Turner had gone to Portland to visit her daughter. But, considering the notice they'd been given, it was a good gathering, Heather thought. She watched Rachel turn a cookie over to examine a burned spot on it, and she wanted to take one of Tessa's canes and smack Rachel in the shin. Rachel bit into the cookie dubiously; her heavy, frowning face quivered like custard. How Poppy, in an orange sweater, orange lipstick, tight jeans, high-heeled sandals, and what looked like half the dime store jewelry in Junket, managed to look remotely glamorous at her age was more than Heather could understand.

They finished their coffee and dessert and gossip; little pools of silence spread until they were all silent, curious faces turning toward Poppy, who was perched on the arm of the sofa, and toward Heather, who was gazing at an old oval black-and-white picture of Evan as a little boy, wearing a sailor suit and shoes that buckled like a girl's. How, she wondered, always with the same astonishment, did he get from being that little long-haired boy to that old man in his grave? How does that happen?

Then the cuckoo sprang out of its doorway nine times, and Heather blinked and saw the faces turned toward her, waiting.

"Who called this meeting?" Tessa asked in her deep, strong voice.

"I did," Heather said.

"For what reason?" Dawn Singleton's young voice wavered a little out of nervousness; her black high-tops stirred the nap on Heather's carpet.

"I've been warned."

"By what?" old Laura Field asked, her voice as sweet and quavery as Dawn's. Poppy almost hadn't got her; she'd been on her way out the door to visit her husband, who had been in a coma at the Veterans Hospital in Slicum Bay for nine years.

"By the moon. By birds. By water."

There was a short silence; even Rachel was looking a little bug-eyed. Then Rachel cleared her throat. "What warning was given?"

"The thing inside Oyster Rock is coming out."

Even the cuckoo clock went silent then. It seemed a long slow moment from the movement of its pendulum back to the movement of its pendulum forth. Dawn's high-tops crept together, sought comfort from each other. Poppy moved, fake clusters of diamonds sparkling in her ears. It was her turn to ask one question.

"What must be done?"

They came to life a little at her voice. Rachel blinked;

Laura Field cleared her throat softly; Sarah Ford, her mouth still open, shifted her coffee cup.

"I have been advised."

"What advice was given?" Sarah asked faintly. Middle-aged, plump, pretty, she looked constantly harried, as if she were trying to catch up with something always blown just out of reach. Having half a dozen boys would do that, Heather guessed. The cuckoo clock stretched time again, suspending Heather's thoughts between its tick and its tock.

"I got to call Storm's children."

Somebody's cup and saucer crashed onto the floor. Heather opened her eyes. Dawn's hands were over her mouth; her eyes looked half-shocked, half-smiling. Rachel, of all people, had dropped her coffee on the floor. Luckily she was sitting over in the kitchen area, where there was nothing to spill it on. Laura Field's eyes looked enormous, stricken; she was patting her hair as if a wind had blustered through the room. Tessa closed her own eyes, looking as if she were praying, or counting to ten.

"Who in hell," Tessa demanded, "gave that advice?"

Rachel, standing beside Poppy while Poppy wiped up the mess, gave Tessa a reproving glance. But no one else seemed to think the profanity unjustified. Heather sighed. Storm had been born out of blistering sun, dust storms, blizzards so thick they had swallowed houses, barns, light itself. But Storm had been the aftermath, the memory of what had passed. She had swallowed the storms, had them inside her, returned them as gifts her children carried—lightning bolts, icicles, streaks of hot brown wind—across the threshold of the world.

"A fish," Heather said.

Tessa pressed her lips together. She was ten years younger than Heather, but heavy and slow; the veins in her legs nearly crippled her. She had kept books for the lumber mill for thirty years. Whenever it closed down, depending on whether the political outcry was for live trees or lumber, she fiddled with an article about how things got named up and down the river between Junket and Crane Harbor, along the coast between Port James and Slicum Bay. She'd be fiddling in her grave, Heather thought privately; she viewed bits of information as suspiciously as she might have viewed something furry in her refrigerator.

Dawn opened her mouth, her young face looking perplexed, as well it might. "What is inside Oyster Rock?" she asked. There was a short silence.

"Don't know; nobody knows. Mask, it's called. Legend is a woman from over Klamath way faced it down and drove it inside the rock."

"If one woman did that," Rachel said tartly, "why do we need to send for Storm's children?"

"Because the trout said," Heather answered wearily. "That's all I know. Advice given by water."

Poppy, rattling fake pearls in one hand, asked Heather resignedly, "Where are they?"

"South," Heather said. "Somewheres. California. Texas. Lydia called me a year ago on Evan's anniversary. She gave me a number to call if I needed them. Said she changed her name to—oh, what was it? Greensnake. She never said where she was calling from exactly. Number's in my book . . ." She leaned her head back tiredly, closed her eyes, wanting to nap now that she'd fed and warned them. She lifted her head again slowly at the silence, found them all watching her, as still and intent as cats. She shifted. "I suppose —"

"Quit supposing," Rachel said sourly. The phone on its long line was making its way toward her, hand to hand. "Do it."


"Call me Lydia again," Lydia said sweetly. Her hair was green; she wore a short black dress that fit her body like a snakeskin and black heels so high and thin she probably speared a few night crawlers on her way across Heather's lawn. Georgie, hauling bags out, turned to give Lydia a sidelong glance out of glacier-cold eyes. Georgie had hair like a mown lawn, quick-bitten nails, flat, high, craggy cheekbones like her grandfather's, and a gold wedding band on her left hand that flashed like fire as she heaved a suitcase into the porch light. Poppy had driven her old station wagon to pick them up at the airport in Slicum Bay. Joining Heather, she seemed unusually thoughtful. Heather, counting heads anxiously in the dark, said, "Where's —" And then the third head came up, groaning, from between the seats.

Lydia said brightly, "Grace is a little shaken."

Grace hit the grass hands first, crawled her way out of the car. She was skeleton thin, with hair so long and silvery she looked a hundred years old when she stood up, haggard and swaying. "I threw up," she whispered.

"In my car?" Poppy said breathlessly.

"Georgie'll clean it up. I can't travel in anything with wheels. Not even roller skates. It's because I'm so old."

Poppy's agate necklace clattered in her hand. "Oh," she said, and stuck there.

"You can't be more than twenty-five," Heather guessed, calculating wildly.

"Twenty-nine," Georgie said succinctly, and clamped her thin lips together again.

"I mean older than the wheel. Deep in my . . . in my spiritual life."

Lydia hiccuped in the silence. "Oh, I beg," she said. She leaned down from a great height, it seemed, to kiss Heather's cheek. As she straightened, Heather caught a waft of something scented with oranges. Her head spun a little: Lydia seemed to straighten high as the moon, as long as the Junket River in her black stockings and heels.

They settled in the living room finally, cups of coffee and tea fragrant with that smell of oranges from Lydia's flask. Heather had some herself; a sip or two, and she could swear orange trees rustled at her back, and she could almost see the fire within Georgie's cold, granite face. In his photo, the last taken, Evan seemed to smile a tilted smile. Poppy, who never drank, had a healthy swig in her cup.

"Oyster Rock," Lydia mused, sliding a heel off and swinging it absently from her toe.

"Mask," Poppy said, "they called it back then." She tapped an agate bead to her teeth, frowning. "Whenever then was, that you call back then whenever they were."

"Uh," Grace said with an effort. She held on to her cup with both hands, as if it might leap onto the carpet. A strand of her white hair was soaking in it. "I'll find out."

"Tessa might know more."

"Tess the one sounds like a sea lion in heat?"

Poppy pushed the agate hard against a tooth. "You might say."

"Uh. She goes back, but not as far."

"As far as—"

"Me. She goes back to when it had a name. I go back to when it didn't."

Grace started to sag then. Lydia reached out deftly, caught her cup before she fell facedown on the couch. Lydia ticked her tongue. "That girl does not travel well."

"She all right?" Heather asked, alarmed.

"Toss a blanket over her," Georgie said shortly. "She'll be back before morning."

Lydia watched Grace a moment. She looked dead, Heather thought, her face and hair the same eerie, silvery white, all her bones showing. Lydia's green head lifted slowly. She seemed to hear something in the distance, though there wasn't much of Junket awake by then. She made a movement that began in her shoulders, rippled down her body to end with a twitch that slid the shoe back on her foot. When she stood up, she seemed taller than ever.

"That place," she said to Heather. "What's its name? Tad's. That still alive?"

"Tad's?" Heather sought Poppy's eyes. "I guess."

"I left something there."

"You—But you haven't been here for seven years!"

"So it's been there seven years. I like a night walk."

"Honey, you can't go in Tad's! You can't go among truckers and drunks with that hair and them shoes. Whatever you left, let it stay left."

"I left a score," Lydia said. She flicked open a gold powder case, smoothed a green brow with one finger, then lifted her lip to examine an eyetooth. "I left a score to settle at Tad's." She snapped the powder case shut. "Coming, Georgie?"

Heather closed her eyes. When she opened them and her mouth, there was only Grace looking like a white shadow on the couch and Poppy wandering around collecting cups. She stared, horrified, at Poppy.

"We got to do — We can't just let — You call Cass, tell him to get down to Tad's and help those girls — "

"No." Poppy shook her head; shell and turquoise clattered with emphasis. "No, ma'am. Those aren't girls, and they don't need our help, and I wouldn't send Cass down there tonight if Tad was singing hymns and selling tickets to heaven. Stop fussing and sit down. Have some more tea."

Heather backed weakly into her rocker, where she could keep an eye on Grace, who looked as if she had bought a ticket and was halfway there. Heather dragged her eyes away from the still face to take a quick look around the room. She said hopefully, "Don't suppose Lydia left her flask . . ."

Poppy gave her a tablespoon of Lydia's elixir in her tea; she was asleep and dreaming before she finished it.

Grace sat upright on the couch. The house was dark. It wasn't even the Junket house, Heather realized; it was more like the old farmhouse where Storm had been born.

"Shh," Grace said, and held out her hand. She had color in her face; her hair glowed in the dark like pale fire. For some reason she was wearing Heather's old crocheted bedroom slippers. "You can come with me but don't talk. Don't say a word . . ."

Heather took her hand. Grace led her into the bedroom where she and Evan had slept over fifty years ago. The bed, under its thin chenille spread, glowed like Grace's hair. Then it wasn't a bedspread at all — it was the sea, foaming pale under the moon. Heather nearly stumbled at a blast of wind.

She opened her mouth, but Grace's hand squeezed a warning; she put a finger to her lips. She turned her head. Heather looked in the same direction and nearly jumped out of her skin. The old rock heaved out of the ocean like a whale in their faces, as black against the sea and stars as if it were an empty hole.

Then she knew it wasn't an emptiness. It was something looking for its face. It was a live thing that couldn't be seen — it needed a face to make it real. Then its eyes could open; then its vast mouth could speak. Heather clung like a child to Grace's hand, her mouth open wide. The wind pushed into her so hard she couldn't make a noise if she'd wanted.

*Heather,* the emptiness said. *Heather.*

She jumped. She opened her eyes, saw Grace rising up on the couch, her hair glowing like St. Elmo's fire, her eyes white as moons. Then her hair turned red. Then blue. Heather, too stunned to move, heard Poppy say, "Guess they finished at Tad's."

It was after one in the morning. Flo Hendrick's son Maury was standing on Heather's lawn talking, while his flashing lights illumined her living room through the open curtains. She couldn't move. Then she heard a strange sound.

Laughter. From Maury Hendrick, who hadn't smiled, Flo said, since his pants fell down in a sack race in the third grade.

Poppy sucked in her breath. Then she grinned a quick, tight grin that vanished as soon as Heather saw it. Maury's car crunched back out over the gravel. Lydia strolled in, carrying a beer bottle.

"Well," she said lightly. "I feel better. Don't you feel better?"

"What happened?" Poppy asked.

"Where's Georgie?" Heather asked.

"Oh, Georgie's still down there helping Tad. Georgie likes tidying things. Remember how she cleaned up the church lot after Grandpa's funeral?"

"What happened?" Poppy asked again. She was so still not a bead trembled; her eyes were wide, her mouth set, the dimples deep in her cheeks. Lydia looked at her, still smiling a little. Something in her eyes made Heather think of deep, deep water, of dark caves hollowed out, grain by grain, by the ancient, ceaseless working of tides.

"A lot of women in Junket suddenly had an urge to drink a beer at Tad's tonight. Funny. There was some trouble over comments made. But as I said, Georgie's helping clean up."

Poppy moved finally, groped for her agates. "Did Tad call Maury in?"

"Nobody was called. It was a private affair. Maury was just cruising Main. He stopped to chat about open containers on public sidewalks. Then he gave me a ride home."

"What'd you say to make him laugh?" Heather demanded. Lydia's smile slanted upward; she turned away restively to Grace, who was sitting motionless on the couch. Heather followed Lydia, still not finished about Tad's, wanting to comb through all the details to get the fret out of her. The wide, moony look in Grace's eyes chilled her.

Lydia stood in front of Grace, gazed down at her silently. Evan, in his sailor suit, looked innocently at them both. Heather wondered suddenly if Evan could have seen them coming, his storm-ridden granddaughters, he would have passed on down the road to peaceable Mary Ecklund and married her instead.

"Grace," Lydia said, so sharply that Heather started. "Where are you?"

"In the dark," Grace whispered. "Watching."

"Watching when? Then? Or now?"

"Shh, Lydia. Whisper."

Lydia softened her voice. "How far back are you?"

"Then. Tide's full. Rock was bigger then. Moon's behind clouds. Seagulls floating on the high tide, little cottony clouds you can barely see. Now—they're all flying. They've all gone. It came out."

Heather's neck crawled. Poppy, walking on eggs, came to stand beside her. Heather clutched at her wrist, got a charm bracelet that clanged in the silence like cowbells. The faint, reckless smile was back in Lydia's eyes.

"What is it?"

Grace was silent a long time. She whispered finally, "I know you." Heather's knees went wobbly. "I know you. I saw you under a full moon ten thousand years ago. You were sucking bones."

Heather sat down abruptly on the floor. For a moment the house wavered between light and shadow; the light from the kitchen seemed to be running away faster and faster. The cuckoo snapped open its door, said the time, but time seemed to be rushing away from her as fast as light. Dark was the only thing not running; it was flowing into the emptiness left by light and time, a great flood of dark, separating Heather from the little, familiar thing that counted off the hours of her life.

*Cuckoo,* said the clock.

*Heather,* said the dark.

*Cuckoo.*

Her eyes opened; light was back in bulbs and tubes where it belonged. "It's two in the morning," she protested to Poppy, who was lifting up the phone receiver. "Who're you waking up?"

Poppy hesitated, receiver to her shoulder, and gave Heather a long look. "I was calling an ambulance."

"I'm all right. I got to go to bed is all."

Lydia was kneeling beside her. Heather groped wearily at her proffered arm. Thin as she was, Lydia pulled Heather to her feet as if she were made of batting.

"Don't be scared, Granny."

"It was eating up everything."

"That's why you called us. We'll handle it, me and Grace and Georgie. But we need you to help."

"I'm too old."

"No. We need you most of all. It's old, too. So's Grace. You get a good night's sleep. Tomorrow you call everyone, tell them to meet us at Oyster Rock at sunset. Georgie, you're back." She smiled brightly at Georgie, who, carrying a couple of empty cans, a flattened cigarette carton, and an old church bulletin, looked as if she had started to tidy up Junket. "Have a good time?"

"Smashing," Georgie said dryly, and did so to a soda can.

"Good. We're about to make another mess."


Between Tessa hobbling on her canes and Lydia wobbling on her spikes, they looked, Heather thought, about as unlikely a gathering as you might meet this side of the Hereafter. They stood on the cliff overlooking the beach and Oyster Rock; they had chosen the Viewpoint Cliff because the sign was so well hidden under a bush that nobody ever saw it. Poppy, wearing stretch jeans and a bubblegum-pink sweater and enough makeup to paint a barn, had driven Heather in the VW. She hovered close to her now, for which Heather was grateful. Georgie had just driven up. She had borrowed Poppy's station wagon earlier and asked directions to the dump. Heather wondered if she had spent the afternoon cleaning it up.

In the sunset, the rock looked oddly dark. The birds had abandoned it; maybe the barnacles and starfish had fled, too. The grass on its crown was turning white. Heather shivered. The sun was sliding into a fog bank. The fog would be drifting across the beach in an hour.

"You all right?" Poppy said anxiously for the hundredth time.

"I'm all right," Heather kept saying, but she wasn't. Her hands felt like gnarled lumps of ice and her heart fluttered quick and hummingbird-light. She could feel the ancient dark crouched out there, just behind where the sun went down, just waiting. It was her face it wanted, her frail old bones it kept trying to flow into. She was weakest, she was easiest, she was closest to the edge of time, she was walking on the tide line. . . .

Maybe I should, she thought, clutching her windbreaker close, staring into the sinking sun. It's about time anyway, with Evan gone and all, and it would save some fuss and bother. . . . Wouldn't get much out of me anyway, I'm so slow; it wouldn't have a chance between naps. . . .

She felt an arm around her, smelled some heady perfume: Lydia, her hair a green cloud, her eyes narrowed, about as dark as eyes could get and not be something other.

"Granny?" she said softly. "You giving up without a fight? After all those blizzards? All the drought and dust storms and poverty you faced down to keep your family safe and cared for?"

"I was a whole lot younger, then. Time ran ahead of me, not behind."

"Granny? If you don't fight this, you'll be the next thing we'll all have to fight. You'll be its face, its eyes, you'll be hungry for us." Heather, stunned, couldn't find spit to swallow, let alone speak. "Am I right, Georgie?"

Georgie picked up a french fry envelope, shook out the last fry to a gull, and wadded the paper. She didn't say anything. Her eyes burned through Heather like cold mountain water. Then she smiled, and Heather thought surprisedly, There's Storm's face. It's been there all along.

"Granny'll be all right," she said in her abrupt way. "Granny's fine when she's needed."

The sun had gone. The fog was coming in fast. Waves swarmed around the base of the rock, trying to heave it out of the water or eat it away before morning. But the rock, black as if it were a hole torn through to nothing, just stood there waiting for the rest of night.

Tessa banged on the VW fender with her cane, which must have brought Evan upright in his grave.

"Gather," she commanded in her sea-lion voice, and Poppy snorted back a laugh. Heather poked her, glad somebody could laugh. They circled on the rocky lip of the cliff: Tessa in one of the bulky-knit outfits she wore so constantly that Heather couldn't imagine her even in a nightgown; Dawn chewing gum maniacally, wearing a skirt as short as Lydia's and high-tops with red lips on them; Laura, fragile and calm, wearing her Sunday suit and pearls; Sarah in a denim skirt and a windbreaker, looking like she was trying to remember what was on her grocery list; Rachel, dyspeptic in sensible polyester; Poppy, her hand under Heather's arm; Lydia in red lipstick; Georgie in jeans; and Grace, who looked like she just might live after all, her hair blown wild in the wind and livid as the twilight fog.

Storm's children revealed what they had brought.

Lydia fanned the assortment in her hand and passed around the circle, giving them to everyone but Heather.

"I don't know what this is," Dawn whispered nervously, holding up what looked to be a size J.

"It's a crochet hook."

"But I don't know how."

"It'll come," Lydia said briskly, handing Laura the daintiest. Poppy was looking dubiously at hers. Tessa gave one of her foghorn snorts but said nothing. Lydia surveyed the circle, smiling. "Are we all armed? Granny, you're empty-handed. Georgie, give her your fishing pole."

"I can't cast in this wind," Heather said anxiously. "It's only got one little bitty weight on it. And the water's way over there. And it's too dark to see —"

"Oh, hush, Heather," Tessa growled. "Nobody came here to fish. You know that."

"Granny did," Lydia said sweetly. Her green hair and scarlet lips glowed in the dusk like Grace's hair; so did Georgie's hands, paler than the rest of her, moving like magician's gloves through the air. The sky was misty, bruised purple-black now, starless, moonless. They could still see something of each other — an eye gleam, a gesture — from the lights in the motel parking lot. "Granny's going fishing. It's Georgie's favorite pole, so whatever you catch, don't let go of it. You just keep reeling in. We'll take care of the rest. Ready, Grace?"

Grace held a bone between her hands.

It was some animal, Heather thought uneasily. Cow or sheep shank, some such, big, pearly-white as Grace's hair, thick as her wrist. Thick as it was, Grace broke it in two like a twig.

She held both pieces out toward the rock. Her eyes closed; she crooned something like a nursery song. Heather felt her back hairs rise, as if some charged hand had stroked the nape of her neck. The bone dripped glitterings as hard and darkly red as garnet.

Dawn bit down on her crochet hook. Poppy held hers upright like a candle; her other hand gripped Heather as if she thought Heather might take to the air in the sudden wind that pounced over the cliff. Heather heard it howl a moment, like a catfight, before it hit. It smashed them like a high wave. Heather wanted to clutch at the sparse hair she had left, but Poppy held one arm, and she had the pole in her other hand. She tried to say something to Poppy, but the wind tore her words away and then her breath.

*Heather,* the dark said, a mad wind crooning in Grace's voice. *Heather,* it said again, a wave now, rolling faster and faster in the path of the wind. *Heather,* it said, sniffing for her like a dog, and she froze on the cliff while it stalked her, knowing she had no true claims to life or time, nothing holding her on earth, even her bones were wearing down, disappearing little by little inside her while she breathed. The circle of shadowy faces couldn't hold her; Poppy's hand couldn't protect her; she was a lone, withered thing, and if this dark didn't get her, the other would soon enough, so what difference was there between them?

"Granny?" Lydia didn't even have to shout. Her voice came as clear and light as if her red neon lips were at Heather's ear. "You can cast anytime, now."

She could feel Poppy's hand again, hear Grace's meaningless singsong. But Poppy's hand felt a thousand miles away; she was just clinging to skin and bone, she could never reach deep enough to hang on to anything that mattered. She couldn't anchor onto breath or thought or time.

"Granny?"

And time was the difference between this dark and death. This thing had all the time in the world.

*Heather.*

"Granny?"

"Honey, it's just no use—" She heard her own cracked, wavery voice more inside her head than out, with the wind shredding everything she said. "I can't cast against this—"

"Granny Heather, you get that line out there, or I'll let this wind snatch you bald."

Heather unlatched the reel, caught line under her thumb, and flung a hook and a weight that wouldn't have damaged a passing goldfinch into the eye of the dark.

The line unreeled forever. It took on the same eerie glow as Lydia's lips, Georgie's hands, and it stretched taut and kept unwinding as if something had caught it and run with it, then swam, then flew, farther and farther toward the edge of the world. It stopped so fast she toppled back out of Poppy's hold; Poppy grabbed her again, pulled her upright.

What she had caught turned to her.

She felt it as she had felt it looking out of the moon's eye.

She went small, deep inside her, a little animal scurrying to find a hiding place. But there was no place; there was no world, even, just her, standing in a motionless, soundless dark with a ghostly fishing pole in her hands, its puny hook swallowed by something vast as fog and night, with the line dangling out of it like a piece of spaghetti. Lightning cracked in the distance; fine sand or dust blew into her face. The wind's voice took on a whine like storms that happened in places with exotic names, where trees snapped like bones and houses flung their rafters into the air. The line tightened again; Heather's arms jerked straight. She felt something fly out of her; the end of her voice, her last breath. She heard Georgie say, "Don't lose my pole, Granny. Grandpa gave it to me."

Evan's old green pole he caught bluegill with, this storm aimed to swallow, along with her and the cliff and most of Crane Harbor. It sucked again; she tottered, feeling her arm sockets giving. Poppy, crochet hook between her teeth, was hanging on with both hands, dragged along with her.

"Heather!" It was Tessa, bellowing like a cargo ship. "Quit fooling around. You've been fishing for seventy years—bring it in!"

She was breathless, her heart bouncing around inside her like a golf ball, smacking her ribs, her side. The line tightened again. This time it would send her flying out of Poppy's hold, over the cliff, and all she could do was hang on, she didn't have the strength to tug against it, she had no more strength, she just didn't—

"Remember, Granny," Lydia said, "not long after Storm was born, when you walked out into the fields with her to give Grandpa his lunch, and halfway back, all the fields lifted off the ground and started blowing straight at you? You couldn't see, you couldn't breathe, you couldn't move against the wind, but you had to get Storm in, you had to find the house, nothing—not wind or dirt or heat—was going to get its hands on Storm. You pushed wind aside to save her, you saw through earth. And then, when you got to the house, the wind shoved against the screen door so hard you couldn't pull it open. You didn't have any more strength, not even for a screen door. You couldn't pull. You couldn't pull against that wind. But you did pull. You pulled. You pulled. You pulled your heart out for Storm. And the door opened and flew away and you were inside with Storm safe."

"I pulled," Heather said, and pulled the door open again, for Storm's children.

It gave so fast Poppy had to catch her. Line snaked through the air, traced a pale, phosphorescent tangle all over the ground. For a second Heather thought she had lost it. Then she saw the end of the line, hung in the air at the cliff edge just above them. She sagged on the ground, her mouth dry as a dust storm, her blood crackling like lightning behind her eyes. She felt the wind change suddenly, as if the world were going backward, and startled, she looked up to see Lydia's blood-bright, reckless smile.

"Georgie?"

Georgie reached behind her to Poppy's station wagon and pulled open the back end. Half the garbage in the Junket dump whirled out, a flood of debris that swooped in the wind and tumbled and soared and snagged, piece by piece, against the thing at the cliff edge. Old milk cartons, bread wrappers, toilet paper rolls, styrofoam containers, orange peels, frozen dinner trays, used Kleenex, coffee grounds, torn envelopes, wadded paper, magazines, melon rinds skimmed over their heads and stuck to the dark, making a mask of garbage over the shape that Heather had hooked. She saw a wide, lipless, garbage mouth move, still chewing at the line, and she closed her eyes. Dimly, she heard Lydia say, "Tessa will now give us a demonstration of the basic chain stitch."

"Dip in your hook," Tessa said grimly. "Twist a loop, catch a strand on the hook and pull it through the loop. Catch a strand. Pull. Catch. Pull."

"Funny," Heather said after a while. Lydia, green hair and lips floating in the dark, knelt down beside her.

"What's funny, Granny?"

"I never knew crocheting was so much like fishing."

"Me, neither."

"You catch, then you pull." She paused. She couldn't see Lydia's eyes, but she guessed at them. "How'd you know about that dust storm? About how the screen door wouldn't open? I never remembered that part. You weren't even born. Your mama was barely two months old."

"She remembered," Lydia said. "She told us."

"Oh." She thought that over and opened her mouth again. Lydia's red floating lips smiled. Might as well ask how she could do that trick, Heather thought, and asked something else instead.

"What's going to happen to it?"

"Georgie'll clean it up."

"She going to put it back inside the rock?"

"I think she has in mind taking it to the dump with the rest of the garbage. It'll take some time to untangle itself and put the pieces back together."

"Will it?"

"What, Granny?"

"Put the pieces back together?"

Lydia patted her hand, showing half a mouth; she was looking at the huge clown face that was loosing bits of garbage as the flashing hooks parted and knotted the dark behind it. She didn't answer. Poppy, at the cliff edge, drawing out a chain of dark from between a frozen orange juice can, an ice-cream container, and a fish head, looked over at Heather.

"You all right, honey?"

"I think so." Beside Poppy, Laura was making a long fine chain, her silver needle flashing like a minnow. Waiting for nine years for her husband to open his eyes gave her a lot of time on her hands, and she could crochet time faster than any of them. Sarah, with a hook as fat as a finger, was making a chain wide enough to hold an anchor. Dawn did a little dance with her high-tops whenever she missed a beat with her hook. Rachel, of all people, broke into a tuneless whistle now and then; Heather didn't know she could even pucker up her lips.

"Nice fishing," Tessa boomed. "Good work, Heather."

"I had help," Heather said. "I had my granddaughters."

Georgie lifted her head, gave Heather one of her burning smiles, like spring wind blowing across a snowbank. Grace had gone to sleep against Georgie's knees, looking, with her hair over her face, like a little ghostly haystack. Heather leaned back against Lydia's arm. She closed her eyes, listened to her heart beat. It wouldn't win any races, but it was steady again, and it would do for a while, until something better came along.

# Star-Crossed

FIRST WATCH: Sovereign, here lies the County Paris slain;
   And Romeo dead; and Juliet, dead before,
   Warm and new-kill'd.
PRINCE: Search, seek, and know how this foul murder comes.

—Shakespeare, *Romeo and Juliet*, V, 3

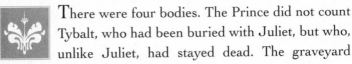There were four bodies. The Prince did not count Tybalt, who had been buried with Juliet, but who, unlike Juliet, had stayed dead. The graveyard seemed frozen after the Prince spoke, in one of those midnight moments when the owls are silent, and the moon itself stops moving. The grass, and the Prince's chain-mail shirt, and the leaves in the great trees around us caught light the color of bone. The vault yawned fire from the torches; everything else shaped shadows alive and coiled to spring. In the torchlight, the dead seemed to move, gesturing and trying to speak, tell. But I couldn't hear them. The Prince was still looking at me. An owl spoke, and then so did I, the only thing I could say, "Yes, my lord."

"There they all were," I told Beatrice later, next to her in the rumpled sheets. "Dead. So young, all of them. Juliet—a child. With a knife through her heart. And the Prince's kinsman, Paris, who was to have married her. Blood still wet from the wound in his belly. And Romeo, not a mark on him, but lifeless, with Juliet crumpled on top of him. And Tybalt. At least he was lying there quietly, without any mystery about him except death. And we know how he died. Romeo killed him, and the Prince banished Romeo. He should have been in exile in Mantua, not killing people in a vault in Verona. Especially people already dead."

"So you think Romeo killed Juliet?" Beatrice asked sleepily. Her eyes, dark as moon-shadow and as mysterious, had that distant, luminous look about them she got when she had us both at both ends of the night: Antonio with the nightingale, and me with the lark. I couldn't begrudge him: he was her husband. I could only begrudge myself for knowing. He rose with the dawn for the day watch, and left that hair like beaten brass, those eyes you could crawl into and hide, those breasts the color of cream and scented with almonds. He left all that treasure alone, for anyone to plunder. For the likes of me, grimy and red-eyed from the night, to stagger home into her bed. I gave up asking how she could, why both of us, who did she love best—those things. She only ever laughed.

I could tell she wasn't listening carefully, but I had to speak anyway, to tell, so that the ghosts would rest in my own head, dwindle back into their deaths.

"He must have come back to dishonor the bodies," I said, puzzled because it was most reasonable and most unlikely. "Maddened by his exile. He stabs Juliet's body and is discovered by Paris, who has come in sorrow to visit her grave.

They fight; Romeo slays Paris. And then—" I stopped, because I could not see beyond. "Romeo dies. But how? Why?"

"I would think he would have attacked Tybalt's body first, since Tybalt was the cause of his exile."

"Romeo was young and could be fierce, but he was at heart a gentle man. I spoke with him, once or twice, when he roamed the streets and orchards at night, plagued to the heart by love of some fair Rosaline. I can't see him stabbing any woman, Capulet or no, dead or alive. But it was his knife."

"Maybe she tried to kill him, in grief for her cousin Tybalt's death—"

"But she was already dead!"

"Apparently," my mistress said with her charming laugh that was the clink of two gold coins, "not dead enough."

So it was, with what the Prince said to me, that day turned into night, and night to day. I had to catch sleep where I could, since I could hardly search and seek during my watch. After a too-brief morning in my mistress's arms, I went out and ate, and then met daylight head-on, bright and painful after such a night. I went to see the friar whose business it had been to bury Juliet and Tybalt in the Capulets' vault. He might remember a flickered eyelid, a sigh without a cause, that would tell us Juliet had not been entirely dead. She had not been, of course; she had bled when she was stabbed. So they had buried her alive, only for her to wake in that terrible vault to find the death she had eluded coming at her yet again, and this time no escape.

But I could not find the friar. He was not in his cell reading, nor in his chapel shriving, nor in his garden with his weeds and wildflowers he calls medicine. His door was latched; so was his gate. The sacristan I finally found in the chapel knew only that the friar had left for Mantua, the day before, but he did not know where or why.

So I went to the palace of the Capulets.

It was noon by then, and hot as a lion's breath. I saw my mistress's husband Antonio, still on watch and scowling like a bear. He caught my arm, but it was not what I thought. "Stephano," he said. "Come with me—there's a fight between servants on Weavers Street."

What we need, I thought wearily. More dead. "Montague and Capulet?" I guessed, as we began to run.

"Who else? They claim the very air that they both breathe. They blame one another for last night. The lordlings keep apart, only eyeing one another, waiting to pick their time. This quarrel shows which way the wind blows." He was panting as we rounded a corner. He was shorter than I, older, rounder, brown, and furry beside my lanky bones and sun-whitened hair. I caught myself imagining him with her, snorting and huffing between her breasts, and I wondered in my own blank fury how she could? How? In my mind, she looked at me over his back and lifted a finger to her lips and smiled.

Antonio gripped my arm again. "There." Still running, we watched two men chasing a third into an alehouse. Another pair grappled on the ground, their livery, the red of one House, the blue of the other, slick with dust and muck tossed out the windows. Even as we came at them, someone emptied a pot from the second story onto their heads. They sputtered, but never noticed much until we dragged them apart. Others of the day watch had come to help; a couple, swords drawn, vanished into the alehouse after the rest of the brawlers. Holding my dirty, bleeding catch by hair and arm, I yielded him to Antonio and his men.

"Thanks," Antonio said. "I'm glad I found you awake."

"I have to be," I explained. "I'm the one the Prince's eye fell on first, last night. Find out who did this, he said. So I'm up at noon, trying to make some sense out of a brawl among the dead in a burial vault."

He nodded. "I'll help," he offered. "These streets will run with blood, soon, if we don't untangle this. What can I do?"

I didn't hesitate. "Come with me. Talk to Lord Capulet, while I question Juliet's mother and her nurse. Women know things, sometimes, that men never see under their noses." I caught a whiff of myself then, having picked up the brawlers' perfume. "After I wash," I added ruefully, and we went together into the alehouse.

Both women, I was told at the Capulets' palace, were prostrate with grief. But I waited, and they roused themselves to speak with me, to shape their horror into words, and to make sure I knew who must be to blame. They came together, the Lady Capulet with her fine face seamed with lines, her hair unbound, a new web of silver glittering over the dark, her eyes red-rimmed, sometimes dry with fury, then spilling sorrow at a memory.

"That Romeo," she said between her teeth. "I should have sent poison to him in Mantua. I threatened to, because he killed our Tybalt. Juliet heard me—she said she would mix it for me." She told me this fiercely, without shame, without thinking. I did the thinking then. Poison might have killed Romeo in the vault and never left a mark on him.

"Did you?" I asked her, since she brought it up. She

stared at me. Her face crumpled then; she turned away, shaking her head.

"I wish I had," she whispered, weeping. "I wish I had."

I looked at the nurse, wondering if she, too, had considered poison. She was plump, doughy, pale as tallow; her eyes, fidgety as magpie's eyes, refused to meet mine. They spent much of their time hidden in a scrap of linen.

"Oh, sir," she wept. "Our treasure is dead, our precious duckling; all we had is so cruelly gone."

"Yes," I said, as gently as I could. "But how? How did you manage, as much as you all loved her, to put her in the vault alive?"

"She was dead!" the nurse cried out. "That morning she was to have married Paris—we found her dead in her bed! The pretty thing, with no more breath in her than a stone has, and no more life. So her wedding became her funeral."

"But she wasn't dead."

Her mother, sobbing into her skirts, turned to me again. "He killed her—that fiend Montague."

"That may be, but for him to kill her, she would have to be buried alive."

"You keep harping on that," she exclaimed angrily, while the nurse's sobs got louder and louder. "How could you think we would have done such a thing?"

"I don't know what to think," I answered, bracing myself stolidly in the full force of their gale. "A young woman about to be married dies mysteriously in her bed, and her bridegroom to be meets his death in her tomb." I could hardly hear my own voice over the nurse's noise. Something was amiss. "Perhaps she tried to poison herself?" I suggested at random, since the word was in the air around us. "She did not wish to be married?"

"She did!" the nurse cried out.

"She didn't," the Lady Capulet said at the same time. They looked at one another. The nurse resumed sobbing. "She didn't and then she did," Lady Capulet amended.

"She didn't at first?"

"I think she fretted—imagined things—the way girls will."

"The marriage bed," I guessed. The nurse had soaked her linen and begun on her apron.

"But she came to peace with the idea," Lady Capulet said.

"So she would not have poisoned herself, that morning, to avoid her marriage. Tried, and failed, I mean. And wakened later in the—"

They were both crying at me by then. It took me a moment to untangle their words, and then their meanings. "Married" they both said, and "marriage" but it wasn't until they finally met each other's eyes again, that we all realized the words they spoke meant wildly different things.

"My poor pet," the nurse was sobbing. Lady Capulet groped for a chair. I could have used one, too.

"What are you saying, Nurse." I half expected Lady Capulet's voice, rasping harshly through her throat, to flame like a dragon's.

"She had no fear, my poor, proud duck, of marriage—she was no maid. She was a married lady when she died."

"Married." Lady Capulet had to stop to swallow. The nurse had hidden her face, trying to crawl into her apron, away, I sensed, from an impending explosion.

"To whom?" I asked quickly, before Lady Capulet found her breath again and scorched the nurse to cinders.

"Who else?" the nurse demanded of her apron. "Of course, to Romeo."

I tried to describe the ensuing chaos to my beloved, the next morning, but I did it badly. It made her laugh: the appalled and furious parents, the distraught nurse, the fury slowly giving way to bewilderment and then fresh tears as they realized what their daughter had done and why.

"She loved him," I said. "That much. And he loved her. Enough for both to defy their Houses. They had some notion, the nurse said, that the marriage might bring peace between their families."

She had stopped laughing at the image of the Lord Capulet chasing the nurse around the room, brandishing a silver branch of candles, while Antonio and I stumbled over chairs trying to catch him. She was silent a moment, dropping kisses like soft petals down my chest until I could no longer think, and reached for her, and she lifted her head, and said abruptly, "But it only answers a single question: Romeo did not kill Juliet. How did he die? How did she? Did she kill herself with his knife? Why? He came to her alive — She was still alive — "

"The nurse kept saying the friar's name — Friar Laurence, who married them in secret barely hours before Romeo killed Tybalt. But the friar has gone to Mantua." I stirred, puzzled by an echo. Coincidence.

"Why Mantua?" she asked, hearing the echo.

"I don't know . . . Romeo had been exiled to Mantua, but . . ."

But what she did then made me forget time and light and duty, until I stood in the streets again, smiling at nothing.

Then time dragged at me, and light roared, and duty called, and I went home to sleep an hour or two before I faced them all again.

I met Antonio at noon, in the tavern where I had my breakfast. He sat with me, and gave me his news, which was little enough, after the previous day.

"I spoke to Lord Montague's nephew, Benvolio, who was Romeo's good friend," he said. "He knew nothing of any marriage. He was stunned by it. He thought Romeo was still brooding over some Rosaline. Walking the fields at night and babbling of love to the moon. It happened fast, his marriage to Juliet."

"Love does, when you're young."

"One advantage of age: It's a relief to be done with such stuff."

I looked at him, startled. "Surely you love. Your wife—"

"If I loved my wife," he said roundly, "I would be walking in Romeo's mooncalf paths. Love's as dangerous when you're older."

"Then what would you call it? What you feel—" I stopped to settle a crumb in my throat. "For one another."

"Use," he said comfortably. "Habit. Familiarity. She won't leave me, though she has her faults and I have mine. She's beautiful, and I let her have what she wants. If she is sometimes restless, that's as it pleases her. She gives herself to me when I want, and she does so smiling. I don't ask about other things that catch her eye, and she doesn't tell. They don't matter."

"But—"

"We are content." He swallowed the last of his ale. "What should I do now?"

He was asking, I realized dimly, about our mystery. I was silent, remembering the open vault, the dead.

"Paris," I said finally. "It was his page who called the watch. Find the page and ask him what he knows."

"What will you do?"

"Break the news to Lord Montague," I said, rising, "of his son's unexpected marriage. Meet me here before my watch begins."

Lord Montague's palace seemed quiet, numbed with grief. He had lost both wife and son within days of one another: Lady Montague had died brokenhearted over Romeo's exile from Verona. Lord Montague, a tall, imposing man with hair whiter than I remembered, greeted me listlessly. He had been told, he said, of the marriage.

"By whom?" I asked.

His mouth tightened a little, eased. He sighed. "By my great enemies, the Capulets. We are left with very little to be angry about, and very much to grieve over. Our faults, especially. Our children might be alive, if we had—if we hadn't—" He stopped, his mouth twitching, then added, "I have made offers of peace to Lord Capulet. Our children tried to love. It seems wrong to war over that."

I bowed my head, relieved. But there were still questions. "Did Romeo go alone to his exile?"

He shook his head. "Balthasar went with him. His man. He was always faithful, very loyal to my son. Why?"

"May I speak to him? He might have been there in the graveyard with Romeo. He might be able to tell us how Romeo died. And why."

"He died—" He stopped again. "He died of love."

So it seemed. I touched my brow, where too little sleep, too many riddles, were beginning to brawl behind my eyes. "I am very sorry, my lord. He was a kind young man, and gentle, unless he was provoked. And then from all accounts brave, and true to his friends."

"Balthasar knows little," Lord Montague said, but sent a page for him. He added, while we waited, "My son was as good at killing as at loving. We taught him to do all things well. I suppose he killed Paris out of some kind of jealousy—"

"It seems unlikely. More likely that Paris attacked him, thinking that Romeo had come to dishonor the dead, in revenge for his exile."

"What was Paris doing there?"

"I'm not sure, yet. But he was young, in love. That's when I would meet Romeo, wandering alone at night, sighing over Rosaline."

"Rosaline." He snorted faintly, and then sighed himself. Better to have lived with a heart broken by Rosaline, than to have died for true love and Juliet.

Or was it better? I wondered.

Easier to think you love than to love.

Easier to tell yourself lies than truth.

"He took me with him to the graveyard, to help him open the vault, but he would not let me stay," Balthasar told us when I asked. He seemed a modest young man, neat and well-spoken. Spidery lines ran across his brow; he blinked often, trying not to see, I guessed, not to remember. "He—he threatened me. That if I stayed, he would kill me." He closed his eyes tightly, as if the light hurt them. "I didn't believe him. But he wanted so badly for me to leave—How could I not do what he wanted?"

"That's all you saw? The open vault and Romeo entering? Where was Paris?"

"I don't know. I was running, by then. I never thought — never for a moment — I only thought he would take some comfort there, with her, and then leave. I thought — he had to see that she was dead, before he could live again." He ground the heel of his hand into one eye a moment, while we watched. Then he added tonelessly, "He gave me a letter for you, my lord."

"What?" we both demanded.

"I forgot about it. I think I lost it when I ran."

"What did it say? In heaven's name, boy —"

"I don't know, my lord," he answered wearily. "I never learned to read. I didn't know it might be important. I never use letters. He wrote it just before we left Mantua for Verona." He lifted his sad, winking eyes, to Lord Montague's face. "I expected that he would be alive to tell you."

I went to the friar's cell again, to see if he had returned, but there was no sign of him, no word, the sacristan said. My steps led me through the graveyard then, back to the vault; I was seized with some vague, nightmarish notion that the dead had wakened again, and I would find the vault gaping open to show fresh horrors, more dead dead again, more mysteries. But it was closed, silent. Trees murmured around me in a hot summer breeze; doves cooed their sad, comforting song. I walked around the vault, searching the long grass, the bushes, looking for something. Anything. What I found was a crowbar one of them had dropped, which only perplexed me more. What had Romeo expected to find if he had brought it to open the vault? A living Juliet? A shiver ran through me, even as I sweated. Was that what they had planned? That she should pretend to die, and he would come into her grave to rescue her? But why did he die, then? Had he not found her alive? She had been alive enough to kill herself at least and fall over his lifeless body.

She had found him dead, then. And killed herself.

But how had he died? And why?

A beggar accosted me as I left the graveyard. A stranger to Verona, I thought; I did not recognize his face. He tried to speak to me, after I tossed him a coin, but I didn't listen; I couldn't hear him over the clamoring mystery in my brain. I went home again, to sleep a while before my watch. I woke at dusk, thickheaded and unrefreshed, still with nothing answered. I had hoped to shape my dreams into solutions, but all I dreamed was what I had seen: Juliet's face, lovely as a flower and ghostly pale, her blood seeping into Romeo's clothing; Paris lying against the wall, trying to coil himself around his wound; Romeo's staring eyes, his parted lips, as if in the end he had seen Juliet alive and tried to speak; great, waxen trumpets of lilies scattered everywhere.

As I ate my meal at dusk in the tavern, Antonio told me where the lilies had come from.

"Paris brought them, his page said." I nodded, unsurprised. "He told his page to keep watch, and whistle if he heard anyone coming."

"Did he bring a crowbar as well as flowers?" I asked.

"No. Why? Was there one?" He answered himself. "There would have to be."

"Then Romeo opened the vault himself. So the page is watching, and Paris is—"

"Strewing flowers in front of the vault and weeping—"

"And what then? Someone comes?"

"Romeo comes. They hide, Paris and his page, and watch Romeo order Balthasar away and open the vault. So Paris—"

"Paris," I said, illumined, "thinks Romeo has come to defile the place. Of course. So he leaps to defend Juliet, and they fight."

"With some reluctance, it seems, on Romeo's part. The page said he spoke with a frantic courtesy, begging Paris to leave. But of course Paris would not. So he died there."

"And the page?"

"He left when they began to fight, and ran to get the watch."

Me. I grunted and chewed a tasteless bite. I felt Antonio's eyes on me, watching, unblinking. I wondered if he knew where my steps led me, at every dawn after my watch. I met his eyes finally, found them smiling faintly, enigmatic. Amused? I pushed my chair back noisily, finishing my meal as I rose.

"What now?" he asked, intent as ever on the mystery. I shook my head.

"I don't know. If Friar Laurence does not return soon, I may have to ride to Mantua and look for him. I'll speak to the Prince tomorrow, tell him what he hasn't heard by now. But there are still those nagging questions. Did Juliet intend to kill herself on the morning of her marriage to Paris? Did Romeo come to the vault to mourn her death, or did he expect to find her alive? What killed him?"

"Poison, likely. He came to die beside her in the vault."

"But why was she still alive?"

He shook his head, baffled. "Star-crossed, maybe. They were never meant to live. Only to love."

He left me with that thought, as if the lovers had been more than human, nothing like us, who, older and growing tawdry with life, could no more have loved again than we could have cut new teeth. He went home to her; I went into the darkening streets.

Another beggar stopped me, just before dawn; I could not see his face. Perhaps it was the same one. I could barely speak by then, with weariness; I only wanted to sleep. He tried to follow me, but I did not want him to see where I was going, and I spoke sharply to him. He faded away with the night. I dropped into my mistress's arms, which she held out to me as generously as ever. I tried to bury myself in her sweetness as in some warm, gently moving sea, but my thoughts kept tossing me onto a rocky shore.

"Do you love me?" I asked her once, without meaning to.

"Of course," she said. "Stephano. Of course."

The beggar was waiting for me when I left her.

I stopped when I saw him, angry and mystified. Maybe he thought to threaten me by telling Antonio what he had seen; maybe he had some notion that Antonio might care. He had started to speak even before I stopped; busy studying him, I didn't listen. He was tall and gaunt as some desert saint; his clothes hung loosely on him, where they weren't holding themselves together by a thread. His hair and brows were shaggy, iron-grey and white. His feet were bare and dusty, cracked, as if he had walked parched roads for some time.

He tried to fill my hand with gold, which is when I began to listen to him.

"He told me to buy food with it, but I found I could not eat his gold. Not with what I gave him. He would not hear 'no.' I will pay your poverty, he said, not your will. I didn't have the will to refuse. Refuse to eat, refuse to live. Until I heard what happened to him. I came to give back his gold. I can't take back what I gave him, but I will not eat his death."

I closed my eyes, opened them, to see if he was still there, if his words made any better sense. "Who are you?" I asked, bewildered.

"A poor apothecary, from Mantua. I wept when I heard. He spoke so courteously to me. He was so young, so bright and vibrant with life. I could not believe he would really want to die. A young woman would smile at him, I thought, and he would wonder how he could have ever thought of dying—"

"Wait." I held up my hand. "Wait." My voice shook; I had to swallow what it was he told me. "You're speaking of Romeo—"

"I didn't know his name," he said. "Until we heard the news in Mantua, about the strange deaths in Verona. Then I knew it must be him."

"He bought poison from you. To kill himself."

"Yes."

"It's death—" My voice rose, broke away from me. "It's death for you to tell me this—If I told them in Mantua what you sold—"

"I know." He peered at me, owl-like, from under his tufted brows, fearless, resigned. "I have done what I have done. And now you must."

I was silent, staring at him, piecing things together. Romeo must have heard of Juliet's death and bought poison in Mantua to die beside her in that vault. I felt something push into my throat, some word, some noise. My eyes stung suddenly. They came alive for me, again: the two young lovers, wanting only time and room in the world to love. We had no time or room, in lives crowded with our empty passions, to give them.

I leaned back against the stone wall of my mistress's house, shaking, dry with sorrow, trying to hear some heartbeat in the stones. I heard only the clink of gold that was her laugh.

"You must take it," the apothecary said. I opened my eyes, stared down at the gold he had let fall into my hands. I moved finally, pushed myself away from the wall.

"Come with me," I said.

"What will you do with me?"

"Feed you. What else? And after that you will leave this city, and I will never see your face again. Will I?"

"Why?" he asked me softly, his bird-eyes, weary and unblinking, holding mine.

"Because," I sighed, "neither you nor I nor the stars themselves could have kept that young man alive without his Juliet." I gave him back the gold. "Keep it. I would have to explain it otherwise. It is not from Romeo, but from me."

I walked him to the city gates, after we ate, to make sure that he did not linger. He seemed bewildered but not, on the whole, unhappy to be still alive. I had no desire to bring the issue up with the Prince. That Romeo took poison seemed obvious; he might have stolen it as easily as bought it. Juliet must have taken some herself, on her wedding morning. I had no idea where she had gotten that. Maybe, I thought, as I watched the apothecary become a shimmer of dust in the distance, we would never know.

But when I went to the friar's cell that morning, his garden gate was open, and so was his door. I walked in. His lean face was harried and wan with grief, but unsurprised, as if he expected me.

"Stephano," he said, and pulled me down beside him. "I have been—"

"I know, in Mantua."

"No," he said, exasperated. "In Verona. I was leaving for Mantua to tell young Romeo that Juliet would only pretend to die—the letter I wrote him had gone astray. But I wound up quarantined along with my traveling companion, Friar John, who had been visiting the sick. Plague, we were told, but it was only measles. They finally let me out this morning. Only to be stricken with this news . . ."

"Friar Laurence, did you give Juliet the poison?"

"It was only to make her pretend to die! So that she would not have to go through that farce of a wedding." He pulled a dusty boot off and flung it across the room, then sat brooding at it a moment. "A foolish old man," he breathed. "Who did I think I was, to meddle with love? Blame me for everything. Let me find my sandals. Then take me to the Prince—I'll tell him—"

"I think we're all to blame," I said softly, and sat on one of his uncomfortable stools. "And maybe it was their destiny to bring Verona peace. Friar, will you shrive me before we go?"

His brows rose in surprise at my oddly timed request. But he only touched the crucifix on his breast and murmured, "Who will forgive me?"

# Voyage into the Heart

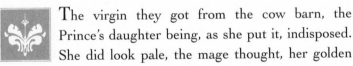The virgin they got from the cow barn, the Prince's daughter being, as she put it, indisposed. She did look pale, the mage thought, her golden skin blanching the color of boiled almonds at the idea. She was to be married within the week; the mage was not without sympathy. Fortunately, the Prince had other things on his mind.

"Just find one," he said impatiently, assuming either that virgins grew on trees or that the word, spoken, would make itself true. "Anyone will do."

Any number of virgins appeared at the mage's summons, all looking quiet, modest, beautifully dressed for the occasion. They became suffused with blushes at the mage's questions.

Lips trembled, eyes hid themselves, hands rose gracefully, silk shaken back from wrists, to touch quickly beating hearts or slender, blue-veined throats wound with chains of gold thinner than the tremulous veins. They saw themselves waiting at the edge of the forest, listening to the wild hoofbeats, the urgent clamor of horns, the courtiers in their rich leathers and furs riding hard, sweating, shouting, slowly closing around the elusive beast, driving it towards its heart's desire. For her only would it stop; to her only would it meekly yield its power and its beauty, while all around her men fell silent, watching the single moon-white horn descend, the liquid eye close, the proud head fall to rest across her thighs.

"Yena," the mage said at one face, startled out of his boredom. "What are you doing here?"

There was no smile in her sapphire eyes, nothing that had been there for him in the dark, scant hours before. She answered solemnly, "My heart is still virginal, my lord Ur. I have not lost my innocence; I have only gained a certain knowledge."

What she said was true; he felt it. But he answered grimly, "You stand to lose more than your innocence." He pitched his voice to be heard, subtly, even by those daydreaming outside the corridor. "The Prince wants that horn to detect poison at his daughter's wedding feast. Despite treaties, he still fears betrayal from old enemies. The betrothal is devoid of romance and so is this hunt. The animal will run from you. I don't know what the Prince will do, but he will not thank you."

He saw her swallow. He heard whisperings through the stone walls, footsteps muffled in supple leather and silk trying to walk on air away from him.

Then he heard rough voices, a woman's pithy curse. The

doorway cleared abruptly at a whiff of barn. A young woman with astonishing eyes, so light and clear they seemed faceted like jewels, hovered in the doorway. A stabler prodded her forward, pushed himself in behind her.

"My daughter, my lord. She doesn't like men."

The mage gazed at her, received only annoyance and some fear from her haunting eyes. They made him turn inward, look at his own past to see what she was seeing in him.

"Well," he wondered, "why should she?"

She didn't seem to know what they wanted of her, why they insisted on washing her, dressing her in silks, making her sit under a tree, just beyond the forest's edge. "A what?" she kept saying. "Is that all you want me to do? Just sit? What about that lot? Did you see those eyes? Like bulging eggs in a pan, chestnuts in a fire. I'm warning, if they touch me, I'll feed their livers to the pigs."

"No one," said the mage's disembodied voice somewhere up the tree, "will hurt you."

She cast a glance like white flame up at him. Not even his spell, he felt suddenly, could withstand that vision. But she said, rising, "Where are you? I can't see you. Can't I be up there with you? They'll run me down, they; with their brains in their breeches and scrambled from bouncing in their saddles—"

"Hush," the mage breathed, weaving the word into the sound of his voice, so that the leaves hushed around him, and the air. His spell did not touch her—the animal might scent it—but the stillness he had created did. She settled herself again, her arms around her knees. A tangle of horns, trumpets, shouts, preceded the hunt. Her face turned toward the sounds, her hands tightening. But she stayed still, biting her lower lip with nervousness. Her lips were full, the mage noted, though she was scrawny enough. Washed and brushed, her dark hair revealed shades of fire, even gold. The fanfares sounded again, closer now. She looked up fretfully, trying to find him.

"This is all—"

"It won't hurt you," he promised. "I'll let nothing hurt you. It will come to you as docilely as a cat. A child."

She snorted, shifting restlessly. "Maybe they come that way to you, cats and barn brats. Then what? Then what after I just sit and let it come?"

"Nothing. You go back."

"That's all."

"All," he said, and then he saw the animal running through the shadows within the wood.

It made no sound. It saw him in the tree; its night-dark eyes found him, pinned him motionless on the branch. It did not fear him. Transfixed, he realized that it feared nothing, not the dogs at its heels, nor the noise, the arrows flicking futilely in its wake, the bellowing men. Nothing. It was ancient, moon-white, and so wild nothing could ever threaten it; nothing else existed with such fierceness, such power, nothing that could die. It was an element, the mage saw, like air or fire. Stunned, he became visible and did not know it. Below him, the woman sat as motionlessly, no longer fretful, watching it come at her. The mage could not hear her breathe. As it grew close she made a sound, a small sound such as a child might make, too full of wonder to find a word for it.

She lifted her hands. The star burning toward her stopped. Something rippled through it: a scent, a recognition. Its horn spiraled like a shell to a fine and dangerous point. It moved toward her, step by cautious step, as if it felt she might run.

Behind it, almost soundlessly, the hunters ranged themselves along the trees, waiting. Even the dogs were silent.

It dropped its head into her hands. Awkwardly, she stroked its pelt, making that sound again, as impossible or unexpected textures melted through the scars and calluses on her hands. It began to kneel to her. The mage felt his throat burn suddenly, his eyes sting with wonder, as they had not for centuries, over something as simple as this: All the tales of it were true.

It laid its head across her lap. She stroked it one more time. Then she looked up toward the mage, found him, tried to smile at him in excitement and astonishment, while tears glittered down her face, caught between her lips. Her eyes held him, held all his attention. They contained, he realized, the same innocent, burning power he had glimpsed in the great beast that had come to rest beneath her hands. Amazed again, he thought: Like calls to like.

And then a blade severed the horn from the head with a single cut. A second drove into the animal's heart.

The mage fell out of the tree. He vanished, falling, then reappeared on his feet as the hunters made way for the Prince, and the woman, screaming, stared at the bleeding head on her knees. The mage, groping for words, found nothing, nothing where anything should be, no word for this: It had never happened before. The Prince laid a hand on his shoulder, laughing, and said something. Then the woman screamed again and flung herself catlike off the ground at the mage.

"You saw—" She still wept, though now her teeth were clenched with grief, her face twisted with horror and fury. "You saw—Your face said everything you saw! But you let them—How could you let them? How could you?" She struck him suddenly, and again, fierce, openhanded blows that gave him, for the first time in centuries, the taste of his own blood.

And then she was quiet, lying across the animal, her face against its face, her arm flung across its neck, as if she still grieved, but silently now, so silently that she cast her spell over all the men. They stared down at her, motionless. Finally, one of them cleared his throat and sheathed his bloody sword. The Prince said, "Take the animal; the hooves might be useful. What do you think, Ur? Are there magical properties in the hooves?"

The mage, beginning to tremble, felt the spiraled horn split his brow, root itself in his thoughts.

"Ur?" the Prince said, from very far away. "Should we bother with the hooves? Ur."

Then there was silence again, as spellbound bone and sinew strained against their familiar shape; the men around the mage grew shadowy, insignificant. Words escaped him, memories, finally even his name. Her eyes opened in his heart to haunt him with their power and innocence and wonder, all he remembered of being human. Seeking her, he fled from the world he knew into the beginning of the tale.

# Toad

 The first thing that leaps to the eye is that my beloved had no manners. She behaved like a spoiled brat once she had what she wanted. If it had not been for her father, where would I have been? Still hanging around the well, instead of dressed in silks and wearing a crown, and being bowed and scraped to, not to mention diving in and out of the dark, moist cave of our marriage sheets, cresting waves of satin like seals, barking and tossing figs to one another, then diving back down, bearing soft, plump fruit in our mouths. "Old waddler," she called me at first, with a degree of accuracy missing from subsequent complaints. She never could tell a frog from a toad.

Why, you might wonder, would any self-respecting toad,

having been slammed against a wall by a furious brat of a princess, want, upon regaining his own shape, to marry her? Not only was she devious, promising me things and then ignoring her promises when threatened by the cold proximity of toad, she was bad-tempered to boot. The story that has come down doesn't make a lot of sense here: why are lies and temper rewarded with the handsome prince? She didn't want to let me into the castle, she didn't want to feed me, she didn't want to touch me; above all she didn't want me in her bed. When I pleaded with her to show mercy, to become again that sweet, weeping, charming child beside the well who promised me everything I asked for, she picked me up as if I were the golden ball that I had rescued for her and bounced me off the stones. If she had missed the wall and I had gone flying out a window, what might have happened? Would I have waddled away, muttering and limping, under the moonlight, to slide back into the well until fate tossed another golden ball my way?

Maybe.

She'll never know.

Her father comes out well in the stories. A man of honor, harassed by his exasperating daughter, who tries to wheedle and whine her way out of her promises. A king, who would consent to eat with a toad at his table, for no other reason than to make his daughter keep her word. "Papa, please, no," she begged, her gray eyes awash with tears, the way I had first seen her, her curly hair, golden as her ball, tumbling out of its pins to her shoulders. "Papa, please don't make me let it in. Don't make me share my food with it. Don't make me touch it. I'll die if I have to touch a frog."

"It's a toad," he said at one point, watching me drink wine out of her goblet. She had his gray eyes; he saw a bit more clearly than she, but not enough: only enough to use me as a lesson in his daughter's life.

"Frog, toad, what's the difference? Papa, please don't make me!"

"Toads," he said accurately, "are generally uglier than frogs. Most have nubby, bumpy skin—"

"I'll get warts, Papa!"

"That's a fairy tale. Look at its squat body, its short legs, made for insignificant hops, or even for walking, like a dog. Observe its drab coloring." He added, warming to his subject while I finished his daughter's dessert, "They have quite interesting breeding habits. Some lay eggs on land instead of water. Others give birth to tiny toads, already fully formed. Among midwife toads, the male carries the eggs with him until they hatch, moistening them in—"

"That's disgusting!"

"I would like to be taken to bed now," I said, wiping my mouth with her embroidered linen.

"Papa!"

"You promised," I reminded her reproachfully. "I can't get up the stairs; you'll have to carry me. As your father pointed out, my limbs are short."

"Papa, please!"

"You promised," he said coldly: an honorable man. A lesson was to be learned simply at the expense of a stain of well water on her sheets, a certain clamminess in the atmosphere. What harm could possibly come to her?

I have always thought that her instincts were quite sound. For one thing: consider her age. Young, beautiful, barely marriageable, she might have kissed—though contrary to common belief, not me—but she had most certainly never taken anyone to bed with her besides her nurse and her dolls. Who would want an ugly, dank and warty toad in her bed instead of what she must have had vague yearnings for? And after all that talk of breeding habits! Something bloated and insistent, moving formlessly under her sheets while she tried to sleep, something cold, damp, humorless—who could blame her for losing her temper?

Then why did she make those promises?

Because something in her heart, in her marrow, recognized me.

Let's begin with the child sitting beside the well, beneath the linden tree. She thinks she is alone, though her world, she knows, proceeds in familiar and satisfactory fashion within the elegant castle beyond the trees. The linden is in bloom; its creamy flowers drift down into her hair, drop and float upon the dark water. Breeze strokes her hair, her cheeks. She tosses her favorite plaything, her golden ball, absently toward the sky, enjoying the suppleness and grace of her body, the thin silk blowing against her skin. She wears her favorite dress, green as the heart-shaped linden leaves; it makes her feel like a leaf, blown lightly in the wind. She throws her ball, takes a breath of air made complex and intoxicating by scents from the tree, the gardens, the moist earth at the lip of the well. She catches her ball, throws it again, thinks of nothing. She misses the ball.

It falls with a splash into the middle of the well, and, weighted with its tracery of gold, sinks out of sight. She has no idea how deep the water is, what snakes and silver eels might live in it, what long grasses might reach up to twine around her if she dares leap into it. She does what has always worked in her short life: she weeps.

I appear.

Her grief is genuine and quite moving; she might have dropped a child into the well instead of a ball. She scarcely sees me. I make little impression on her sorrow except as a means to end it. In her experience, help answers when she calls; her desperation transforms the world so that even toads can talk.

All her attention is on the water when she hears my voice. She speaks impatiently, wiping her eyes with her silks, to see better into the rippling shadows. 'Oh, it's a frog. Old waddler, I dropped my ball in the water—I must have it back! I'll die without it! I'll give you anything if you get it for me— these pearls, my crown—anything! So will my papa."

She scarcely listens to herself, or to me. I am nothing but a frog, I while away the time eating flies, swimming in the slime, sitting in the reeds and croaking. Her pearls might resemble the translucent eggs of frogs, but I would have no real interest in them. Yes, of course I can be her playmate, her companion; she has had fantasy friends before. Yes, I can eat out of her plate; they all do. Yes, I can drink from her cup. Yes, I can sleep in her bed—yes, yes, anything! Just stop croaking and fetch my ball for me.

I drop it at her feet. I am no longer visible; I have become a fantasy, a dream. A talking frog? Don't be silly, frogs don't talk. Even when I cry out to her as she runs away, laughing and tossing her ball, that's what she knows: frogs don't talk. Wait for me! I cry. You promised! But she no longer hears me. All her fantasy friends vanish when she no longer needs them.

So it must have been with a first, faint sense of terror that she heard my watery squelching across the marble floor as she sat eating with her father. They were not alone, but who among her father's elegantly bored courtiers would have questioned the existence of a talking frog? The court went on with their meal, secretly delighting in the argument at the royal table. I ate silently and listened to their discreet murmurings. Most took the princess's view and wished me removed with the salmon bones, the fruit peelings, and tossed unceremoniously out the kitchen door. Others thought her father right: I would be a harmless lesson for a spoiled daughter. Most saw a frog. A toad with its poisonous skin touching the princess's goblet, leaving traces of its spittle on her plate? Unthinkable! Therefore: I was a frog. Others were not so sure. The king recognized me, of course, but, setting aside the fact that I could talk, seemed to believe that for all other purposes, I would behave in predictable toad fashion toward humans, desiring mainly to be ignored and not to be squashed.

But the princess knew: to journey up the stairs with me dangling between her reluctant fingers would be to turn her back to that fair afternoon, the sweet linden blossoms, the golden-haired child tossing her ball, spinning and glinting, toward the sun, then watching it fall down, light cascading over leaves into shadow, until it fell, unerringly, back into her hands. When the ball plummeted into the depths of the well, she wept for her lost self. Faced with the future in the form of a toad, she bargained badly: she exchanged her childhood for me.

Who am I?

Some of the courtiers knew me. Their wealth and finery did not shelter them from air or mud, or from the tales that are breathed into the heart, that cling to boot soles and breed life. They whisper among themselves. Listen.

"Toads mean pain, death. Think of the ugly toadfish that ejects its spines into the hands of the unwary fisher. Think of the poisonous toadstool."

"If you kill a toad with your hands, the skin of your face and hands will become hardened, lumpy, pimpled. Toads suck the breath of the sleeper, bring death."

"But consider the midwife toad, both male and female, involved with life."

"If you spit and hit a toad, you will die."

"A toad placed on a cut will heal it."

"If you anger a toad it will inflate itself with a terrible poison and burst, taking you with it as it dies."

"Toads portend life. Consider the Egyptians, who believe that the toad represents the womb, and its cries are the cries of unborn children."

"She is life."

"It is death."

"She belongs to the moon, she croaks to the crescent moon. Consider the Northerners, who believe she rescues life itself, when it ripens into the shape of a red apple and falls down into the well."

"She is life."

"It is death."

"She is both."

To the princess, carrying me with loathing up the stairs, a wisp of linen separating the shapeless, lumpy sack of my body from her fingers, I am the source of an enormous and irrational irritation. I rescued her golden ball; why could she not be gracious? I would be gone by morning. But she knew, she knew, deep in her; she heard the croaking of tiny, invisible frogs; she recognized the midwife toad.

If she had been gracious, I would indeed have been gone by morning. But her instincts held fast: I was danger, I was the unknown. I was what she wanted and did not want. She could not rid herself of me fast enough, or violently enough. But because she knew me, and part of her cried *Not yet! Not yet!* she flung me as far from her as she could without losing sight of me.

Changing shape is easy; I do it all the time.

The moment she saw me on the floor, with my strong young limbs and dazed expression, rubbing my head and wondering groggily if I were still frog-naked, she tossed her heart into my well and dove after it herself. She covered me with a blanket, though not without a startled and curious glance at essentials. She accepted her future with remarkable composure. She stroked my curly hair, whose color, along with the color of my eyes, I had taken from her favorite doll, and listened to my sad tale.

A prince, I told her. A witch I had accidentally offended; they offend so easily, it seems. She had turned me into a toad and said . . .

"You rescued me," I said gratefully, overlooking her rudeness, as did she. "Those who love me will be overjoyed to see me again. How beautiful you are," I added. "Is it just because yours is the first kind face I have seen in so long?"

"Yes," she said breathlessly. "No." Somehow our hands became entwined before she remembered propriety. "I must take you to meet my father."

"Perhaps I should dress first."

"Perhaps you should."

And so I increase and multiply, trying to keep up with all the voices in the rivers and ponds, bogs and swamps, that cry out to be born. Some tales are simpler than others. This, like pond water, seems at first glance as clear as day. Then, when you scoop water in your hand and look at it, you begin to see all the little mysteries swarming in it, which, if you had drunk the water without looking first, you never would have seen. But now that you have seen, you stand there under the hot sun, thirsty, but not sure what you will be drinking, and wishing, perhaps, that you had not looked so closely, that you had just swallowed me down and gone your way, refreshed.

Some tales are simpler than others. But go ahead and drink: the ending is always the same.